THE I[...] CONNECTION

A Jemima Fox Mystery

Josie Goodbody

For my mother, Trisha Goodbody
1947 – 2011

THE
DIAMOND
CONNECTION

Prologue

October 1953 - Rethabiseng, Pretoria, South Africa

Irene du Plessis heard shouting coming from her husband's office at the other side of the house. She reluctantly got up from her faded chintz armchair, where she had been sipping an iced tea and reading the latest issue of *Vogue*. The latest being June 1953 and was sent by her younger cousin Louise, who had emigrated to America. It took several months for the magazine to arrive by boat. Every parcel Louise sent also contained a letter telling Irene she should emigrate too. This issue was all about Queen Elizabeth II's Coronation and Irene was transfixed by all the stunning clothes and jewels. She read the magazine for times like this, when she felt fed up and depressed at the lack of luxury living in a backwater.

Leaving the parlour, Irene walked down the cool, dark corridor, past her daughter's playroom, from which she could hear voices.

"Damn, why is that kaffir child always with my Marta?" she murmured to herself. Normally she would have gone into the room to tell Sarah to go back to the servants' block but she wanted to find out what this noise was with Marnix.

Sarah, named after Marnix's mother, who had died a week before the child was born, was the daughter of their housekeeper-cook Lulama and a year younger than Marta. The two girls provided each other with friendship. Irene would have preferred her daughter to befriend the girls from the wealthy white family at the neighbouring farm who came to visit their grandparents for weekends and holidays.

By the time she reached the office doorway, the noise had quietened to a loud conversation. She stood outside, listening to a voice she vaguely recognised as Lulama's brother's. He was trying to sell her husband what he said was a special diamond. Irene tried to squint through the crack in the door to see this 'diamond' but the candlelight was bad and all she could see was what seemed to be an ugly glassy stone sitting on the desk, on top of an old paper bag.

She heard Marnix firmly and angrily say no and order the man to leave. As he did so, his footsteps falling heavily on the stone floor, Irene jumped back into the shadows. The man opened the door, slamming it shut as he walked away towards the servants' block, no doubt to take his anger out on his sister.

Irene opened the door and entered to see her husband squinting over his accounts. "What was that about?"

"He said that he had a diamond that was the other half of the Cullinan," Marnix sighed.

Irene's heart jumped. She remembered, just before the war, her grandmother telling her stories which had at the time resurfaced, about this 'other half' of the world's largest diamond, found not far from their home in Pretoria. The old lady had said cynically that ever since the diamond's discovery in 1905 there had always been stories of the mythological other half: one that it was with the old Magato tribe in Zoutpansberg in the north of the country; another of a well-known criminal tricking a native who had found the missing diamond into selling it for what turned out to be a bag of fake money. When Irene asked if there really was a second half, her grandmother had laughed, saying that finding the other half of the Cullinan was as likely as finding a pot of gold at the end of a rainbow. Irene had been so disappointed then and she felt disappointed now, that her husband had dismissed this man. Perhaps it was the real thing and this was the luck Irene had been hoping for. She had given up praying. Her life was not meant to be like this. Why should they have so little money and her daughter have no chances compared to the English family next door? Her husband had always let her down and now he was about to do it again. With a sudden anger inside her, she left him without a word and made her way to Lulama's room to speak to the brother.

"Lulama, where is your brother?"

Her maid was sitting on edge of the narrow bed, looking very vexed.

"He has left, Mrs du Plessis. He was upset and said that he had to sell to your husband something as a bad man was after what he had and he wasn't safe to keep it."

"To keep what?" Irene feigned ignorance.

"A strange stone. He thinks it is worth some money. It must be if someone else wants it that bad. He said something about a famous royal diamond. But I don't know; he has always made up stories."

"Did he take it with him, Lulama? I don't want dangerous people coming here looking for it." Irene's heart was beating fast.

"He left it with me for safekeeping. Said he'd come back in a couple of days when he had found a buyer. He didn't want to carry it around with him as it is quite big to hide on his person."

"Well if Mr du Plessis thinks it is nothing then perhaps you should get rid of it. Throw it in one of the fields. I'll take it now and do it, as you must go to make dinner. The sooner it is out of the house, the better."

"I don't know, Mrs du Plessis. He said that he would be back to get it in a couple of days."

"I am sure it is nothing, Lula," Irene spoke unusually kindly, trying to placate her upset maid. "Why would he have such an important stone? It would be with diamond dealers if it really was a diamond. He won't be back. He was illegally trying to sell false goods to Mr du Plessis."

Lulama nodded and got up off her bed, lifted the old thin mattress, and handed over the brown paper bag with the rock inside.

Irene took it from her and walked towards the door. "Now hurry with dinner. Mr du Plessis will be hungry and I want Marta to go to bed before too long." She reached the door and without turning around said, "And Lulama, please remind your daughter to stay in the servants' quarters."

In her bedroom, Irene sat at her dressing table and took the rock out of the bag. It was fairly heavy - she guessed around two pounds in weight. It didn't look to her like a diamond, which she'd thought were bold, beautiful and bright, but even she could see it was not just any old rock from the fields; it had two coarse sides and then a third side that was sharp and straight; virtually gleaming, though not as she imagined a diamond would gleam.

She had little experience of diamonds. Her engagement ring was just a small opal that had been Marnix's mother's. She should have known then that he wasn't the right man for her. She had travelled to Johannesburg and seen the stores selling sparkling diamond jewellery and of course she had seen the pictures in her copy of *Vogue* of the British Crown Jewels. The huge diamond in the Crown itself didn't look at all like this ugly thing and it definitely was from the original Cullinan Diamond.

4

She put the rock in the back of the table's deep drawer and returned to her soft chair to carry on reading. She particularly wanted to finish re-reading the bit about the Crown Jewels now that she might have the missing part hidden in her drawer. However, she couldn't stop wondering what she would do if the rock really was a diamond, and the Cullinan's other half at that. How would she sell it without causing a big furore? She smiled to herself as she thought that she would be able to buy everything in the magazine. She would move to America to live, as Louise had so often suggested. She and Marta would have the life that was rightfully theirs. Irene thought then that she would persuade Marnix to go to Pretoria the next day so she could go to look in the National Library about diamonds, especially this famous Cullinan one.

Two days later, having done some research and realised that there was every possibility that the rock in her dressing table drawer really was a diamond; though of course no idea if it was the sister of the Cullinan, Irene was already making plans to leave and go to New York City. She had spoken to her husband, without mentioning the rock, and showed him the letter from Louise. She implored him to sell the farm and start a new life for the sake of their only daughter. Marnix laughed at her and said she was mad, that she should start helping him with the farm instead of drinking tea and reading silly magazines which only put ideas into her head. However, Irene had survived 32 years of living in a way that she knew she was not meant to. Why should she not have the life of those women in *Vogue* with beautiful clothes and shoes? She had given up helping on the farm years ago but still her hands looked like maid's hands. It was too much. Just as she thought she might cry, she pulled herself together and decided that she would leave Marnix and the farm. Take her daughter and diamond and start again in New York City with a new name and a new life. She would send Louise a telegram to wire her some money. She could pay her back tenfold with the sale of her lucky charm. For that is what she felt it was.

Once she received the money from Louise, she would give Lulama what she was sure was more than enough for her brother.

She was just about to go to her writing desk to start making plans when she heard a deafening gunshot, followed by screaming, coming from the direction of the kitchen. She ran to find Lulama on the stone floor, blood pouring out of her head. Little Sarah was screaming and crying while shaking her mother. Marta was standing at the door to the kitchen, staring dumbfounded.

"What has happened? Who did this?" cried Marnix who pushed past Irene as she stood holding onto her daughter.

Marta now spoke in such a gentle voice you could hardly hear it, "We were on our way to the kitchen to get some lemonade when we heard Sarah's uncle shouting and then we came in and saw him fire the gun at Lulu."

"What was the shouting about? Why did he kill her?"

"He was shouting something about a diamond." Sarah sobbed, looking at her mother.

1

December 2010 – London

Jemima was waiting on the ground floor of Vogel House for the lift which would take her five floors up to the press office. As per usual it was taking forever. She pulled her BlackBerry out of her black Christian Dior bag and began tapping away frantically. She wanted to finish the email that she had started on the bus on her way into work.

<<*So basically, after much begging, I went down on him. After all, he had made the most delicious scrambled eggs and smoked salmon and I had managed to avoid doing it since we got back together. But it was awful. I was so hungover and I had to be in the office in an hour and just as I was moving up his very long but not very toned torso, Fritz said...*>>

The lift doors clunked open. Fortunately it was empty so she stepped straight in but just as the doors were closing, they jolted back open with such a force and noise that she jumped, dropping her phone. Before she'd had a chance to retrieve it she was joined by three other members of staff squeezing in around her.

"Oh, I am sorry, I don't think that there's enough room," she said, looking down at her phone which was about to be trodden on and hoping that the lack of room in the tiny lift would deter them. She was also worried that her breath might smell of the glass of wine she'd had at lunch at Cecconi's.

"That's OK. We'll breathe in!" joked one of the girls, putting Jemima's urgent email to her flatmate Flora on pause once more.

They were squashed in like sardines for the ride up in what Jemima was sure was the slowest lift in Mayfair, if not London.

Once they had shuffled out at the third floor, she picked up her phone, which she saw had a couple of missed calls from an unknown number. When she finally arrived at the fifth floor, Jemima made her way to her desk. Throwing her heavy bag on the floor, her BlackBerry still in her hands, she slung her grandmother's mink on the back of the chair, kicked off her beautiful black Nicholas Kirkwood heels, which she still hadn't paid off on her credit card, and sat down to continue. Just as she was getting to the punchline of her email, the phone rang on her direct line. It was Mr V.

"Hi Mr V... sorry ... yes, I'll pop down now," she said, tapping as fast as she could:

<<*"Was intending not to drink this week, but I've got a date tomorrow night." Can you believe he said that!?*>>

Jemima put the phone down on her desk, retrieved her heels and, telling her assistant Zoe where she was going, started to walk back out of the office again, wishing that she had not had that drink with Ariana, the jewellery editor of *Tatler*. Hair of the dog only made her more exhausted and irritable.

"Oh yes, Mr V did call a few times, as did Anna – sorry, I forgot to tell you..." drawled Zoe, very unapologetically, looking at her Facebook page. Jemima only just managed to ignore her and, taking a deep breath, walked towards the lift. She would not let Zoe annoy her today.

Jemima Fox-Pearl was Global Head of Communications at Vogel;

8

one of the most exclusive jewellers in the world. Mr V was Sidney Vogel, the eponymous founder of the firm, who had begun his life living behind his father's barber's shop in Liverpool, as a child sweeping up the hair that his father cut from the seamen who worked in the docks. He now spent his life, when not flying around the world in his private jet, buying beautiful diamonds and precious stones to create even more beautiful pieces of jewellery.

The Vogel global headquarters were housed in a large townhouse, at 22 Arlington Street, behind the Ritz hotel and overlooking Green Park. It had once been home to a Prime Minster, something which Jemima always imagined Mr V quite liked. The press office was on the top floor, which in the prime minister's day would have been the maids' attics, and was very low and poky. As you descended the floors, however, they became increasingly large and luxurious, with expensive pieces of art adorning the high walls. Mr V's private office was in what would have been the drawing room on the first floor and overlooked the rose beds between the building and Green Park. The Vogel store was on the ground floor next to the reception with a separate entrance from the street. They were in the process of buying another bigger store on the corner of Piccadilly and Bond Street.

Damn, I should have locked my BlackBerry, she thought whilst waiting for the lift, *I bet Zoe will look at what I am doing and I definitely do not want her seeing that email to Flora.*

Zoe Weinberg was an American Park Avenue Princess. Jemima had been so nice to her; too nice probably, when she arrived, and now the former intern was clearly out for her job. Jemima hoped she would not get her way. Mr V had once said he thought Zoe was quite stupid, although he had only met her twice, which was music to Jemima's ears. Nevertheless, there was something about Zoe, which Jemima knew needed to be nipped in the bud. If she was honest it also infuriated Jemima that not only were all her friends engaged, if not already married, but so was her 24-year-old assistant, who loved to show off her Vogel ring which was bought in Manhattan from the store on Fifth Avenue.

Also part of the press office was Noémie Rousseau who was out of the office that day at a fashion shoot. Noémie was a beautiful French woman who had been working for Vogel for some six years. She was part time and only came in to deal with magazine shoots, being normally very occupied with her three beautiful blonde sons.

Flora Fairfax, who Jemima had still not finished the email to, was one of her best friends, her flatmate, and going out with Benjy Pocock – brother of Jemima's on-off boyfriend Fritz. Flora often giggled in delight when hearing of Jemima's rail crash of a love life, now that she had such a stable life of her own.

Fritz, although very good-looking, was very stupid. He desperately wanted to get into finance to prove something to his father but as well as being stupid he was much too lazy to do so. Despite this, Jemima had been happy enough to re-kindle their relationship, but what he'd said that morning had put paid to her dreams of a double wedding with Flora.

Standing waiting for the lift once again, Jemima could feel herself getting more and more worked up at both Zoe's attitude and what Fritz had said to her earlier.

I just cannot believe he said that to me. Once inside, she looked at her reflection in the lift's mirror as she started the slow descent. *I know what Flora will say – I shouldn't have jumped back into bed with him so quickly - but after all the drinks he poured into me I didn't even know I had until I woke up the next day... urgh, I must stop this, harden up and move on. He will only continue to hurt me.*

She looked closely at herself, thinking that despite the late night and horrid morning she didn't look so bad that she should be single at her age. She was tall and slim with golden highlights in her shoulder-length hair which she always wore swept up off her fairly pretty face. She wasn't perfect but she wasn't completely imperfect and she was determined to get a Vogel rock on her finger before too long.

2

The lift arrived at the first floor with a jolt and the noisy doors slammed open, bringing her back to her senses. Jemima crossed the heavily-piled carpet, passing a couple of Picassos, and knocked on Sidney Vogel's door. This was his new office, just refurbished from being a private client salon, and she had not as yet been inside.

The door was opened by Anna Smith, Mr V's PA. Anna was a pretty, petite but neurotic woman in her mid-40s with bobbed brunette hair à la Anna Wintour, her heroine and the Editor-in-Chief of American *Vogue*.

"He's not happy, Jemima, he's been calling your office for hours," she whispered accusingly.

"Zoe didn't mention anything, until I said I was coming down just now. Why didn't you call my mobile? What does he want?" Jemima replied nervously, realising that the missed calls must have been from them. She sometimes forgot that 'Unknown' numbers were more often than not from a Vogel line and not just the bank chasing her for an unpaid credit card bill.

Butterflies playing havoc in her tummy, Jemima wished again that she hadn't had that glass of wine earlier.

"Sit down, I'll be with you shortly," came an eerily calm voice from somewhere Jemima couldn't tell. Other than a huge beautifully polished David Linley oak table, an Apple MacBook, a pretty sparse sideboard, and four huge pieces of what some people might call art on each of the walls, there was nothing else in the room. There was the outside of course; huge French windows looked out over beautiful rose beds to Green Park, but it was raining and she could not imagine Mr V was out there. Anyway, due to the noise of the rain and density of the bullet-proof security glass, no outside voice would be heard.

Jemima sat down on one of the two chairs on the opposite side of the table to the laptop and looked about her. She had never seen such orderliness. The sideboard, also oak, had a candle burning and a selection of colour-coordinated invitations leant against the wall. The candle gave off quite a pungent smell and she recognised that it was the same as those in the boutique. Slightly heady. Tempting. *Diamond-buying-tempting.*

The artworks were definitely of a certain taste. One looked like a giant KitKat wrapper, only omitting the words 'KitKat'. Red and silver foil taking up some three square metres of wall space above the sideboard. On another wall, what could be described as a *trompe d'oeil* was an exact replica of the French windows opposite but rather than reflecting the park outside, the 'view' was of a desert island amidst a sea made from sparkling gems and a shark nose-down in the crystal-simulated sand. It reminded her of the world famous diamond-encrusted shark which was in the Vogel reception – fitting for a company which boasted several sharks amongst its employees. It had been in Mr V's previous office and always reminded her to keep cautious. There was a huge portrait of the man himself by Lucian Freud – more to her liking - and one of Andy Warhol's famous silk screens of Marilyn Monroe.

Suddenly, part of the wall opened and Mr V appeared. He was a fairly tall, slim man with a shock of thick white hair and a faint hint of a Liverpudlian accent. Sidney Vogel was dressed more casually than normal, with a well-pressed white shirt tucked into a pair of stone-coloured Levi jeans. He smiled at her in his usual way and she felt immediately at ease, kicking herself for always thinking the worst. She wondered why everyone appeared so in fear of him; Anna was like a rabbit in the headlights in his presence.

"Jemima," he said slowly as he sat down and, opening a drawer by his waist, pulled out an auction house catalogue, "are you busy this evening?"

Although it was a Monday and she had woken with a hangover, Jemima had been intending to be busy as she was thinking of going over to Fritz's again, putting to death any ideas of his Tuesday night date. But the more she thought about the way he had behaved that morning, the less keen she was on the idea and thought she would actually prefer a night on the sofa chatting with Flora or now, perhaps, a date with her boss?

"No... well, not really."

Mr V raised an eyebrow and she immediately thought she had not given the right answer.

"I would like you to accompany me to an auction at Bothebie's so perhaps you can rearrange whatever plans you may have had?"

The question appeared rhetorical.

"Of course, I am sorry. What time would you like me to be there?"

"We'll leave from here at 7pm, so I will see you downstairs in the reception. I presume you have something to change into? The invitation says Lounge Suits." He looked her up and down whilst pushing a white, embossed invitation across the table. Her outfit of skinny jeans, despite them being her friend's luxury label MiH, with one of Fritz's smaller Savile Row shirts which she had thrown on that morning at his flat, was clearly not up to a Bothebie's *soirée*.

"Of course, I'll pop home." If she was quick she could fit in her blow-dry and really look the part at the auction. Mr V was now pushing the catalogue across the table, open at a page showing a huge rough diamond.

"Good. Now this is what I am interested in. It is a remarkable and mysterious diamond that has come onto the market officially as a rough diamond, although it has been worked on, in so much as it was part of a larger stone. However, it has never before been seen publically."

"Yes, I have read about it; the Vanderpless Diamond. I read that it has the same gemmological origin as the Cullinan."

"Ha!" Mr V laughed. "That probably came from Bothebie's PR team trying to make it go for more. Have you been to an auction before?"

"It's so interesting," Jemima continued, "I love history and it is such a mystery, this old lady auctioning off a huge rough diamond. I wonder how she happened to have it? And no, I haven't ever been to an auction but have been to several of the preview events at Bothebie's."

"Whatever the rumours, I am not that interested in the history of a stone – it is the future which is important. Now, by the time my driver gets us there the auction will be about to start. I will introduce you as my PR. Do not answer any questions, before or after. Smile and leave them to me. Just watch and learn."

"OK. Thank you so much, Mr V. It sounds really exciting."

"It is exciting but also very important that you, being my Head of PR, convey the correct image." Thank goodness she had that Neville's appointment. "Very well. Now run along and read up about the gem if you like. It may, or may not, come in useful."

Just before she opened the door he spoke again. "One more thing Jemima, where were you earlier when I was trying to find you?"

"At a PR lunch with the jewellery editor of *Harper's Bazaar*." Jemima hoped he'd not smelled the wine on her breath.

"I do not want you wasting your time or my money lunching with journalists. I employed you for more important reasons than sitting in Cecconi's as you no doubt were."

With that, she was dismissed. Goodness, what else would she do if she didn't take journalists to lunch? And more importantly, what should she wear later?

3

Paul Pratt was in Anna's office. Paul was the Company Secretary and Head of Human Resources at Vogel; he was relatively new to both the company and the country. He had arrived in early September, with a strong, Jemima suspected largely fake, Irish-American accent, and an air of arrogance more suited to an oil baron. His titles seemed to mean to him that he was second in importance to Mr V; even more important than Alexa Vogel, Mr V's daughter and heir of Vogel, and Danny Vogel, Alexa's son.

Paul was probably someone who had been bullied at school so he used his power to treat Jemima and everyone else as though they were idiots. He would brag about his accomplishments and bore people with tales of his outdoor pursuits as a climber. Social climber more like. He was consequently already not popular in the company and thought of as a meddler by some of the long-standing staff. Paul deemed it important to know about everything that anyone was doing, particularly those things that did not have any relevance to him. Danny and Alexa had very little time for him.

"Aha Jemima, I hear you may have had a Mr V knuckle-rapping session?" Paul sneered, sitting slumped in an uncomfortable-looking chair, his grey suit so shiny that it seemed to reflect the strip lighting above.

Jemima looked at Anna, who was avoiding her by pretending to read a pile of papers on her desk, then back at Paul, who was smirking at nothing in particular.

"No actually, not at all. He was so nice. He invited me to go to the

Bothebie's Christmas auction tonight with him," she said lightly, not unintentionally scratching her head with the corner of the catalogue.

"Really... he seemed pretty agitated that he couldn't find you earlier on," Anna perked up, trying to focus on the catalogue over the top of the glasses which sat at the end of her tiny nose. "I wonder if he is going to buy that diamond I have been collecting articles about, and why he is not taking Danny?"

"He did say that my time was very valuable and that he had lots of plans for me here." Jemima was beginning to enjoy Paul's increasingly worried expression. "Anyhow, I had better get back as I have some research to do before tonight. Have a lovely evening, both of you."

She walked back out of the office and along the corridor to the lift, trying very hard not wobble too much in her uncomfortably high heels.

By the time she had got back to her office, Noémie was there, sitting on the corner of her desk with a cup of tea and chatting to Zoe. Noémie was the person who had warned Jemima about employing Zoe, for exactly the reasons Jemima now felt worried about.

"Tea? I am about to make another – I'm freezing after my day and got soaked coming back from the store." Noémie seemed to drink more tea than the English.

"Oh no, is it raining now?" Jemima asked, worried that having a blow-dry would be a waste of time after all. "And yes thanks, I'd love one but I have to be quick as I have a date with Mr V and need to go home to change!"

She sat down at her desk with her BlackBerry in hand to finally finish and send the email off to Flora:

<<Wish he'd said it while I was sucking the life out of him and I would have bitten it! Anyway, I'm going to go over later in my mink and that La Perla I bought to screw his brains out.>>

"Really!? What are you doing?" Zoe seemed unusually interested, much to Jemima's amusement.

"You know that huge diamond, the Vanderpless? Well tonight is the auction of it at Bothebie's and he's asked me to go along with him. I feel honoured! Anna and Paul were shocked he'd asked me. They're as thick as thieves, aren't they?"

"Oh, I'd be careful with anything that you say to her. Very careful," said Noémie, "Although now she knows that you are the favourite, she'll start courting you! Anyway, tonight sounds great – what are you going to wear?"

Noémie was one of the best-dressed girls in the company, always wearing high street clothes like Top Shop and French Connection but adding a towering pair of designer heels. With her long, glossy dark hair and petite frame, she looked like she had just stepped off a Parisian catwalk. Jemima was sure that she was more interested in clothes than diamonds.

"I have a blow-dry at Neville's which," looking at the clock on her phone, "I am running late for and just a… little black dress!"

Hurriedly, Jemima typed 'F' into her BlackBerry to find Flora's address and pressed 'Send'.

"Oh Jemima, do you want the latest *Tatler* to take with you?" Zoe asked unusually generously. Normally she took all the glossy magazines home with her, once she had pulled out any Vogel press cuttings, which infuriated Jemima who never got to see them.

"Oh thank you, Zoe," Jemima said, smiling, and slipped the magazine into her bag. "Bye, girls!"

"Good luck!" Noémie and Zoe shouted in unison as Jemima grabbed her things and walked towards the lift.

"*Merci*! Ahhh!" she shrieked back as the lift door caught her Christian Dior bag, reopening and closing again with such ferocity that Jemima wondered if even the lifts were programmed to keep employees on their toes.

As she scampered outside, a taxi sped up and almost passed her as though hoping to pick up a wealthy guest, and therefore a handsome tip, at the Ritz. Reluctantly, the driver stopped, and within seconds Jemima was on her way to her first big Vogel occasion, via the most glamorous of hair salons - Neville's on Pont Street.

4

Jemima lived in a mansion block behind the department store Peter Jones, just off Sloane Square in Chelsea, Central London. It was a ten-minute walk from Neville's so she hoped the rain would stop before she had to head back to her flat to change. Being on the top floor, she and Flora liked to think of it as their penthouse apartment, though it was actually a tiny attic flat, with no lift and six flights of stairs to walk up - not quite as glamorous as it sounded. In fact, Jemima seemed to spend most of her life in pokey attics, but at least both her office and her home were in good addresses and easy to commute between by foot or bus. In fact, her flat was in her favourite area and her legs had become toned walking up all the stairs, keeping her fit and saving her from forking out on a gym membership which her paltry salary couldn't afford, so it wasn't all bad.

As she pushed open the heavy glass door into the salon, the noise and hot air from the hair dryers and a plethora of London's poshest chattering away hit her. She walked up to the reception desk to sign in and then sat down momentarily to check her emails before she was taken off to have her hair washed. There was no reply from Flora but she hadn't expected one yet - Flora worked at Stella McCartney and was no doubt busy with the Christmas shopping season. Jemima also remembered that her flatmate was going to a cool fashion party that night in East London.

"Hi Jem," she looked up to see Charlie, her favourite stylist, waiting with a younger boy with bright ruby-red hair. "Dion is going to wash your hair and then we'll do your blow-dry."

"OK, amazing." Jemima got up awkwardly from the low chair and towered over the two guys in her heels. They walked over to the basins, passing a couple of TV presenters and a duchess reading magazines mid-treatment. Jemima handed her coat over to Agnes, the cloakroom attendant, before sitting down and leaning her head back over the washbasin.

Dion must have been new to Neville's. He turned the water on very hot and Jemima squealed as he scorched her head before apologising and turning it down. He then put shampoo on and started very roughly scrubbing her scalp with it.

"Oh Dion, please can you be a bit more gentle?" Jemima asked politely, hating to complain.

"Yeah sure," he said without apologising and she made a mental note to make sure he didn't wash her hair again.

Eventually she got up and, with a towel wrapped around her head, she went over to Charlie's chair and sat down, taking the copy of *Tatler* out of her bag. *Tatler* was by far her favourite magazine. She had been in the social diary, *Bystander*, a few times and she just loved its sense of humour and articles, which were often about people she knew well. There was a page sticking out slightly as though it had been already pulled out and stuck back in so she opened it there to see what it was: <<*What do girls, who have it all, want for Christmas?*>>

There were the usual It girls before she saw a picture of a beautiful girl whom she didn't recognise sitting in a very gold-and-marble-looking apartment.

<<*Petrina Lindberg. 27 years old. Lawyer at NyLon firm Nortakers.*

I am spending a few months working in the London office this Christmas season and I am excited to go down Bond Street to look at all the beautiful jewellery shining out of the windows, but what I really want is for someone to buy me a Vogel diamond.>>

Oh gosh, another spoilt Daddy's girl, Jemima thought, wishing for the millionth time that someone would buy her diamonds.

"Jem – how was your wash?"

"Charlie, he was quite rough and practically scalded my head with the super-hot water."

"Oh babe, I am sorry – it was his first day. I'll have a word with him."

"Don't worry. Anyway, can you just do me a simple but sexy blow-dry. Not too big. Thanks darling!"

"OK, you got it!" Charlie started to get his hairbrushes out while looking at the page open on Jemima's knee. "She was in here a couple of hours ago with her mother. Petrina, that is. Her mother is from Montenegro. I only know that as one of the trainees is also Montenegrin and commented on something they were saying to each other. The father came to collect them - I remember as he ended up paying the bill! He was much older and American."

"How annoying. London doesn't need any more beautiful girls!" Jemima laughed to betray how she felt, although she had known Charlie long enough to know he would see through it.

"Babe, you're beautiful, you just don't see it. And you'll look even more so when I'm done with you."

"Mmmm. Thanks, Charlie!"

Half an hour later, Jemima thought Charlie, almost true to his word, had made her look half way to beautiful. Having paid her heavily discounted bill, she saw that the rain had stopped so she walked back to the flat in Culford Gardens.

As she was now walking up the stairs, she realised that the music she could hear getting increasingly louder was coming from her flat. And it was what only Benjy, Flora's 'very cool' DJ boyfriend and Fritz's brother, would play. That meant he was back from New York and obviously staying with them. For how long? Last time it was a month and the flat was just too small for a third person – particularly such an *obvious* third person. He had better not be smoking weed. She did not want to turn up at the first event she had ever been invited to by her boss, whom she was determined to impress, smelling of marijuana.

"Jem Jem!" he exclaimed, greeting her with open arms. He was definitely on something, although there was no horrid smell lingering around. "I've missed you. Great hair! Neville's, I take it? Date? Finally over Fritz?"

"Ahhh, thanks for the compliment! Neville's, yes of course - where else would Flora and I go?! Fritz and I have actually been seeing each other again; didn't he tell you when he was with you last week?" She wondered if Benjy's face would give anything away when she said this but he remained expressionless. "Anyway, I must run in and out as I'm going to an event with my boss at Bothebie's."

"You know Fritz and I don't chat about love, but that sounds great," Benjy replied unconvincingly. "Listen, I'm driving to meet Flora at a party in Shoreditch. I'll drive you there on the way."

"Really? Are you OK to drive? You seem a little... how should I put it? Stoned? Drunk?"

"Stoned? Jet-lag more likely, though I did have a glass of *rouge* on the *avion*." Clearly Benjy's Franglais hadn't abated since living in New York.

She raced into her room, praying that Flora hadn't borrowed her divine new Reiss dress. It was so perfect. Half Roland Mouret, half Hervé Leger. Opening her wardrobe, which was crammed with clothes, she could just see that it was there on the hanger. It was normally hidden under her grandmother's mink, which she would wear again that night. Jemima congratulated herself on having hidden it there. Flora had become loyal to Stella McCartney's mantra of not wearing any fur or leather - well fur, at least; Jemima had recently found her black leather jeans in Flora's wardrobe.

Having slipped into the dress with her new La Perla underneath, Jemima reapplied her Chanel make-up and chose a pair of shoes which she wouldn't walk awkwardly in. She looked in her long mirror at herself.

She constantly wished she were thinner and fitter. Though her hair needed a good cut, fortunately Charlie had given her a great blow-dry so she didn't need worry about that. Looking closer at her face, she smiled at the memory of splurging in the Chanel concession in Harvey Nichols. She loved the black and white iconic packaging almost as much as the product. But her greeny-brown eyes were looking quite bloodshot and she should have washed her face before reapplying but there was no time so she left her bedroom to find Benjy waiting with his jacket on and speaking to Flora on the phone.

"So I guess I'll get to you at 7.30. Dropping Jem off somewhere on the way. That's good? Cool – see you then, baby."

"Benjy – thanks for this. I guess we're taking Flora's car? I saw it at the top of the street. Here are the keys."

She handed him the Alfa Romeo keyring from the sideboard.

Flora had been given a beautiful vintage Alfa Romeo Spider by her parents for her 30th birthday and only let Benjy drive it with extreme care. Clearly he only obeyed this rule when she was with him, as a hair-raising ten minutes later he screeched up to the Vogel headquarters and almost collided with Mr V's Rolls Royce which was waiting patiently outside with its 'SV1' number plate.

"Right, hon – here you are. See you later, or tomorrow maybe!" Benjy added with a wink.

"Let's see! You had better not let her see you driving like that!" Jemima said, laughing as she attempted to get out of the car elegantly. It was not an easy feat. Despite wearing only kitten heels, her dress was too clingy and the car too low.

Once she had walked inside the main entrance, Jemima used the telephone to call Mr V up in his office.

"Hi Mr V, I'm downstairs and your car is outside."

"Very well, I'll be down in a few minutes."

She thought that she would have a proper look at the diamond-encrusted shark but just as she was gazing at his teeth, her BlackBerry beeped. A text from Fritz. Unusually, she'd forgotten that she hadn't heard from him all day; she normally waited for his texts with bated breath.

<<Can't wait for the fox fur, or will it be granny's mink? Teeth sharpened?>>

Flora wouldn't... she thought before scanning her emails, red-faced. Oh god, the last sent email was to Fritz Pocock, entitled 'AKA NOCOCK'!

Before she could pull out her powder to smother her flushed face, Paul Pratt appeared out of the shadows.

"Jemima, I take it that when you say Mr V, you mean our Chairman?" he asked accusingly.

"Yes, why?"

"It is very disrespectful to call him that in person. You gotta address him as Mr Vogel like everyone else does."

"But that is what everyone calls him."

"Not to his face, Jemima. You really are out of place here, aren't you?"

"Come along, Jemima." Mr V arrived just at the right moment, dressed immaculately in a dark suit and ignoring Paul, who seemed to have slipped back into the shadows.

She couldn't help wonder what on earth Paul was doing, lurking around when everyone else had gone home. He was as dodgy as one of the evil characters from Dallas. She was sure she saw his shadow race up the stairs as she closed the door behind them.

5

Jemima was pleased with her choice of shoes as she chased Mr V up the stairs to the main galleries and the auction. She was relieved that she had managed to hand the mink into the cloakroom while Mr V was being greeted by the auctioneer, Michael Talbot. The redness caused by Fritz's text and her stupidity hadn't been helped by sitting in a fur coat with the Rolls' heating on in the chilly December evening.

The biggest relief was that during the journey to Bothebie's, opposite the American Embassy on Grosvenor Square, which had taken all of seven minutes, Mr V had been on the phone to Danny, talking about the diamond. Jemima was able to calm herself with silent but very deep breaths. She just couldn't believe she could be so stupid, sending the email to Fritz, its subject, rather than to Flora. Bloody predictive text.

On the one hand, she thought that she should rise above it, make it into a joke and go and have another night of love-making. But on the other, maybe she should start to pull back and not be so available - make Fritz think he had lost her. She was still madly in love with him and although to him she played along with them having this on-off relationship, she was truly devastated that he was going out with someone else the next day. The way he had told her was as though she was just a casual thing; his friend even, but with benefits.

Fritz had been her life for a whole year but just after they had split (he had dumped her), she'd got the job at Vogel and so far it had been so intense that she hadn't been able to think of him so much.

Just a few times a day instead of a few times an hour. But then they 'got back together' and she was a bag of nerves from the start, most of the time waiting for any contact from him. She even checked his Facebook page periodically throughout the day to see if he had 'friended' any new girls and if so, who they were.

Jemima snapped back to attention. At the top of the stairs there was a waiter holding a tray with several glasses of champagne and water. She accepted one of the delicious-looking chilled glasses of champagne and smiled at Mr V, following him through the large doors into the galleries. She took a sip and the frothy, creamy liquid slipped down her throat, taking away any thought of what she had done that morning to Fritz, and that silly email. She was at one of the highlights of the Christmas calendar, on the arm of one of the VIP guests. She didn't need small fry like Fritz Nocock tonight.

The auction was not only the Bothebie's Annual Christmas Jewellery Auction but hugely significant this year, due to the inclusion of the mysterious Vanderpless Diamond. It was one of THE events in the London social calendar, attendance by invitation only of course, and included most of London's Russian contingent who, the auction house hoped, would be vying with each other to be seen to spend the most money and therefore bidding up the prices of the pieces of jewellery and watches.

Sidney Vogel was the one of the most important people in the room and he, as well as everyone else, knew it. His purchasing power meant that he and two others were often said to set the global price of diamonds. With such an important diamond coming up for auction for the first time, it was also an indicator to the luxury goods industry of how well, or badly, it was doing. It was also unusually coming onto the public market as a rough diamond; normally a diamond would have been cut and polished but due to its atypical appearance, Bothebie's were auctioning it as it was given to them.

The room was very full. Jemima glanced at the glamorous guests, already sparkling like the Bond Street Christmas decorations. Two seats had been saved for Mr V at the front of the room under the auctioneer's podium. She noticed some sneering looks from women wondering who this diamond-less girl was, making her way to the front row. Being a young woman on the arm of a man old enough to be her father was the only thing which Jemima had in common with the rest of the room. She wished Mr V would let her borrow jewellery when she was representing the company.

Their seats were on the left of the central aisle, Mr V in the right hand chair, and as she turned around to pick up the catalogue from the seat, Jemima noticed the supermodel Sahara Scott sitting two rows behind them. She was one of the most famous models in the world, as well as being the first black supermodel. She also had a reputation for being a diva. Jemima could not help but be blown away by her beauty, despite the model being in her late 60s. Sahara was dressed in a black silk jumpsuit with a white fox fur stole strewn across one shoulder so that only one long dangling diamond earring could be seen, appearing brighter than those on anyone else in the room.

Sahara must have known someone was staring as she looked up and Jemima noticed what looked like a badly covered scar across her left temple, as though it was a line from her eye to the earring below.

How lucky there was airbrushing in magazines; she'd never noticed the scar in any photography. Jemima wondered how Sahara had got away with it before airbrushing was invented and hoped she'd remember to look up some old photography of her on the internet.

Back at the front of the room, Michael Talbot was welcoming everyone to the sale, his polite jokes only attracting a few laughs from the small number of English guests amongst the deadpan Russians. Sidney Vogel was also not laughing, his attention taken by typing an email into his BlackBerry.

Of all the lots in the auction, Jemima had only seen details of the Vanderpless. Alongside images of the diamond there was a copy of its GIA certificate. The GIA (Gemmological Institute of America) is the world's authority on diamond quality and grading. All diamonds have a GIA certificate which includes the Four Cs: grading of cut, clarity, colour and carats, to advise as to its value.

Jemima was still not completely *au fait* with the grading and had so far managed to bluff her way through any difficult questions from journalists. Danny had promised to go through the Four Cs and explain Vogel's criteria when buying diamonds, but each time they had provisionally arranged to do so, one or other was called down to Mr V's office or had to cancel for another reason. She hadn't really minded as the idea of being alone with Danny unnerved her – equally due to his mean reputation as to his devastatingly good looks.

Whilst flicking absentmindedly through the rest of the auction's catalogue, Jemima couldn't help thinking about the fact that she had never gone out with anyone who would buy her any of those pieces of jewellery. Maybe she should be practical and start looking for a man who would actually treat her like a princess. Perhaps she should just forget trying to stop Fritz going on his date; after all, if it wasn't tomorrow it would only ever be another night.

The auction was well underway when she stopped day-dreaming.

"We now come to lot number 15; a lady's Belle Époque diamond and aquamarine wrist watch by Cartier..."

Jemima thought again of Sahara Scott and that terrible scar on her face. It was slightly annoying sitting at the front as you couldn't see what was going on; she would much prefer to be standing at the back to see who was buying what – not that she would know who anyone was. Many were no doubt Vogel clients but the press office and other members of non-sales staff were rarely welcome in the boutique so had next to no contact with clientele.

The gavel came down suddenly and Jemima almost jumped. The main part of the auction had come to an end and, from the pleased faces of Michael Talbot and the members of staff taking telephone bids next to him at the front of the room, it appeared the sale had gone well. A break of a few minutes was announced while the night's star attraction was being fetched from the building's vaults.

Jemima turned to Mr V who was back on his BlackBerry. Goodness, he was BBMing. She was surprised at how technologically up-to-date he was.

"You didn't bid for anything?" she asked.

"I am not here for the small pieces - it is only the Vanderpless which is of interest. Anything take your fancy?"

"Lots of things," she didn't want to admit she had spent most of the last half hour day-dreaming, "but sadly I have not the resources, financially nor romantically, to pay for anything."

"I wouldn't worry. They'll come."

Damn – no Christmas bonus then, she thought as she pulled her own BlackBerry out of her bag. Nothing more from Fritz. Probably a good thing. She decided once and for all not to spring a surprise on him. She just wanted to go to bed early and not be hungover the next day. If Mr V was going to buy the diamond, no doubt she would have to be on the ball tomorrow.

Michael Talbot was back on the podium, trying to get his audience's attention. Jemima glanced over her shoulder and saw that Sahara was still there, glued to her Blackberry. From an entrance to the right of the room came the diamond in its glass box, on a blue velvet cushion, carried by a member of staff and flanked by two security guards.

"Now Lords, Ladies and Gentlemen, we have the star attraction – the Vanderpless Diamond. I need not inform you, as I am sure you will have read all about this mysterious diamond in the newspapers, that at 723 carats it is one of the most important gemmological discoveries of recent years, equal to that of the Cullinan which was discovered in South Africa in 1905. In fact its provenance and appearance is very similar to that of the world's largest and most famous diamond."

"Good luck, Mr V," Jemima whispered excitedly, wondering if he was right about Bothebie's inventing the similarity between the two diamonds. She really did hope that he would 'win' the Vanderpless. She would love to work on the press relations stories and she was fascinated by the mystery, whatever Mr V said.

He nodded without looking at her, his gaze being firmly on the auctioneer who had just lifted the gavel to indicate the start.

"I have a starting telephone bid of… any advances on £35 million?"

The cool Russian crowd gasped as the estimate had jumped from £20 million to nearly double that, before the bidding had even begun. For the next few minutes, Michael Talbot's voice shouted out increasingly high numbers from two bidders. One seemed to be at the back of the room and the other was on the telephone. Jemima looked incredulously at Mr V. She was pretty certain that he had not even tried to bid for this diamond, so why had he come, and why had he brought her? She was also very disappointed, having expected a huge bidding war between Mr V and the Russian oligarchs behind them.

Suddenly there was an extremely load bang from just above her. This time she did jump, thinking it was a gunshot. She was about to fall to the ground, pulling Mr V with her, when she realised it was only the gavel again, smacking down on the rostrum above them.

"That is £55 million from Diana's caller! Tonight we have set a world record in diamond sales!"

"Shall we go?" Mr V said very calmly to Jemima whilst getting up from his seat, the crowd behind them gasping and chattering away in Russian. "Remember, Jemima, watch and learn – not everything is how it appears."

"But…"

"I thought that we would go out for dinner. Danny will join us. Can you get a good table at Annabel's?"

"Yes, of course I can."

"Very well, that is why I hired you. I'll meet you outside where Ivo is waiting with the car."

6

As Jemima made her way past people gathering up catalogues and handbags, she noticed that Sahara had already left her seat. Walking through the next room to the stairs, she saw the model alone, speaking on her BlackBerry in quite an agitated way, her free hand making wild gestures. Had Sahara wanted the Vanderpless Diamond for Christmas, like the girl in the magazine? She had read that Sahara had a much younger Russian boyfriend. She was sure he was an oligarch and had no doubt bought Sahara something almost as expensive, if not the Vanderpless itself.

Jemima pulled out her BlackBerry, scrolled to Annabel's Club, and just as she was about to press the call button she noticed the girl from *Tatler*, Petrina Lindberg. She was with someone who could only be her mother and – could that handsome man be her father? The girl was beautifully dressed, in a peacock-blue knee-length silk dress and sparkling diamonds at both her ears and wrist. She was the spitting image of her mother, who was in a green silk suit. The man looked as though he would have been extremely dashing in his day but must have been in his 70s by now. Petrina was scanning the room like a hawk before she slipped away down the staircase after her parents. Jemima wondered if perhaps someone would buy this beautiful girl a Vogel diamond for Christmas after all

"Hi Douglas, it's Jemima Fox-Pearl. How are you?" Douglas was the first person to greet clients on arrival at Annabel's. He knew every member by face.

"Good Jemima, and yourself? We haven't seen you for a while."

"Actually I am with my boss, Mr Vogel – can we get a good table for dinner tonight?"

"Hold on, I'll put you through to the dining room. See you in a bit I hope."

"Thanks!"

"Good Evening. Annabel's dining room."

"Hello – I am hoping to get a table for three in ten minutes, so around 9.30pm? For Mr Vogel."

"Let me see – we're very busy tonight; although it's a Monday, it's December... but I am sure we can help you when you get here."

Jemima found it amusing that even being one of London's richest and most successful men did not automatically guarantee you at place at London's most glamorous venues.

"Thank you – see you in a bit."

She looked at her messages and a wave of embarrassment came over her once more as she thought about her mis-sent email. It was probably a good thing that she was going out for dinner with her boss, as she couldn't then turn up at Fritz's. She would be distracted from thinking of him by the irresistibly good-looking Danny and arrogantly Fritz would be expecting her, so it would serve him right for being so callous that morning. Let him have his beauty sleep before his big date the next night.

She grabbed her grandmother's mink coat from the cloakroom and went outside, noticing that Mr V was already out of the cold and in his Rolls.

"We did buy the diamond," he announced as she sat down in the warmth. "Danny was the telephone bidder. I was there as a smokescreen; I like to play a game with the other buyers. If they see I am not bidding then they are less likely to, so then we get it at a better price. It is true that people follow my lead when it comes to diamonds and I am very lucky – I have rarely been disappointed by any I have bought."

"But you bought it at nearly three times the estimate."

"The estimate was much too low. But these Russians don't know anything. By going in at that price no one was going to compete and I actually got a bargain."

"A bargain?!"

"Yes. I told you I have a seventh sense when it comes to diamonds. I started thinking about what you said about its provenance. Maybe I was too hard on Bothebie's. It might well come from Cullinan but even if not, its perfection and size make it worth at least what I paid and by paying that much now, when we cut it and turn it into a piece of jewellery, we can charge whatever we like."

Jemima marvelled at the sheer brilliance of her boss. Her crush was purely admiration; nothing more. There was water fountain gossip that he had a way with the ladies but Sidney Vogel had been married for 45 years to Sophie and, as they said in Hollywood, theirs was one of the strongest marriages in the business. Alexa was their only daughter and according to office gossip she had not been so lucky in love. There were rumours that she had once been married and that the marriage produced Danny. Others that he had been conceived during a one-night-stand when she was just 20.

They pulled up at Annabel's, the infamous restaurant-cum-nightclub in Mayfair named after the founder's wife. Jemima's father had been a founding member of the club back in the early 1960s and all the most important family occasions had been celebrated there. Jemima had even managed to split open her chin there, having tripped over a piece of carpet and landed on a silver champagne bucket, blood spewing over a well-known celebrity's table. When asked which plastic surgeon she had gone to, enquirers were amazed to learn that it was the Chelsea & Westminster Hospital A & E who had preserved her looks.

"Good evening Jemima, Mr Vogel," said Bruno the doorman who, having been there for as long as Jemima could remember, was probably the one who had deposited her in the ambulance after her accident.

"Hi Bruno – how are you? Freezing isn't it!"

They made their way down the narrow stairs to the club, which was in the basement of a townhouse on Berkeley Square. Douglas was there to greet them and while Mr V was handing his coat in she saw Danny walking towards them with a huge grin on his face and a glass of champagne in his hand. He was also dressed immaculately in a razor-sharp suit, his chiselled dark features accentuated by the shadows of the corridor.

Jemima, along with having a bit of a crush on him, was quite shy of Danny. The overwhelmingly good but hard looks seemed to go hand-in-hand with his reputation of ruling his department with the same rod of iron as his mother. Like his grandfather, he was a boy wonder in the bling business. Unlike his grandfather, he had been offered it on a plate.

Having returned from Antwerp, where he formally learnt his

predestined profession, Danny was immediately put in charge of the Creative and Production Teams, much to the antagonism of those he was now directing, who did not fancy being told what to do by the 25-year-old grandson of their boss. But he was the apple of his grandfather's eye and could do little wrong. And now, Danny had just secured for his grandfather the most expensive diamond in the world.

"Hi Danny, congratulations!" Jemima said, embarrassingly high-pitched.

"Jemima! How nice to have you with us tonight. I think my mother is coming too – so you will really be part of the family celebration."

Jemima's excitement at spending the night away from the philanderer Fritz, with her boss and his hot grandson, suddenly turned to fear. She had not spent any time with Alexa in the six months that she had been at Vogel. She'd only spoken on the phone a few times with her, and passed her at various times in the boutique, when her smile had more often than not been met with a curt nod.

"Pop, I've got us a bottle of Krug, would you like a glass?"

"Danny, where are your manners? You should ask Jemima first if she would like a glass."

"I'm sure I don't need to!" Danny joked, handing Jemima a very chilled glass of champagne and then one to his grandfather.

The trio raised their glasses before being led to their table, tucked away in a dark alcove.

Jemima loved Annabel's. The service and food were impeccable. She was sure that her 'tripping over an old carpet' was actually management's polite excuse for the fact that she was too drunk. She hadn't remembered what had happened until she awoke the next day and looked in her bathroom mirror, seeing four huge black stitches appearing from her chin like a witch's facial hair. Mortified by her appearance, she had jumped into her car and driven home to her parents' house in the countryside until the stitches were ready to come out.

When Danny's bottle of Krug was brought in a silver champagne bucket to the table, Jemima examined its rim to see if there were any indentations. It had been eight years but if the scar was still there then maybe the dents were too.

The waiter brought the large A3-sized menus and announced the dinner specials.

"For the Christmas season tonight, we have as a starter Pressed Terrine of Goose Liver, Pickled Beetroot and Granny Smith Apple Purée. We have two special Mains this evening: Roast Norfolk Bronze Turkey with Chestnut Stuffing or Venison Wellington with Swede Purée and Red Wine Jus."

Jemima was unusually sober for a night out in Mayfair and incredibly hungry; however, wanting to impress the Vogels, she decided to go for much lighter choices and chose a mushroom *consommé* with quail egg, followed by *filet* of halibut and baby leeks. She also wanted to make sure that, should Alexa arrive, she did not look greedy. Women were often competitively interested in what other women ate.

As if on cue, in walked Alexa and, not having to walk up and down endless stairs that evening, she strode into the dining room in the highest of heels as though she owned the place. She wore a knee-length black silk Yves Saint Laurent dress, backless with only a thin strip of diamonds running down her spine. In her ears were a pair of diamond hoops and around her left wrist a bracelet with huge diamonds more usually set in a necklace. Jemima felt like the poor relation again, sitting once more amongst a room full of diamond-clad women. Again, she wished that, like her contemporaries at other fine jewellery houses, she had a few signature pieces to wear.

Alexa thanked the *maître d'*, who brought her to the table and waited while her father and son stood up to greet her before sitting down and turning to Jemima.

"Aah Jemima, finally we get a chance to talk. What do you think about our news?"

"I think it is really exciting," Jemima was desperate not to say the wrong thing.

"It will be, yes. We are going to have to decide how to announce it," Alexa said then, turning to her father and son, "I think that we may get complaints when we say that we intend to re-cut it. People are ridiculously protective and interfering about things like this. Jemima, tomorrow we will talk about all of this. For the moment, let's enjoy the evening. Danny, please pour me a glass of that Krug. I don't know why the waiter hasn't done it already. Have you all ordered?"

The next hour went by quickly. They talked a little about work but mainly what plans they had for Christmas. Jemima said that she was going to Cape Town on Boxing Day for ten days.

"Cape Town? Good for you, getting some sun in this dismal winter."

41

Alexa put Jemima's fears that this was the wrong time to be taking a sunny break to rest.

"I used to live there and try to get back when I can. It is one of my favourite places and I've got lots of friends there," Jemima explained.

"You must visit the Cullinan mine when you are there. I don't suppose you have been to a mine before?" Mr V said, interested and relaxed after a glass of champagne.

"No, I haven't – but I would love to."

"Yes, you must. Speak to Anna in the morning and she can organise it for you."

"Thank you – it sounds brilliant!"

"Good. Now I am going to go home. Tomorrow will be a busy day and at my age, I need to sleep!" Mr V joked. It was well known that he needed very little sleep and often woke in the early hours to do business deals with the Far East.

"I'll come with you, Dad. Danny, will you make sure Jemima gets a taxi home, and don't be too late, you two – as Dad said, it's going to be a big day tomorrow."

"Thank you so much for a lovely evening, I hope that I won't put too many backs up in the office tomorrow," Jemima answered, slightly drunk from the champagne and the evening's excitement.

"You don't have to tell anyone, Jemima. What you do outside work hours is no one's business but yours." Alexa smiled.

With that, they left Jemima and Danny at the table with another, almost full, bottle of Krug to share.

"So have you got a boyfriend?" Danny asked, almost before his mother was out of earshot.

"Wow, that was to the point, Danny! Not really, no." Jemima was feeling increasingly attracted to Danny who, although he had barely said a word during dinner, kept on looking at her. Earlier, when he went off to talk to a beautiful girl at the bar, she had felt oddly jealous. "Have you got a girlfriend?"

"A few!" he replied

"Oh," she said, disappointment ringing in her head.

"Here, have some more champagne," he said, laughing and pouring her a huge glass. "Let's have a dance."

"Danny, you are much more fun than I was led to believe," Jemima teased, taking such a huge gulp of Krug that the bubbles went up her nose. She followed him from the table, trying not to sneeze.

As they weaved their way through the tables to the tiny dance floor at the back of the room, Jemima looked about her. Annabel's was always decorated so beautifully for Christmas. Fairy lights covered the ceiling like a sky full of stars, the various pillars dotted around had ivy wrapped around them and holly berries strewn amongst it, giving the impression of a sort of Christmas garden. She recognised several faces of friends, and those of London figures; the latter group with women who were definitely not their wives, and some from the auction that night.

It was only as she was dancing with Danny that she noticed Fritz's parents having dinner with a group of friends. She hoped that they hadn't seen her; she really didn't want Fritz knowing that she was there, although she should not care what he thought of her. After several tracks, they went back to their table and Jemima saw Petrina Lindberg, sitting near the back of the room. Petrina's feline eyes appeared to be following Danny as he led the way back to their table. After a few minutes, Jemima said that she should go home. She was worried that this strange but beautiful girl would come and take Danny off for a dance. She also wanted to do a good day's work the following day. Danny got the bill and, having retrieved their coats from the cloakrooms, they headed up outside to get a taxi.

"Thanks for such a fun night, Danny. See you tomorrow."

"I'll drop you home – where do you live?"

"Sloane Square – you?"

"St John's Wood – different direction but no matter!"

"Don't worry, it's easy to get a taxi back home."

As she was about to get inside the taxi waiting at the kerb, the doorman holding open the door, Danny leant forward to kiss her and placed the most arousing kiss on the corner of her mouth.

He whispered, "Come back with me."

"No Danny, don't be silly. You're drunk and I work for your grandfather. It will only end in tears."

She quickly jumped inside the black cab and went home, her heart beating fast in excitement and a huge smile on her face.

7

"Jemima, Mr Vogel would like to see you in his office." Anna's voice trilled down the line.

Jemima had woken that morning with such a hangover and she could just about remember Danny attempting to lure her back to his flat in St John's Wood. Thank god she had been sober enough to resist. She hoped that his crashing and burning would not turn against her and that she was not being called down because of some issue to do with the previous night.

She rushed to the bathroom to apply the make-up that she hadn't had the time to do before leaving her flat. She'd even taken a taxi into work as she just could not face the cold while waiting for the bus. Now she wished she had as it always woke her up after a late night.

Zoe was sitting smugly at her desk. She rarely wore any makeup and still looked bright-eyed and bushy-tailed, but then she did seem to have such a boring life, even though she was seven years younger than Jemima.

Jemima was relieved that she had worn her brightly-patterned Diane Von Furstenberg wrap around her dress so it would distract from her tired face.

Five minutes later and five floors lower, Jemima knocked at Mr V's door, only for it to be opened by the peremptory Paul Pratt.

"Paul, how nice to see you," she said sarcastically, which fortunately seemed to pass him by, probably because he believed that no one would dare to be anything but obsequious towards him.

She walked into the room to see both Danny and Alexa there too, seated in the permanent chairs on the other side of the table to Mr V. She managed to avoid looking at Danny and immediately turned to her boss. "Good morning."

"Hello Jemima, can you go next door and get a chair so you can sit down? We need to talk about how we are going to announce our purchase of the diamond."

As she went through one of the side doors to the boardroom, she realised that Danny was behind her.

"Let me help you," he said, loudly enough for it to be heard back in the office, then more quietly, "I'm sorry that you didn't come back with me – I was lonely when I woke up this morning in my big bed."

"Danny, please. You're putting me in a very difficult situation," Jemima whispered back quietly. "I love working here, I have wanted to since I gazed in wonder at the yellow diamonds in Harrod's years ago, knowing that I would never own any. I really don't want to screw it all up because of a fling with you."

"It might not be a fling; then you would get to wear them - whatever you like, for that matter - forever."

"Stop it. We both know that is impossible! And I can carry my own chair," she replied, intentionally grumpily. An affair with Danny could only go one way – with her having to leave the company.

"Shut up! Let me carry your chair."

Back in the office, both father and daughter were on their respective BlackBerries. Alexa was standing by the big windows, again towering in high heels. Mr V was in his swivel chair, facing away from the rest of them so that he looked like a Bond villain. Paul didn't have his phone so sat looking awkward.

"OK," Mr V said at last, swinging around in his chair, "so far all that has been said is that an unknown buyer bought the diamond via telephone last night at Bothebie's. Of course speculation is rife that it was me and all of our telephones have been ringing off the hook. Jemima, I believe you have received several calls to this effect from the press?"

"Yes. I've got Zoe to take messages because I've not as yet been briefed as to what I should say - so this meeting will be helpful. Someone even asked if it is similar to the Cullinan and suggested you should give it to the Queen for her Diamond Jubilee in a couple of years!"

"Who is Zoe?" Alexa asked.

"Zoe is my press office assistant." Jemima replied.

"Jemima, you have your assistant answering your calls?! I wonder if perhaps the reception should direct all calls through to me?" Paul Pratt said slyly, "We want to make sure that the right message is relayed and we do not want anything to be said that isn't true."

Jemima looked at him, dumbfounded. She could feel Danny staring at her for her reaction. She flicked her eyes to see him smile knowingly and shook her head slightly in disbelief.

"Paul, this is a press matter and Jemima is quite up to dealing with it," Alexa said, with no facial expression.

Maybe I made a good impression on her last night, Jemima thought with some relief. Ignoring the put-down, she turned to Mr V.

"How would you like to release the story? And what should we say about its mysterious provenance, as I am sure that will be a point that keeps arising?"

"I think that the best thing would be," Alexa stepped in, "to ignore all rumours, except saying that it was part of a New York family estate, the Vanderplesses'. That we will be re-cutting it because the current cut is very antiquated, so much so that it could have been done centuries ago and that not only is it chipped but it is too huge at 723 carats to be worn. I do not think we will make any reference to its origins. And with regards to its name, it is the Vogel Vanderpless."

"I agree with you, Mum," Danny replied. "Jemima, any help that you need, please just call me. And this all reminds me that I have never gone through the Four Cs with you. Can you come to my office around 4pm today?"

With all eyes on her there was no chance to say no but after last night she didn't really want to be with him in his office alone.

"Of course." She smiled.

"Good," Mr V said, clearly finishing the meeting. "Jemima, will you also please prepare me a draft statement? I think that we need to release something before noon."

"Yes, I'll get onto that straight away."

Sitting at her computer with the auction catalogue by her keyboard, instead of concentrating on the release, she started thinking about Danny. He was so different from her usual boyfriends. Why not have a 'no strings attached' affair? Except of course there were strings attached. Vogel strings that, if damaged, could prove detrimental to her career.

She was brought back to reality by the light on her BlackBerry flashing red. She'd just checked her emails so clearly it was a text. For the first time all day she wondered if it was Fritz. It was.

<<What happened to the fur n'fuck??>>

She suddenly felt very sorry for the girl Fritz was going to take out later that night. If she knew who it was, she could put her off wasting a night out with such a cad. She probably did know the girl; the London single scene was increasingly small when you got to your 30s and Fritz didn't go for 20-year-olds! She should probably ignore him but she just couldn't resist replying.

<<It fucked off.>>

<<Shame>>

What an answer, she thought. Oh well, same old story. She just hoped that whoever the girl was shared his sense of humour. Jemima knew that she needed to move on and find someone like Danny Vogel, who would help her make a success of her life.

Back to the press release. After several drafts and lots of running up and down the stairs to Mr V's office, the release was ready to go out to the press. Within minutes of putting it out on the internet newswire, her email inbox had filled up with requests for interviews or more information. There were lots from people complaining about Vogel re-cutting and renaming the diamond, saying that it had been like that for too long and would be losing its history.

Then there was an email about the diamond being the lost part of the original Cullinan Diamond. Jemima stopped scrolling through the others and opened this one immediately.

<<Dear Ms Fox-Pearl, Please, I have reason to believe Mister Vogel has purchased the missing part of the famous Cullinan

Diamond found near here over a century ago. We would like to interview Mr Vogel about this. Sincerely, Mr Walter Nquyu>>

His email stated that he was the editor of the *Pretoria Post*. Mr V would never agree to the interview but she was sure he would give a quote.

How interesting that this man said that it was not only from the same mine but also had actually been part of the Cullinan Diamond. How could that be? Jemima was about to Google the new lead, as she was apt to do with anything, but she decided she would first get a quote from Mr V and then bring up the story in the meeting she had with him later. He was sure to be interested as this would be an incredible story. The diamond he had bought not only came from the same mine but was from the same diamond. Maybe she would finally get a front cover news story; the pinnacle for any PR.

She phoned his direct line, too excited to wait until their 3pm appointment. "Hi Mr V, I know that I am coming down to see you in a bit but it would be great to get a quote from you about the diamond and that it…"

"Who wants a quote and about what?" he replied in an unusually brusque tone.

"Ummm," suddenly the idea of asking him for a quote about a long lost diamond for a man from the *Pretoria Post* seemed like it would sound better being asked for in person.

"The… *Financial Times* have asked for one and I know how you much you regard the paper," Jemima lied, knowing that the only paper he would think worth answering was the *FT*.

"Put the journalist through," he said impatiently.

"There isn't one to put through but am sure I can get hold of her, she just emailed me." Jemima kicked herself under her desk for lying.

"I don't have time to think up these things, Jemima, that is what I pay you for."

"Ummm, OK..." she knew that whatever she said, she would be told later that it was wrong. She didn't understand why his mood had monumentally changed. Wow. The guy had just bought the most important diamond in the world for a so-called cut price... he should be happy!

"OK Jemima, just say what Alexa said this morning, that we are re-cutting it as it is much too big and the current cut is too old; it doesn't do the diamond any justice. It is all in the release we have just written. These journalists are very stupid."

"OK, thanks Mr Vogel," she spoke more formally than normal due to his mood, but to an empty line, as he had already slammed the phone down.

She hoped that he would be less impatient in their meeting later.

However, at 2.50pm she got a call from Anna and was smugly told that Mr Vogel had left for the day but would call in the morning. Jemima was relieved, however, as her hangover was getting worse and Zoe was out at a jewellery shoot - a pain as Jemima could have really done with some help fielding calls before her meeting with Danny. She was also starving, having been unable to pop out to Prêt à Manger and she knew that they had her favourite Classic Tomato Soup on, having seen it on the board when she got her morning soya cappuccino.

"Tea?" Noémie asked, having just walked in from a different shoot, looking as chic as ever in high-waisted charcoal velvet palazzo pants and a matching cropped velvet jacket. Jemima couldn't help but wonder why she never found these items in TopShop.

"Yes thanks! I would love one! And are there any custard creams? I'm starving."

"Here you go, I grabbed some on my way in! The shoot was very dull."

"I've been here for six months and I still haven't been on a shoot – I really should one day. Which would be fun?"

"Well we've got a *Russian Vogue* one with Sahara Scott coming up in the New Year."

"Oh my god – Sahara Scott was at the auction last night... I think with her Russian toyboy. The room was full of Russians, anyway. It seems that they are the only ones who buy jewellery nowadays, even at auction. Us Brits are so poor! Except Mr V who, by the way, bought the diamond after all."

"Goodness, I forgot! You must tell me all about it. Hang on though, while I make our tea."

Five minutes later, Noémie was perched on Jemima's desk, listening to her regale about the previous night. Not missing out a single detail, Jemima couldn't help mentioning that she was almost pounced upon by Danny Vogel. She could trust Noémie, who was above office politics. Noémie also knew all about Fritz and had always teased Jemima about her crush on Danny.

As if he could hear her three floors down, Jemima's line rang, Danny's name appearing on the display.

"Damn, I'm late for Danny!" before picking it up, "Hi Danny, sorry - just coming, I was on the line to Mr V."

"Well that is odd as so was I, on the phone to him in his car. So are you avoiding me?" He feigned hurt.

"Not at all! Coming down now!" she said, dropping the handset on her desk in haste, getting up from her chair and then replacing the phone in its base.

"What are you going to see him for? To carry on where you left last night?" Noémie teased jokingly.

"Shhh – you mustn't tell anyone. Particularly not Zoe. I don't trust her with anything."

"I told you... but of course I won't, as long as you promise to keep me updated on all and any developments!" Noémie winked at Jemima.

"There will not be any developments. I am sure he has a girlfriend and is playing with me for his own weird amusement. Anyway, gossip girl – I am going to come on that shoot with you. Let me know when it is, asap. Hopefully it's not when I am in South Africa. See you in a bit!"

8

The security at Vogel was extremely tight. Each door had its own code and on some floors the code was kept secret, known to only a select few. Anyone else had to press a buzzer to gain entrance - which could be denied of course, thanks to the CCTV cameras situated above the doors. These were the gemstone floors.

Having been granted access to the third floor, where the Design and Merchandising departments worked under Danny's beady eye, Jemima crossed the floor to where his office was. As she walked past each person, their heads barely moved, bent over papers, or pieces of jewellery being weighed or looked at through a jewellery loupe.

"Come in," he said when Jemima knocked.

She pushed open the unusually light door to a room that looked like it would have fitted well in the depths of a bank vault. Opposite were three thick safe doors, some eight foot in height and one foot thick, standing ajar, each revealing a column of small drawers. A couple of drawers were open to reveal examples of Vogel's jewellery.

Danny was on the phone with the speaker on and, with a smile and a wink, waved her in to sit down on the other side of his desk while picking up the handpiece for privacy – not that the call seemed to need it.

"So, what are we going to do tonight? Hit some bars? I'm over Movida and Cavendish, I'm always bumping into the kids of clients... OK sure, but are you a member – I guess they're strict, what is it like?... Sounds a bit dull?... Done, we can check that place out and then see what we feel like? See you later, mate."

Danny called off and casually dropped the handset into its base. As Jemima had just done with hers, it missed and clattered onto his desk. She couldn't help but giggle. Perhaps they weren't that dissimilar after all.

"Jemima," he said, pretending nothing had happened and with the air of someone much older than a 25-year-old, "how is it all going with the press?" Before she had a moment to answer he continued, "Are you a member of Soho House, by any chance?"

"No, just the Electric in Notting Hill, but my friend is Nick Jones's PA."

"And who is he?" Danny spoke as though he was obviously someone with little or no importance.

"The owner."

"Aaah. Well if you can get me membership then I won't try to kiss you again."

"And if I don't?" Jemima smiled. She could give as good as she got, and wasn't sure that she didn't want him to try and kiss her again anyway. "They're quite strict on who they let become members. You have to be in the media or be creative, they don't like City guys. Plus there's a committee and quite a list to get through each month." Jemima knew this because Etty, her friend, was always explaining the process to people when they found out what she did and wanted immediate access.

"Well if you are as good as my grandfather thinks you are then I am sure you can fix it for me."

"I'll look into it. You might find it a bit different to what you're used to."

"You do that. Now, before our lesson begins... are you sure you won't come out for a drink with me one night soon? What are you doing later?"

"I'm having an early night. I was tired when I woke up and today hasn't really helped – I've had endless emails from the press and calls. And I have been the only one in the press office."

"It's tough at the top, Jemima. Don't I know it!" he laughed at himself. "I am not going to let you go on a break without coming for a Christmas cocktail with me, so pick your night. Tonight it would be safety in numbers as I'm going out with that mate I just spoke to."

"Not tonight Danny, and anyway, I am perfectly able to defend myself from your clutches. Now we must get on with this as I need to find out what is going on with the news stories around the Vanderpless."

"OK, you're right. Let's get on so you can spread the word to the millionaire masses! What do you know of diamonds?"

"I did start a gemmology course, but when I mentioned that to Mr V he said that I would learn more on the job. Anyhow, I was a bit frustrated with how slowly it seemed to go. We hadn't progressed on to diamonds or gemstones; we were just looking at pieces of glass really. So I gave up."

"Fortunately I knew enough from my grandfather and mother to bypass that part of gemmology, but it can be helpful. Anyway, I'll take you through the basics, what we call the Four Cs. Then we can go through what Vogel is about – the smaller signature pieces, and have a look at some larger pieces which are exceptional to us."

With that, Danny diligently went through what made a diamond a Vogel diamond.

"Diamond grading is based on Carat, Clarity, Colour and Cut, which also define what the diamond is worth. The Carat of a diamond, or any gemstone or pearl, is its weight. The word comes originally from the Greek *kerátion*, meaning carob pod or seed, which were used in the ancient times as a unit of weight. So, the higher the Carat, the larger the gemstone. The Clarity of a diamond is measured by how many natural inclusions or markings the gem has in it. The fewer the inclusions visible under a jeweller's loupe or microscope, the higher the clarity grading. We only deal in the highest categories – Flawless or Internally Flawless." Danny passed Jemima a ten-carat brilliant cut white diamond and his tiny loupe. She looked into the stone, which was as pure as ice, seeing its facets which created such light.

Because Jemima's initial obsession with Vogel was down to the enormous sunflower-like yellow diamonds she had seen in the display cases in Harrod's, she already knew about the importance of colour, and the many variations other than white or colourless. A white diamond allows more light to pass through it than a coloured diamond and sparkles more. The cut of the diamond accentuates the sparkle even more. The millennia-old creation of a diamond ensures that only a few rare diamonds are purely white. The whiter a diamond's colour, the greater its value.

"However," Danny continued, "fancy coloured diamonds do not follow this rule. They can be any colour, from blue to red to bright yellow, and are very rare and very expensive. They are in fact all the more valuable for their colour. Red being the rarest and most valuable. My grandfather was always annoyed that he lost out on the largest and most valuable red ever found! I think it was one of the only diamonds he ever really wanted that he didn't get!"

"Why, who got it?" Jemima asked

"Moussaieff has it. They bought it about ten years ago. It is worth about £15 million and apparently is incredible."

"Red doesn't really suit me," Jemima said vacantly.

"Well that is lucky!" he laughed, making her face flush. "No, you're right, it doesn't suit you! Stop blushing and concentrate. The grading of white diamonds is done against the GIA's colour scale; beginning with D, as the highest rating, and travelling through the alphabet to Z. Vogel only deal with the top two: D and E. However, it is the cut of a diamond that many believe is the most important of the four criteria. A good cut gives a diamond its brilliance, which comes from the very centre of a diamond. The angles and finish are what determine its ability to handle light and consequently brilliance."

Of course Vogel had some of the best diamond cutters in the world, who all the other diamond houses tried to poach. Mr V used a team on Saffron Hill in Hatton Gardens, the less glamorous epicentre of London's diamond industry, which would be home to the Vogel Vanderpless as it took on its new form and the same brilliance as the other Vogel diamonds.

After half an hour or so, Danny asked if she would like to have a look around the workshops, somewhere she had not yet been.

"I'd love to!"

"Great, but beforehand I am going to show you a secret which only four of us in the family, plus the head designer, have seen."

"OK..." she replied, unsure of what on earth it could be. She followed him out of his side door to the back stairs and down a floor to where the head designer worked alone whenever there was a special secret commission.

Danny opened another key-coded door. Inside, bent over a high drawing table, was Sally - the tall, dark-haired designer.

"Sally, hi – I want to show Jemima your drawing for the Vogel Vanderpless necklace."

"Oh yes, sure," Sally said, frowning slightly, probably due to the utmost secrecy in which she had been working. She was effectively locked into the room without her mobile phone and its camera so she had to call to be let in and out. This was Vogel's way of ensuring no one found out about the destiny of the world's most expensive diamond before it was revealed. Jemima looked at the drawing and was blown away by its sheer beauty. She would be happy enough to have just this watercolour design, let alone the necklace itself.

It was a huge diamond necklace painting drawn with such precision, each facet of each diamond was marked and she could see each as though it were real. It really seemed as though the necklace sprung off the page, almost longing to be worn. At the bottom of the piece, an enormous pear-shaped diamond hung low and Jemima wondered if its weight might pull down the head of whoever the lucky woman was who would eventually wear it.

"But Mr V; well you, Danny, only just bought the diamond last night. How could you have done this so quickly?"

"We always knew we would get this so Sally has been working on the design since the moment Bothebie's announced the sale," Danny proudly explained. "We wanted it to go straight to the workshops so they could get on and cut the stone to create this in a matter of months."

"Oh my goodness!" Jemima exclaimed, her eyes unable to move from the drawing.

"Well you must not mention a word of this to ANYONE or we will both be fired. I am sure my grandfather didn't want me showing you! Anyway, we had better go before he discovers us in here!"

They said goodbye to Sally and headed off to find a taxi to take them to the workshops in Saffron Hill.

Jemima couldn't believe how different the street was to where the head office and store were. It was narrow and dark with rubbish on the ground and a small greasy spoon café on the corner. They pulled up outside a small, insignificant-looking door and got out. Once through the heavily-coded steel door entrance and signed in by a security guard, they made their way down a narrow, dirty stairwell to the workshops in the basement. Jemima had never seen anything like them. On the worktops there were piles and piles of both polished and unpolished white diamonds, coloured diamonds, pink, yellow and blue sapphires, emeralds and rubies. They really did look like piles of coloured sweets. There were settings of necklaces which had not as yet been set and looked like pieces of scrap metal. Calendars and pictures of Page 3 girls adorned the walls, eyes gazing down at the jewels that they would never wear. Danny took her around the different stages of making a piece of jewellery and she saw how the metal started to take shape once filled with the colourful stones which had looked so unreal in their unpolished, unfinished state.

The men's eyes followed her through the rabbit warren that was the work studio, seemingly undressing her as she marvelled at their wares, as though they had never seen a woman before. It reminded her of Fritz. He had made her feel so cheap. She felt like having a fun night and moving on from him. He was, after all, out on a date later.

"OK Danny," she said as they were getting a taxi back to the office, "let's go for a drink after work. Where shall I meet you? We can't be seen leaving the building together."

"I knew you couldn't resist me after seeing all the diamonds! Ha! Let's go to the Dorchester for champagne and then we'll go and find my mate, wherever he is."

"See you there!" she said as they were pulling up under the big green flags, Mr V's Rolls arriving at the same time. Danny got out to talk to him so she dashed through the staff entrance.

By the time she got back up to the press office, Noémie had already left, but Zoe was back from her photo shoot, sitting at her desk again, glued to Facebook.

"Zoe, how did the shoot go and which pieces did they use?"

"Hey Jemima, it went really well. They used the emerald ring and earrings and also the white and yellow diamond tennis bracelet. I've got to go as Ned is downstairs waiting for me. We're going to a show later with my Mom who's over from the US."

"OK great, well, well done today. I hope it wasn't too boring. Though you do seem to enjoy reading magazines all day! Have fun tonight."

"Thanks!" Zoe said, not noticing the jibe Jemima had made. She almost ran into Paul Pratt, who was coming out of the lift. "Sorry Paul!"

Oh goodness, thought Jemima, *what does he want now?*

"Hi Paul."

He came into the room as Jemima was glancing through her emails. She looked up and again couldn't help noticing that he was probably the worst dressed employee at Vogel. With his high salary she was always surprised at what he wore. He was dressed in a very grey, very shiny suit, with a black shirt underneath, and black trainers.

"Jemima. Would you please give me an update on all press enquiries." This was an order rather than a question.

"I've not had a chance to update Mr V yet as he had to go out and I have to run off to a meeting. Can I do it tomorrow?"

"Who are you meeting?" As if it was any of his business.

"A journalist." She spoke through clenched teeth.

"Has our Chairman given you permission to meet a journalist about this yet? I think not."

"It has nothing to do with this. I am meeting a jewellery editor who is also a friend." She really was infuriated when he used 'our Chairman' when everyone else called him Mr V and anyway, why on earth was Paul so incredibly determined to be so involved?

"And expensing it?"

"No Paul," she sighed obviously, "but it is important to keep up relationships with these people so they include us in their magazines. This is part of my job," she replied, knowing that Mr V had actually said that he didn't want her to waste time with magazines. "I'll email you a list of who has expressed interest first thing tomorrow."

"Good, Jemima, I am sure our Chairman will be expecting it."

"Yes, Paul. I am seeing him first thing. In fact I want to tell him about an interesting email that I got today."

"Why, what was interesting about it?"

"Someone from South Africa sent me an email saying that the diamond was part of the famous Cullinan and asking Mr V for a quote!" Immediately she knew that she shouldn't have told him.

"Who have you told about this?" Paul replied rapidly.

"Paul, what is it with the 20 questions? I'll tell Mr Vogel all of this in the morning," she said as patiently as impossible, amazed by his persistent interest. "Let's leave – I need to lock the office."

"Please forward me that email."

"OK." Of course she wasn't going to forward him the email; she didn't want him nosing around upsetting nice humble journalists from Africa.

She walked past him to the lift, wondering for the millionth time since she had started at Vogel why, with such a senior position, Paul didn't have his own business to deal with. She was relieved that it was not just herself he bothered, but most heads of department. She might even mention it to Danny later and ask his advice.

It was raining again as she stepped outside into the dark December night. The downpour only increased her excitement about going to the beach in Cape Town and seeing her South African friends. Lots of the familiar London social crowd would flock to Cape Town for New Year too. This year she was invited to Carter Lewis' New Year's Eve party, the invitation of the Cape and always guaranteed to be an amazing night.

Fortunately, and unusually for a rainy December night, there was a cab passing, having dropped off people at the Caprice, the infamous restaurant next door, so Jemima flagged it down and jumped inside, directing the driver to the Dorchester. She was looking forward to some flirting with the dangerous Danny.

When they arrived at the impressive hotel on Park Lane, Jemima paid the cab driver and thanked the doorman, who chivalrously held the heavy door open for her to go inside. Like Annabel's had the previous night, the hotel gleamed with Christmas decorations, the pinnacle of which was the enormous tree in the foyer. She wondered as she walked past if she would ever have a room that would require such a big tree. Opposite the entrance was a long walkway, called The Promenade, from which the various bars and restaurants sprung. She had forgotten to ask which bar Danny meant but assumed it was the champagne bar half way up on the left.

Jemima had butterflies again flying around her tummy and the feeling that what she was doing was not a good idea. She knew that things were going to become more than just a few glasses of champagne but it felt like the train she had got herself on wasn't going to be stopping anytime soon.

Walking into the bar, she saw him sitting with a bucket of ice and a bottle of champagne - a glass, half full, in front of him while he sat fiddling with his BlackBerry. Goodness, he was sexy. It wasn't just the arrogance he epitomised. He dressed so well and had the most chiselled cheekbones imaginable with a big but elegant Greek nose. He could quite easily have made it as a Ralph Lauren model if his grandfather hadn't lured him into diamonds.

As though sensing she had arrived he looked up, smiled, and came over to her, kissing her on the cheeks. Wow, he even smelt amazing

– she recognised one of Dior's men's fragrances.

"I wondered if you were actually going to come," he teased, although half serious.

"I was cornered by Paul. Why has he got it in for me? I don't really understand his criteria. It's as though he is trying to catch me out on something but what, I just don't know. Mr V seems to really like me so why is Paul - and sometimes Anna too - being so annoying?"

"Have a glass of Krug and it'll seem less of an issue, but basically I think that they are both jealous that Grandpa rates you highly. Particularly Anna, who wants to be the office darling and in on all his affairs. She's probably pissed off that it is you that he chooses for events like the auction. I guess Anna has Paul's ear, and vice versa."

"This is delicious, Danny, thank you – just what the doctor ordered!" Jemima sighed after taking a huge glug of Krug. "It seems so silly. He was demanding to know who from the press had been requesting information about the diamond. I don't really understand why he was hassling me about it all."

"Yes, he was asking me about when the diamond was coming to the office as he wanted to see it. I thought it quite odd when it is at Saffron Hill – obviously my grandfather hadn't told him. However, I would just go along with what he wants and don't antagonise him. Everyone has problems with him, though - I've heard he slags me and my mum off and likes people to think that he is Grandpa's confidante. Which he is not, by any means. Anyway, enough of him and work. Let's have some fun."

Jemima felt a sense of warmth spreading through her body, despite the cold champagne. Danny seemed to be so sweet but she just wished he was a little kinder to his staff. She was determined to enjoy the evening and put aside any morals she had about work relationships. She'd just see how the evening panned out and anyway, his friend would be joining them before too long.

The bar was heaving with pre-Christmas drinkers but fortunately Jemima hadn't spotted anyone she knew. After some time, it appeared that Danny's friend was not going to turn up, which she couldn't help but not mind. She was having so much fun with Danny, although her mind did occasionally wander to Fritz. She wondered what he was doing with this new girl and where they were.

"I'm just going to the bathroom, sweetheart," Danny said, bringing her back to the present.

She pulled out her BlackBerry and saw that she had a Facebook message from Marike, her best friend in South Africa with whom she was staying after Christmas.

<<*Babe, howzit? So happy you're coming to stay so soon. Already tons of hot boys on the beach and a bunch of new places opened up for summer. See you in three weeks!*>>

Jemima was going to reply but saw Danny was walking back and, although he was talking to one of the waiters, she didn't want to look as though she wasn't totally focused on their date, which it seemed to have become.

"We're leaving," he said, standing by the table

"Oh, is something wrong?" she asked, always assuming the worst. She grabbed her things and stood up unsteadily, the champagne going to her head.

"No. I've got a key," he announced, as though it was the most normal thing in the world.

If Jemima hadn't had more than half a bottle of champagne and nothing to eat, she would probably not have giggled, blushed, and ended up following him out of the bar and into the lift. But she had, and before she knew it, Danny was unlocking the door of the Terrace Suite. She stepped inside and immediately sobered up.

This was the most beautiful hotel room she had ever seen; admittedly that wasn't difficult as she had never before stayed in a five star hotel, but nevertheless this was stunning. The curtains were open so that, through the huge French windows leading onto the terrace, she could see the city was ablaze with lights from the Christmas decorations lighting up London and the trees along Park Lane. Inside, the room's colour scheme of white, beige and gold was beautiful.

"Danny – this must have cost the earth?!"

"We have it on hold for important clients coming to London. It just so happened that tonight it is free."

"It's amazing!" she shrieked, jumping on the huge bed and then getting up to explore the enormous suite. The bedroom with its delicate smoky grey and gold furnishings had an *en suite* bathroom and dressing room. It was big enough to fit both her and Flora's wardrobes. The bathroom was stunning, with a large jacuzzi bath and French windows leading out onto the terrace. There was a beautifully appointed sitting room with a marble fireplace, the fire was lit, and there was a dining room with space enough for six people.

"I want to live here! Just think – I would never be late for work, I could walk to the office in under 15 minutes!"

"OK, don't get too used to it. Would you like another drink? Shall we have some room service? I'm starving and do not want too much of a hangover tomorrow morning."

Danny picked up the phone, ordering a bottle of Chateau Latour and two burgers, without consulting Jemima.

"I don't eat meat!" Jemima protested.

"Well that had better change." He winked.

"Oh shut up! Right, I'm going outside to check out the view properly."

"I'm coming with you so you don't fall…"

It was freezing outside and she only had on a small thin jacket but he could see her shivering next to him so he took off his beautiful camel overcoat to put over her shoulders. Suddenly, feeling reckless from the champagne, Jemima turned around and on tiptoes kissed him briefly on the lips. He put his hand behind her head to pull her lips back to his and kiss her so delicately but so passionately that any suggestion of refusing what was about to happen went over the balcony.

The doorbell of the suite rang, as if on cue, so Danny went in and opened the door for the room service waiter. In came the trolley with the two metal domes and the bottle of wine.

"May I open the wine for you, sir?" said the waiter.

"Yes thanks."

Jemima, having followed Danny back inside, felt a huge chill making her skin tingle but it was not from the freeze outside - she was still wrapped up in Danny's cosy camel coat. She was nervous about what she was about to embark on with her boss's grandson. If she

68

didn't handle it properly she would be out of a job more quickly than she was drinking the delicious glass of wine.

She found she could barely touch her burger, feeling full of liquid and on edge. Her light-headedness was getting worse and when Danny went to the bathroom, she moved towards the bed to lie down, the room spinning faster and faster as she did so.

9

December 26th 2010 – London Heathrow Airport

Three weeks later, Jemima leant back in her Virgin Upper Class seat, which would transform into a much-needed bed for her night flight to Cape Town, and let out a long, silent, but smiling sigh.

One of Vogel's VIP clients was spending the winter in the sunny Cape and he wanted to propose to his girlfriend on New Year's Day at Cape Point. Having only thought of this once out there, he needed Vogel to deliver a ring to him in his villa. So, rather than paying for a security guard to take it out, Jemima was asked if she would, and for security purposes, her steerage seat was upgraded and the ring tucked safely amongst her Accessorize beads and earrings in the overhead locker. Looking about her, she thought that she was very unlikely to be the only one with such jewels stashed away in hand luggage. Although, looking at what she was wearing, it would appear very unlikely that she was carrying anything valuable at all. She looked very untidy in contrast with all these elegant people. Cape Town was still a glamorous destination for Europeans at Christmas and the New Year.

Not wanting to miss out on any part of the Virgin experience, once they were airborne Jemima waited for the seatbelt sign to turn off and then made her way to the bar on the lower deck of the Upper Class. Sitting uneasily on a high bar stool, she ordered a Virgin Vespa, loving the name and not even thinking to look at what was in it. Three of those later, on an empty stomach, she realised that before she told the barman about the huge diamond in her bag she had better go back to her seat and go to sleep.

She got her wallet out of her bag and asked how much her bill was, eagerly flashing her Vogel Amex card which she had been given earlier that day in case of emergency. She slipped as inelegantly as possible off her stool to the ground, still clutching her card.

"Can I help, madam?" she looked up and through hazy eyes all she could see was glossy red. Rubbing her head, which had hit the side of the bar, Jemima realised that the red was a very glossy pair of lips belonging to a woman dressed in an equally glossy red suit who was looking knowingly down at her.

"Yes, I need to go to bed but have to pay my bill first," she heard someone say before realising it was her own dry lips and parched mouth talking.

"Hi, I'm Debbie. It's OK, let me take you to your seat, I've already made it up as a bed as it is past midnight GMT now."

"You're so kind, but what about my bill?" Jemima whispered, happy to be escorted up the stairs to a cabin of sleeping passengers.

"It's all free here!" Debbie replied kindly, handing Jemima a bag with Virgin pyjamas and inflight cosmetics.

Scuffling off to the tiny bathroom, Jemima pulled off her clothes and put on the very comfortable, if very unflattering, pyjamas then brushed her teeth – all with eyes half closed - before scuffling back to her bed. It took a while to get comfortable and she was feeling pretty dizzy. Wondering if it was the bump on the head or the alcohol, she eventually fell asleep thinking it was perhaps both.

The night with Danny at The Dorchester had ended in her passing
out on the bed, waking up to a huge hangover and a note next to her
telling her not to be late for work. She had gone into the office the
next day half expecting to be summoned to Paul's office (in his role
as Head of Human Resources) and let go with some excuse that she
had done something wrong at work. Fortunately not. Danny joked
that he would never forgive her and would not leave her alone until
he had properly bedded her.

He tried again the next night. The one after that, she relented. Her
after-work life had become one of secret dates in the top hotels
around London. It had all been such fun but she was exhausted and
terrified someone in the company would see them. She had missed so
many of her friends' Christmas parties, with no excuse other than
that she was working, which was not too far from the truth. Not that
she was doing anything because she wanted a promotion or a pay
rise; she knew that even Danny had no say in that, and she couldn't
rise higher than head of department in any case. For some reason, he
wanted to hang out with her, and they were having fun. He was
incredible in bed and she was really enjoying herself for the first time
in ages. Danny treated her like a princess. She didn't know if he
might want more but maybe things would be different when she got
back from Cape Town. He had even given her a Christmas present; a
very unassuming pair of diamond earrings which were probably the
smallest thing that Vogel had ever made, but they were Vogel
nonetheless. It meant that she could wear them without fear of being

caught out, although she never did so at work. The earrings were also amongst her Accessorize muddle.

Jemima had managed to keep the affair from Flora, who would only tell Benjy, who in turn would tell Fritz, and she just didn't want him to know, but she couldn't wait to tell Marike. Unusually, Jemima hadn't told anyone else because it was quite fun doing something so secretive.

What felt like a few hours of sleep must have been much longer as, before she knew it, Jemima was being awoken by Debbie, who advised her that they would be landing in Cape Town in just under an hour.

"Would you like any breakfast?" Debbie asked, putting Jemima's bed back into a chair. "There is a Full English or Continental style."

"I'd love the cooked breakfast please, and a strong cappuccino?"

The three cocktails she'd had in the bar had given Jemima an almighty hangover and she barely wanted to look up in case she caught disapproving looks from her fellow Upper Class passengers. A cooked breakfast would hopefully sort her out, she told herself while changing out of her pyjamas and squeezing painfully into her skin-tight jeans. The mixture of alcohol and altitude had made her legs balloon with water retention. She just hoped they would deflate before she had to hit the beach.

By the time she got back, the delicious breakfast had arrived. Whilst eating it she looked around at her fellow Upper Class cabin passengers. There was a very geeky-looking guy glued to his laptop; a hugely fat and old man, who had perhaps been wearing his Panama hat all night, eating what seemed to be more than one cooked breakfast; a couple who she had overheard telling Debbie that they were off on a romantic break, and a very glamorous elderly lady who was reading *Fifty Shades of Grey*, trying to hide it behind a magazine.

Eventually the captain announced that it was 15 minutes to landing and they were all told to put away any electrical equipment. Jemima felt her heart beat fast with excitement to be soon in the sun after months of relentless rain.

10

Having got through Passport Control and collected her ridiculously large and heavy suitcase, Jemima pushed the trolley through to where Marike would be waiting for her.

"Marike – hi!" she screamed when she saw her pretty, skinny, and very tanned friend looking around keenly.

"Jem! How are you? So exciting to see you!"

They hugged each other hard and made their way to the car park and Marike's huge 4x4.

"Nice car, sweetheart – wow!"

"I know – not mine – my new boyfriend's!"

"Why didn't you tell me – what's he called?"

"Stuart. He has an IT company. I met him when he came to sell some new software at work! It's such a cliché!"

"Great, I'm really happy for you. I have a lot of gossip to tell you but…" Jemima took a deep breath in of hot air as they got into the car, "I am so happy to be here – London is very cold, wet and grey."

"So nothing changes? And what gossip? Have you got a boyfriend or are you still holding out for Fritz to change his mind and tell you he's madly in love with you?!"

"Mmmm… I've finally realised that it would never work with him. We're really very different and anyway, most importantly I want to get married in the not so far future, he doesn't. Besides, I haven't heard anything from him since the beginning of December when he was an idiot. He's probably got a new girl to mess around. So…" taking in another deep breath as this was the first time she had admitted her dalliance with Danny, "I have been having a very dangerous fling with my boss's grandson, who works at Vogel too. I worry that I am falling for him. But he is fun and generous and makes me feel so sexy all the time."

"No! Really?" Marike laughed.

"Mmmm… yup!" Jemima laughed back. "I hadn't ever slept with a Jewish boy before," she added as she knew that Marike usually only dated rich Jewish boys.

"They're the best!" her friend laughed teasingly. "It all sounds amazing but please take care – that is such a great job you have, you don't want to blow it, and the longer it goes on the worse it will be to end it."

"I know, I know! Thank god I am away here for a bit to diffuse it all. Anyway, let's not think about that now. What plans have you got for us, other than being on the beach every day? It's great that you've got time off work to hang out with me. And we're both going to the party on New Year's Eve?"

"I want to of course, but what about Stu? Obviously I want to spend it with him and I doubt we can get him invited along too?"

"I'll ask but you know what these Carter Lewis type guys are like – they never like you bringing along boyfriends. Anyway we've got a few days to work it out. I'm going to be away for a day on 3rd January as going up to Jo'burg to visit the mine where they found the biggest diamond in the world! The Cullinan... Mr V just bought a huge diamond that is supposed to have originally come from around there and as I've never seen a working mine he suggested that I visit this one while I'm here."

"How interesting! You might even find one!"

"Sadly that is very unlikely!"

The two girls carried on nattering, all the way back to Marike's flat in Camps Bay; a coastal suburb of Cape Town with a long beach strip and restaurants and bars lining the beach road. Jemima had lived on the other side of the strip from Marike in an incredible apartment overlooking the ocean. Many a night they had carried on partying into the early hours, sitting in the jacuzzi on the terrace, glugging bottles of Graham Beck sparkling wine. Now, as they headed over Kloof Nek, the part of Table Mountain which led down to the bay, Jemima inhaled quickly at the view. It always took her breath away. Being greeted by the endless blue water with sun flickering on it was such a perfect way to arrive in Camps Bay.

"So, tell me, what's your favourite bar this year and is Caprice still up and running?" Caprice had been the after beach place to be and be seen in when Jemima had lived there.

"Yes, Caprice is still going as strong as ever. There's a cool place just opened up in Green Point – another sushi place but amazing cocktails too! I thought we'd go there tonight. Right, here we are!" Marike said, pulling up to her apartment block.

Marike had a sweet one-bedroom apartment and a small single sofa bed that she put up when friends came to stay. There was a wonderful view looking down over the Camps Bay strip and Clifton, the next-door suburb, plus the huge expanse of the ocean stretching out for as far as the eye could see.

"Do you want to go to the beach for the day? We're meeting Stu at this new place, Sushini, in Green Point later."

Within the hour, the girls were lying on the beach, reading the magazines Jemima had picked up at Heathrow and discussing the various pointless points of celebrity gossip.

"Goodness! I completely forgot – I've got some jewellery to give to a client..." Jemima whispered, not wanting to be overheard.

"Where is it? And what is it?"

"A huge diamond engagement ring! Worth about 1.2 million!"

"Pounds?!"

"Yes, and it is in my hand luggage in your sitting room. I am going to email him now."

"OK, but before you hand it over please let me try it on – maybe it will give Stu some hints..."

"Or make him run a mile! It's beautiful but huge, not the kind of thing we'd wear. It's for girls who go to the beach for lunch in full make up, not to lie on the sand on towels and then actually swim. Talking of which, I know the water's always cold but this year it is a whole new level of ice!"

"GW."

"What?"

"Global Warming. That's why your summers are so bad..."

"Shut up – they've always been like that!" Jemima said, rolling her eyes behind her new Ray-Bans that she had bought in Duty Free.

"Don't email - call him now so we know what the deal is."

"OK," Jemima dialled the number she'd been given, "Hello Mr Rubenstein? It's Jemima Fox-Pearl from Vogel."

"Hello Jem Fox & Pearls from Vogel, how are you? You sound like a Bond girl!"

Jemima was well used to these remarks and rolled her eyes but she did like the Bond girl bit. "When is it good for me to come with the ring? I am in Camps Bay. You're in Fresnaye – would it be convenient to come by this evening?"

"Yes, come by and have a drink and we can see how foxy you really are."

"Well, I will be coming with a friend of mine," she said, winking at Marike, who was shaking her head and smiling. "See you there."

"So we've been invited to his house for a drink, is that OK? It's next to Carter's I think – I bet they're friends. He sounds a bit creepy to be honest."

"I could tell! I think I know this guy – yes, he is a bit of a sleazebag. He's been on the Cape Town party circuit for ages. So he has finally popped the question - I wonder what she is like? I bet she wouldn't like him saying what he said to you! But no doubt she's a Swedish model!"

"Well we won't see her tonight – she's not arriving until New Year's Eve."

The rest of the day was spent chattering away and then they headed back to shower and dress. Some girls really dressed up in Cape Town but most just wore a hot pair of jeans and a nice top with some pretty flat sandals or thongs. The girls chose the latter option, jumped back into Stuart's truck, and sped off to Fresnaye. The huge diamond ring was back in its beautiful Vogel box, in Jemima's evening bag, having been on Marike's finger for the previous hour.

11

Ralph Rubenstein was exactly how Marike had described him. He was in his late 40s with a dark tan and his shirt open too low to reveal a very hairy chest and a shark's tooth around his neck on a gold chain.

"Girls come in, Vogel have done well with their diamond courier service! Couldn't believe the name when you called! Better looking than the FedEx man too!" He winked. "What can I get you to drink – champagne? Martini?"

"Champagne please," replied Jemima. Marike said she'd have the same.

"Coming right up." As he walked over to the bar he carried on talking, "What do you think of the view?"

The girls walked over to where vast glass sliding doors opened to a sprawling deck and long lap pool that seemed to spill down the hill into the sea. The view over the rooftops and streets all lit up was so impressive. High ceilings enabled the huge pieces of, mostly, erotic art to be displayed for all to see. It all seemed very Zen, modern and expensive.

"What can I say – it is extraordinary, particularly the colours of the sea with the sun setting and all the lights below."

"Yes, I am lucky to have found this place. I just hope my girlfriend likes it! So Foxy, is this your first time in Cape Town?"

"Do call me Jemima," she said, smiling and hoping that he would get the hint. "No, I've been here lots of times. I used to live in Camps Bay about eight years ago; that's how I know Marike. I come back as often as I can. I love it here."

"Yah, it is a pretty awesome place, particularly around now – lots of parties and pretty girls! But I am sure you must have a boyfriend who whisks you off to exotic places?" he asked sleazily.

"Mmmmm… sadly, no. But Vogel did pay for me to fly Business on account of carrying the ring!"

"Well, that is something I guess. Although they will probably have added it to my bill!" He laughed more in annoyance than amusement. "Marike, you look familiar?" he continued when Jemima said nothing.

"So do you – I think that we must have met over the years. Wow, this champagne is delicious. Thanks!"

"I only buy proper champagne. None of this local sparkling crap!" he said arrogantly. "Let's go and sit outside and enjoy the sight."

When they were seated on the terrace, conversation turned to the Vogel Vanderpless Diamond.

"So, Jemima Fox," Ralph said, "Tell me about the big South African rock Vogel has bought. Do you think it was really worth £55 million?"

"Well I think if Mr Vogel paid that much for it then he must believe that is what it is worth. It is the Vogel Vanderpless Diamond, named after its owner Mrs Vanderpless, and of course Sidney Vogel. But that is all I know."

"Ralph, your girlfriend is really lucky," Marike said, noticing that Jemima was feeling uncomfortable talking about the diamond. "I am afraid Jemima allowed me a peek at the ring. When is she coming to Cape Town?"

"Andrea is Swedish and a model. Sounds a cliché I know!" he admitted sheepishly. "But she is more than just looks. She trained as a lawyer at Harvard before she got spotted by a booker in Manhattan. She is coming down with a lawyer friend for New Year. Maybe you would have time to meet them – Andrea could do with some nice girlfriends down here."

"Yes, of course – we may be going to Carter's for New Year – will you both be there; he is your neighbour after all?" Marike said.

"We will. I like Carter though I don't know him that well. I only bought this place in October but he sent around an invitation, which was hospitable. How would you both like to come here before the party and we can all walk around there together?"

"I don't know if I can go – my boyfriend hasn't been invited, yet." Marike looked at Jemima, who nodded to confirm she would ask.

"But if I don't come – Jem, you could go with them to the party?"

"Sounds great, thanks Ralph, and I really look forward to meeting Andrea."

"Right, I think we'd better be going," Marike stood up. "Thank you Ralph, we're off to Sushini for dinner with my boyfriend. Maybe I'll see you on Friday night. Otherwise I am sure we'll bump into each other out and about. And good luck with the proposal – Jem told me you're going to Cape Point – it's very impressive there!"

"I hope she'll say yes."

"I am sure she will!"

With that they said their goodbyes and the girls made their way to Green Point.

"Actually – he wasn't too bad, except about the champagne, what an arrogant line!" Marike exclaimed. "I felt a bit mean not inviting him to dinner but you never know - Stu might know him and not like him! I could see you were uneasy talking about that diamond, by the way."

"Yes, the Vogels are so funny about staff socialising with clients ... I'd probably get the sack for just having a drink with him, let alone talking about the VV."

"Haha. But they don't mind you screwing the boss's grandson!"

"Touché. Anyway, he led me on. At least I haven't hooked up with the office IT man!"

"Hey. You had better be nice to him. I think he's the one."

"My god – you sound like me. Danny is definitely not the one, though. I haven't heard anything from him since Christmas Eve. In fact when we were on the beach just now all I could think of was Fritz."

"You need a good South African roasting. Stu's got so many hot mates. Oh, and there he is," Marike said, pointing to a very good-looking guy walking towards the door of the restaurant.

"Hey babe!" she shouted out of the window, "we're just going to find a parking space."

He waved and nodded, gesturing that he would head up to the first floor bar.

Five minutes later, they joined him and, having made the introductions, Marike handed Jemima a cocktail list and suggested she try the passion fruit martini.

"It is to die for!"

"OK, cool – I'll have one of those then, thanks."

"Great. Girls I'll order and why not go and get one of those free tables out on the deck, I've got James joining too now," Stuart said, smiling.

"Thanks hon," Marike turned to Jemima and whispered as they made their way to the deck, "Oh my god, James is so hot! Work at being roasted by him!"

"No, I am off men this holiday. I have more important things to think about. Not least going to the mine and something I want to investigate there."

"Investigate?" Marike asked as Stu came back and put the drinks down on the table.

"Remind me to tell you tomorrow." Jemima didn't want to bore them with her theories, however exciting she might think them to be.

"Good table! And I've brought us some sushi menus. We can eat here or go up to the restaurant and the conveyer belt?"

"Oh let's stay here! It's rare I get to eat outside!" Jemima laughed.

"Stu, why don't you order for us? Jem, you like all sushi don't you?"

"Yup, except eel."

As Stu walked back up to the bar he stopped to talk to the most good-looking man Jemima had ever seen. He was tall and lightly tanned, wearing a pale blue t-shirt and jeans. He could quite easily have been a younger Brad Pitt.

"Mari, is that James?" she whispered, almost breathless.

"Yah! Hot, hey?! James, hi – we're over here!" Marike shouted, standing up - much to the annoyance of the other girls in the bar, who had their eyes on him for themselves.

"Hey Marike, howzit going?" he said, hugging her in a brotherly way and smiling shyly at Jemima over her shoulder. He had short dark blonde hair and bright green-blue eyes.

"Great, thanks. Jimmy, meet Jemima from London."

"Hi Jemima from London!" he smiled, giving her a kiss. "Your drinks look finished already, would you like some more? I'm going to the bar to get myself a beer, I reckon Stu will forget it with the amount of food he'll probably order..."

And with that he headed back to the bar with a multitude of mascaraed eyes following him.

"You are right, he's the hottest guy I have ever seen!"

"He is super intelligent and plays polo!" Marike gushed. She always thought of polo as such a glamorous sport.

After several more passion fruit martinis, a bottle of chilled Haute Cabrière and more sushi than Jemima thought Nobu probably served on a daily basis, Stu paid the bill and took the wheel of his SUV from a very tipsy Marike. Jemima jumped into James' truck and they all headed back to Stuart's Clifton beach-front villa for nightcaps. Jemima knew what Marike was like after a few drinks and was pleased that James was there so she didn't have to play gooseberry to the couple.

On the way back from the restaurant she found out that he wasn't a professional polo player but worked for Investec. He had spent a decade working in London, living in a mews house in Notting Hill with his then girlfriend but they had split up when he had decided to move back to South Africa. He actually lived mainly in Johannesburg but was down in the Cape for New Year, staying with Stuart who he'd known since school. James played polo for fun and had spent that day out on the field at the Cape Town Polo Club, half an hour outside the city.

When they eventually got to the entrance and left their trucks on the road, Jemima quickly discovered that there was quite a precarious walk down to the villa and, being unsure of the path, she was relieved when James took her hand to help her. It was almost midnight and there was not much of a moon to guide them.

"This is an amazing place!" Jemima exclaimed when they were finally down at the bottom of the steps and in the villa only a few metres from the water. "I have always wondered who lived here and now I know! Oh my god – is that a hot tub?" she exclaimed, walking towards the terrace.

"It sure is and we're going in! Jem come here and I'll lend you a bikini!" Marike said excitedly.

Jemima followed her friend into the bathroom to find a plethora of colourful bikinis hanging off the towel rail. She chose a black Heidi Klein and put it on, then the girls went outside to find James and Stuart already in the jacuzzi, Stu pouring champagne into glasses.

"Bit clichéd but why not? Welcome to South Africa, Jemima!"

As James was staying at Stuart's house and Marike obviously was too that night, it left Jemima with two choices: sleep on the sofa, or with the most good-looking guy she had ever laid eyes on...

12

Jemima awoke feeling confused. She couldn't remember the noise of the sea being so close the last time she had stayed at Marike's apartment... nor the sofa bed so comfortable. She stretched her legs out under the duvet and felt herself kick another leg. Goodness, who was that? She felt the familiar stirrings of panic in her chest. She'd been in the country less than 24 hours and already she was going to have a reputation. At least she wasn't naked; she noticed that she was wearing a pair of boxer shorts and a t-shirt.

"Morning Jemima, sleep well?" a sexy voice spoke next to her, bringing her back to her surroundings.

"Erh, yes thanks, and you?" she knew she sounded a little squeakier than usual.

"Good, but those drinks have wrecked me," James grinned, "And without sounding presumptuous, I think you're probably feeling the same. If you've lived here I am sure you know what the best hangover cure is?"

"I am not going in the sea! I'll die!"

"No you won't. It's the only way to get through today. Come on. You hung your bikini in my bathroom. Go and get changed and I'll meet you on the terrace. I'll make us a flask of coffee."

"James... we didn't...?" she paused just outside the bathroom door.

"No we didn't, don't worry! Not that I didn't want to – but I am a gentleman. Now hurry before you change your mind."

Inwardly breathing a sigh of relief, Jemima laughed, "I think it was you who made up my mind, not me!"

A few minutes later, having cleaned her face of smudged mascara and washed her mouth out with mouthwash, Jemima was on the terrace, already scorching in the 8am sun.

"Right, come on."

They walked the few metres to the sea and James just ran straight in, having dropped the flask of coffee on the towels. His body was out of this world, tanned and toned.

"You're mad!" Jemima shouted, running after him and shallow-diving into the ice-cold water. "It's freezing! But you're right, my fuzzy head has almost gone."

"Cool. Now do a few ten metre laps with me and we'll go back to the beach for a coffee!"

She was so numb from the cold that she knew the only way to get any feeling back in her body was to do as she was told. The sea that surrounded the Cape of Africa was made up of the Indian Ocean on the Eastern side and the Atlantic on the Western. Cape Town welcomed the Atlantic and the temperature was so low because it was the first land mass that water encountered after the South Pole.

The next few minutes got better as they completed his challenge. Before she knew it, they were out wrapped in the towels he'd brought and sipping delicious fresh coffee while looking out at the sea in which they'd drowned their hangovers. Chattering about this and that, she told him what she did at Vogel and about her life in London, without mentioning Fritz. Although he was so easy to talk to, she realised as she was speaking how exhausting her life sounded.

"Are you happy?" he asked.

She paused before before answering. "Yes, I think so. I love my job but I find it very nerve-racking the whole time. I am constantly worrying that I have messed up. The company secretary is always trying to trip me up. But I guess if I can get over that then I am getting great experience. I think I need to be harder, though. The Vogels are so tough and don't suffer fools gladly. But I am lonely and fed up of being single whilst all my friends are getting married and having babies."

"It's good to be tough at work. Try only to get involved in things you need to do and forget about people being difficult. But why are you so lonely?" he asked sympathetically. "You're gorgeous, you must have men falling at your feet?"

Jemima took a deep breath and couldn't help hoping that he was asking to find out her romantic status. She was determined not to wax lyrical about Fritz. "My relationships never seem to last very long and I just don't know what the hell is wrong with me. Other than that, I drink too much and maybe men don't like that. But it's London – everyone I know drinks too much."

"I doubt that there is anything wrong with you but drinking too much too often isn't pretty or cool. But the guys in London drink a lot too, as I remember?"

"Well. I guess. None of my exes are married though, and some are in their early 40s now!"

"There you go. I'm not much better. I have only had really short-term relationships since I got back from London. South African girls can be so tricky!"

"So can British girls," she said, now looking at his face. His eyes seemed more blue than green, being near the sea. "Right, let's stop this miserable chat and go have some breakfast. I am starving!"

Laughing together, they went back up to the house to find Stuart and Marike already in the kitchen and cooking a fry-up.

"We thought that you might like an English breakfast so you don't feel like you're too far from home, Jemima!"

"My god. I never have them. Can't you tell?!" she laughed, twirling in front of them all.

"Babe, you're huge!" Marike teased back with a slice of toast in her hand. "Now stop showing off and what shall we do today? More beach?"

"Definitely. I really need to soak up as much sun as possible after months of grey skies."

Yes and can you speak to Carter about Stuart coming - if you would like to?" Marike turned to Stuart, "And you too, James?"

"Well, we kind of have plans for New Year but tell me about this party?"

"OK, so Carter has an amazing house up at the top of Fresnaye. Huge. And each year does incredible parties with live acts, so much food and booze. The evening normally ends with a firework display. Do let me know if you'd like to come and I can ask him?"

"Sure sounds good. We were just going to go to a few bars with a bunch of friends!" James laughed. "This sounds much more sophisticated! Jemima, I am going to take a shower - or do you want to go in first?"

"Yes OK," she said, walking towards the bedroom. The house was mainly on one floor with a big TV room downstairs at beach level.

"Be quick. Breakfast will be ready in five!" Stuart shouted after her before loudly whispering to James, so Jemima couldn't help but hear, "So Jimmy, she stayed with you in the same bed? Why didn't you sleep on the sofa?"

"She's too pretty to let sleep alone!" This caused Jemima to smile from the other side of the door. "But nothing happened, just a very cold swim."

"Well you've always got New Year's Eve!" Stuart teased.

"Guys, this is my best friend we're talking about…"

"I know babe," Stuart tried to appease Marike, "and I'm saying how pretty and cool she is."

By the time Jemima got back, they were sitting at the table eating a cooked breakfast which wouldn't have looked out of place in any top London hotel.

"Yours is in the oven," Marike told Jemima.

"Thanks," Jemima said, still glowing from the earlier conversation that she wasn't supposed to have heard. "Mari, I was thinking that I'd love to go to Kalk Bay one day – I love all those little shops there. I still have those pretty halter neck tops I bought in India Jane all those years ago!"

"Yah sure – I've not been there for ages. We should go to Harbour House for lunch or an early dinner. It's amazing. You must have gone there before?"

"Absolutely, I love it!"

"Great. OK, I'm going to have a quick shower too and then let's go back to mine?"

Ten minutes later they were in the car, headed along the beachfront with Marike laughing about the night before.

"What do you think of James?"

"He is utterly amazing. I am embarrassingly head over heels in love. I mean, who is Fritz and who is Danny?!"

"Haha Jem, I knew you would be. He is so like all the guys you used to fancy when you lived here. Do you remember that other James you had a huge crush on?"

"Yes, and then you dated him when I left..."

"Oh yes, not a good move for a friend to make."

"No but anyway, you have made up for it by introducing me to this one!" Jemima said excitedly. "Let's see what happens. If anything."

13

They spent the next few days on the beach, shopping, eating, and drinking. Jemima hadn't felt so happy since the early days of her relationship with Fritz.

The boys weren't working so when James wasn't at the polo club, the four of them hung out together. Once they went to watch him play a few chukkas and Jemima felt as though she really was falling head over heels in love with this handsome, kind and intelligent man. Her nights were spent in James's bed in Stu's beachfront villa; mornings swimming in the ice cold water below. She and James had only kissed and cuddled and she couldn't help wonder why he hadn't tried anything more, as most men would if they had a girl in their bed. He was the most incredible kisser and she was sure it was only a matter of time before they made love. In fact the waiting was making it all the more exciting.

New Year's Eve came and after a post-beach sundowner at Caprice, the girls headed back to Marike's apartment to have a sleep and then to get showered and dressed. Carter's party always had a theme and this year it was 'The Beautiful and Damned', the title of Scott Fitzgerald's famous 1922 novel, but Jemima was sure very few of the guests would know that. She remembered years earlier gate-crashing Kate Moss's legendary 30th birthday of the same theme at the artist Sam Taylor-Wood's house, along with Flora whose boyfriend at the time was a friend of Kate's. Ever since that party, Jemima had thought of Kate's amazing midnight blue sequinned dress. Then one day when she was in Rellik, a vintage dress shop in London which she had read Kate frequented, she saw the dress and bought it immediately, knowing that one day she would have the chance to wear it.

"That dress is stunning, Jem – my goodness, where did you find it?"

Jemima told Marike the story. "What are you going to wear?"

She was worried that her friend was still walking around the apartment with nothing more than her knickers on and it was already 9.30pm. They were supposed to be meeting the boys downstairs before being at Ralph Rubenstein's in 15 minutes.

"Oh, a vintage Chanel of my mum's," Marike said casually. "I can't believe that you found Kate Moss's dress in a second hand shop! I remember the pictures. You should put a gold star around your eye like she did. I've got some gold face paint somewhere. Are those Vogel earrings too?"

Although small, the diamonds shone brightly like only real, well-cut diamonds would.

"Yes! A present from Danny. Goodness, I've not thought about him once until now... James is completely occupying the space I have in my brain for boys! Yes, good idea re: the star, but we had better get going if we are going to get to Ralph's on time and then to Carter's before 10.30pm. I don't want to miss out on any of the fun before midnight."

Carter always had incredible caterers with delicious food and cocktails, and just before midnight a band would come on before everyone joined in, counting down the last minute of the year. While Marike slipped into her Chanel, Jemima painted on the star a bit haphazardly, hoping James wouldn't notice how bad it was.

They ran down the apartment block's stairs to find the boys having a beer, leaning on the bonnet of James's truck and staring out at the moonlight glistening on the sea. They both looked so good-looking, despite not having come in costume; both were in jeans and shirts.

"Wow, you two look stunning!" Stuart said as James just stared lustfully at Jemima so that her stomach turned several somersaults.

They drove up the hill to Fresnaye and parked outside Ralph's house where they were already able to hear the music and noise coming from Carter's.

"I wonder what Ralph's ladies will be like!" Jemima whispered to Marike mischievously.

"Girls!" The door opened before they had a chance of ringing the bell and out came Ralph, looking as though he had just stepped out of the Roaring 20s, in a white jacket, black shirt opened to reveal his tanned, hairy chest, and an untied black bowtie hanging around his neck in place of the shark tooth. The look was finished off with a pair of black trousers and shoes that would not have gone amiss on Fred Astaire. He had a huge Cuban cigar in his fingers and a puff of smoke seeping from his mouth. "You both look great. And you lucky guys must be their boyfriends?"

"Hi Ralph, you look dressed for the part yourself!" Jemima said, laughing. "This is Marike's boyfriend Stuart and his friend James." She didn't know how best to introduce James - however much she might like him to be her boyfriend, he wasn't. "Where is Andrea? And have you asked her yet?"

"Oh, the girls are coming down in a moment and yes, she is wearing the ring tonight," Ralph replied proudly. "Come in, I have martinis ready to pour."

They followed their pre-party host inside and as he was pouring his concoction into tall martini glasses, his girlfriend walked down the stairs with a girl whom Jemima recognised from both *Tatler* and the auction at Bothebie's. The girl who had been eyeing up Danny at the club. Petrina Lindberg.

"Oh Andrea baby, this is the girl from Vogel I was telling you about. And her friends, who all live here." Ralph handed martinis to Stuart and James and champagne to the girls.

"You work at Vogel?" Petrina asked Jemima before Andrea had a chance to respond.

"Yes I do," Jemima smiled. She noticed how beautiful this girl looked close up. Her face had feline features and there was not a blemish on her olive-coloured skin - of which a lot could be seen. Andrea couldn't be more different in looks. As Scandinavian as they come, with hair which could have come straight out of a bottle of bleach but obviously hadn't, and the bluest of eyes set wide apart in her lightly tanned face.

Andrea and Petrina towered over Jemima and Marike in their five-inch heels. Jemima didn't want to look at James for fear he would be staring at them with his eyes on stalks. They both wore incredible designer dresses, which she couldn't help recognising as they had both been on the Net-a-Porter site which Jemima often spent several hours each week scanning. She had been ogling Andrea's Gucci silk cocktail dress when she had thought she might get a Christmas bonus from Mr V. Sadly it was not to be.

Petrina looked like she was wearing a Victoria Beckham number in bright white, which highlighted her flawless olive skin. Jemima imagined their bedrooms were strewn with the dream-like black and white Net a Porter bags that 'Father Porter' had delivered for Christmas. The pair looked exquisite with the requisite sparkles at their ears and wrists. Andrea had the immense Vogel yellow diamond on her engagement finger and Jemima could see Petrina's huge classic Cartier Roadster watch with diamonds around the face. Under the watch she saw what looked like part of a tattoo on the inside of her wrist, but she couldn't make out what it was.

Out of the corner of her eye, Jemima glanced at James and blushed when she saw he was not staring at them but at her, with a huge smirk on his face. Damn, she had been busted! She smiled sweetly and moved over to the drinks tray as she had almost finished her champagne.

Marike walked towards Andrea and Jemima hoped she wouldn't let on that she had been wearing the huge ring a few days ago.

"That ring is amazing! Jemima wouldn't let me have a look at it before she brought it to Ralph." Jemima thought that sounded such a lie.

"Jemima, is it?" Petrina purred whilst Jemima was putting the bottle of Cristal back in the ice bucket. She practically jumped.

"Yes. And sorry, I don't think we've been introduced..." She was not going to feel intimidated by this beautiful, mysterious catwoman.

"Petrina," the girl put out a long, elegant hand, adorned with a white diamond and onyx Cartier Panthére ring on its index finger. "So what's it like working with Danny Vogel?"

Jemima pulled her hand back from Petrina's cold bony one and tried to pretend that she hadn't just frozen on hearing that name, whilst wondering how this girl knew Danny.

"Oh, do you know him?" she asked innocently.

"*Of* him. Of course. Who doesn't? He is so sexy, isn't he? You must find it difficult to concentrate at work."

Petrina smiled seductively and Jemima smiled back, happy that Petrina didn't know him quite as well as she did. But just as she was about to reply protectively, James came over and she felt guilty of her jealousy.

"Hi darling," he said, kissing her just below her ear. As a shiver ran down her spine, Jemima saw Petrina stare at him in lust. Her confidence empowered her.

"Hey. This is Petrina. She was just asking me about my boss."

"Sidney Vogel? He's a bit old for you, isn't he?" James teased.

Petrina moved her lips into a smile without her eyes following suit.

"A little…" she said, winking, and slunk off to talk with her friend.

"Was she OK?" James asked Jemima kindly. "Your face went pale for a second."

"Oh really?" she replied, hoping he hadn't read her mind about Danny as she hadn't told him about her office fling. "I don't trust her."

"You've only just met her."

"I know, but I have seen her before. At the Bothebie's auction when my boss bought that diamond. She looked like she was up to something then and I am sure that she is now."

"OK, Miss Marple. Stop your investigation now. It is New Year and we had better be going."

Jemima was feeling a little bit tipsy and realised that she'd had no water for a while so she made her way to where she imagined the kitchen would be. Just before she pushed open the door she heard someone speaking in hushed tones on the other side. She looked through the little window to see Petrina speaking into her cellphone whilst looking at her reflection in the fridge's mirrored door. Jemima heard the word 'Vogel', and her own name, but Petrina was speaking in Montenegrin. Jemima spoke four languages fluently but unfortunately Montenegrin wasn't one of them.

"OK, will do," Petrina replied in English to whoever it was on the other end and Jemima wondered what it was she would do and what it was she was saying about her and Vogel. Forgetting the water, she walked quickly back to the others, who were all getting ready to walk to Carter's.

"There you are!" James, noticing her worried expression, frowned. "All OK?"

"I hope so!" Jemima replied, smiling and putting her arm through his. "Come on, let's go."

"I'll wait for Andrea and Petrina. You guys go ahead. You never know how long these beauties will take," Ralph said patiently, although it was clear he was keen to go to the party sooner rather than later.

"OK, bye Ralph – see you in there! Don't be long!" Marike gave him a kiss before the four of them set off towards Carter's house.

"Wow, what a house!" Stuart said. "And I really liked Ralph. He's a bright guy."

"Your house is amazing," Marike said sweetly. "I'd much rather be down on the beach."

"Me too," Jemima smiled at James. She suddenly wanted to be as far away from Petrina as possible.

Having got through the high security gate and past a hefty Afrikaner bodyguard, they arrived inside Carter's complex and what seemed like a party already well underway. Outside the house were several vintage cars parked up and music blasting from the other side of the house. Candles lit the path from the drive up to the big open oak door and waitresses stood with trays full of champagne bowl glasses and martini glasses.

As the group made their way into the house, they each took a glass and walked through the large hall which led to a gallery overlooking the terrace below. Already there were lots of people. An ice bar stretched along one side of the gallery, with an abundance of crayfish, oysters, sushi and sashimi. Waiters were hulling fresh oysters to whoever wanted them and topping up champagne or pouring shots of iced vodka.

The four looked over the edge and saw all the guests in beautiful dresses or suits, dancing and chatting. It was such a sight, as though part of a movie set. They wandered down to join in but after an hour or so, Jemima left dancing with her friends to get a much-needed glass of water and go to the loo. As she was passing the sushi bar, Petrina Lindberg stepped out from behind a pillar.

"Are you having a nice time?" she asked in the same low, purring voice that had chilled Jemima earlier.

"Yes, it's amazing isn't it?" Jemima hoped that she sounded as normal as possible. Despite the now numerous cocktails, the phone call she had overheard stuck in her head and she just wanted this girl to leave her alone.

"Yes, very good, but I wish I was here with a boyfriend like yours. Tell me more about Danny Vogel. Could you set me up with him?"

Jemima thought it odd to ask someone you had just met to introduce you to their boss with the intention of hooking up with him. Petrina had said in *Tatler* that she wanted a Vogel diamond though; maybe dating Danny seemed an easy route to achieve this.

"I don't really know him very well I am afraid," she lied. She couldn't help but feel as jealous of this beautiful girl as she was suspicious. Petrina Lindberg was up to no good and she was also exactly the sort of girl Danny Vogel would go for. It made Jemima's skin prickle with goose bumps despite the heat of the night.

When Jemima got back to the others, pandemonium had broken out. The iced sushi and oyster bar had melted all over the guests below. Most of them were furious that their expensive dresses and hair were soaking wet and covered in pieces of sashimi and seaweed, even though they were from the best sushi place in Cape Town.

She saw James chatting to Ralph and Andrea whilst Stu and Marike were still dancing, having fortunately missed the sushi shower. Petrina was nowhere to be seen. Jemima hoped that she had gone home, forgoing the countdown to midnight. She made her way over to James, who smiled as he saw her coming over.

"Where have you been? I was worried you'd done a Cinderella on me and I would have had to welcome in the New Year on my own!"

The band stopped playing and began the minute countdown.

"Of course not! I wouldn't miss it for anything. I was getting some water as I'm feeling quite drunk."

"Well done! We've had quite a few days of drinking."

"Yes – I need to stop drinking for a month or so. That will be my New Year's resolution, I think!"

"Mmmmm. Let's see." James laughed at her as the last five seconds came.

"Five, four, three, two, one... HAPPY NEW YEAR!" Everyone shouted and the most incredible firework display started from a boat out on the ocean below.

James kissed her so intensely that she thought her knees would buckle and was relieved that, thanks to the water, she had partially sobered up. He was so amazing and she dreaded having to say goodbye when she went back to London and had to face Danny in the office. Unless, of course, Petrina had managed to orchestrate an introduction and distracted his attentions away from her.

14

Jemima's flight to Johannesburg on 3rd January was too early for her liking but James said he'd take her to the airport before heading to the polo club.

As she sat in his truck and he picked up take out coffees at the petrol station, she again wondered about this perfect guy who she had spent every night kissing in bed but who hadn't gone any further with her.

"OK honey – I hope today is interesting. It's a long way to go for just the day. If I am still out here when your flight gets in, I'll SMS you."

"James – thanks so much."

She kissed him goodbye and hopped out of the truck to make her way to the domestic departures area where she checked in. Within the hour was headed up into the atmosphere. The plane was full with people heading back to Johannesburg at the end of the Christmas break. Jemima was thrilled that she had managed to reserve a window seat as the view of the ground below was intriguing. Mile upon mile of empty land punctuated by the occasional farm settlement, it was amazing how clear it was from so far up in the cloudless sky.

The two-hour flight passed very quickly and soon she was walking through the arrivals gate towards where she had been told her driver would be waiting to take her to the mine.

"Jem!" she was sure she heard. "JemImaaaah…"

As she turned to look around, she realised whose voice it was and the excited flutter in her chest was instantly quelled when she saw who he was with. Fritz was walking towards her alongside a very beautiful blonde girl with glaringly obvious expensive travel clothes – she could have been Victoria Beckham if her hair was darker and she'd been wearing heels as opposed to her elegant, expensive-looking Greek sandals.

All Jemima could think of in her own defence was that she was amazingly sun-kissed after a week on the beach and thank god she had borrowed a very cool khaki jumpsuit from Marike, although for practical reasons she was wearing plimsolls to cope with the rough terrain.

"Fritz, hey," she said, smiling – not too widely, just friendly enough.

"What are you doing here?" he asked, kissing her so close to her mouth she couldn't help but feel another stirring inside her.

"I'm on my way to a diamond mine. I've been in Cape Town since Christmas." She reached her hand towards the girl who was now standing practically on top of Fritz. "Hi, I'm Jemima."

"Oh sorry!" Fritz grinned, "Anoush – this is a... an old friend of mine from home, Jemima."

"Hallo Jemima," Anoush replied coolly.

"And what are you doing here?" Jemima asked.

"Anoush's parents are taking us on safari. We're catching a flight to Sabi Sands Game Reserve in a couple of hours. We're staying at Richard Branson's place, Ulusaba!" Fritz's eyes were wide with excitement "Do you want a coffee?"

Jemima noticed Anoush's eyes also widened, in annoyance. Although she would have loved to annoy the girl further, the last thing Jemima wanted was to spend any longer in the presence of this ice maiden and the (once?) love of her life.

"Thanks but I've got to go. I am on a really tight schedule. Have fun." She gave him a quick peck on the cheek, said goodbye and walked towards the man holding up a board with her name, tears stinging her eyes.

15

Jemima was relieved and soothed on finding that the car she was travelling in was a very comfortable, air-conditioned Mercedes Benz E Class and not like the taxi she'd taken once from the airport in Gambia. Then, she had thrown up most of the way over the broken roads.

Having not slept on the plane because of the unmissable scenery below, Jemima put on the eye mask she had been given on the Virgin flight and willed herself asleep, not wanting to think of Fritz and that girl. Anoush must have been the date he had told her about. What quick work by him, to be taken on safari by her parents. Of course Fritz liked Anoush. She must have lots of money and could afford to keep him as he dreamt of being kept. How annoying that she hadn't agreed to James's suggestion of accompanying her – that would have put a bee in Fritz's pretentious Panama hat.

Jemima was shaken awake and, lifting her mask, she saw that they were now off road and driving slowly along a rough dirt track. The whole Fritz experience had made her quite sick with anxiety and this bumpy ride was now not helping. Tears sprung again in her eyes which not even this beautiful landscape spread out on all sides of her, nor James waiting for her back in Cape Town, could cancel out.

She remembered the text she had got from Danny on New Year's Eve, saying how he couldn't wait to see her when she got back. All it did was make her cringe and panic. Why did she get herself in these ridiculous situations? She needed to be much cooler and more sophisticated.

Fortunately she was brought back to reality again when the driver, pulling up in a little car park area, said to take her time and that he would be there waiting for her when she needed a lift back to the airport. Jemima stepped out of the cool car to be hit by the hot, dusty air. Although she had of course not spent the whole year that she had lived in South Africa on the beach, she had never been as far inland as she was now. At even 11am it felt hotter and drier than mid-afternoon in the breezy Cape. She looked around her and saw that leading away from the car park was a tree-lined avenue of cottages, at the end of which were some large industrial-looking buildings. Just on the other side of the car park she saw a sign saying 'Reception' and followed its arrow to a little wooden house with the sounds of a radio drifting from an open window. Inside were a couple of elderly ladies chatting at what could only be described as the reception desk.

"Good day," one of them said. She had a lovely pretty face with blue, sparkling eyes. "How may I help you?"

"Hello. I'm Jemima Fox-Pearl. I am booked into a tour."

"Well, you are too late for the full tour," the other woman replied brusquely.

"Oh dear, I have just flown up from Cape Town and got here as soon as I could."

"Not to worry my dear," the kind lady replied. "The full tour includes going down into the mine. The experience is much nicer being watched from the comfort of our video room. It is really the gentlemen who are keen on the full tour package. Anyway, I am free at this time so we can start when you are ready."

"You are so kind. Yes you're right. I'm not really brave enough to go underground!"

"Right, well here's a bottle of water. Shall we go?"

"Thank you." Jemima followed her guide out of the door and down the little wooden steps onto the avenue.

"I'm Hannah and I've lived in Cullinan for 50 years. My husband used to work at the mine and soon we'll see the house that we lived in. All these houses were built for the miners and mine managers over the years. The higher the position and also, if married, the bigger the house."

As they walked up the pretty, aptly-named Oak Avenue, which was lined with jacaranda trees as well as oaks, Jemima looked more closely at the cottages and houses of this quaint village which seemed more like something out of a Western movie than what she had imagined a South African mining village would be like. The buildings were a mix of Edwardian and Cape Dutch, with picket fences and verandas, although they were now mainly cafés and gift shops. They were so pretty and well-kept, with lovely gardens full of roses contrasting with the dusty road.

At the top end of the avenue there was a large locked iron gate to go through and then they were in the mine area. Hannah showed Jemima around the huge warehouses, which contained machinery that made up the modern industrial Cullinan Diamond Mine. She explained that when the world's biggest diamond was found, mining had been a very much simpler process. It had been an open mine and her husband's grandfather had been there when the rock was discovered.

"Both the village and its famous find – the Cullinan Diamond – were named after a Sir Thomas Cullinan who, in 1903, after many years of trying, purchased the farmland underneath which the mine was then developed. For many years he believed there was a huge wealth of diamonds to be found but the farmer who owned the land was adamant he would not sell. Eventually the old man died and his family, needing to raise money, agreed to sell to the prospector." Hannah told the story as though it were a fairy tale. "Then one afternoon in June 1905, a mineworker discovered what turned out to be the largest diamond ever found. He saw a shiny object in the wall of the open mine; it was visible because of its reflecting in the evening's sun. The surface manager was called to inspect and managed to prise it out of the earth, albeit breaking a tool or two, to reveal an enormous object. Tests revealed it was a flawless diamond weighing over 3000 carats. Up until that time the largest diamond found was just less than 1000 carats."

"Goodness!" Jemima's eyes were wide with amazement. The Vogel Vanderpless was 723 carats and that had looked huge.

"Yes, it was quite a thing, and within days it became a global sensation, with news crews turning up at this tiny village! It went on display in Johannesburg and then in London - its delivery there was something that would make your James Bond proud!"

Jemima laughed. "How come?!"

"Well, it was hidden in the hatbox of the wife of an employee of the South African postal service. She was travelling by train from Johannesburg to Cape Town, where it was transferred to a ship travelling on to London. As a safety precaution, a bogus stone was also aboard a mail ship, in the captain's safe and guarded all the way to London. Both arrived in Britain safely, the real one taken to Buckingham Palace for an audience with the King, Edward VII, before going on public display. For two years it remained on view, as no one came forward with the asking price. Eventually the diamond became a problem for the Transvaal Government, who had bought it from Thomas Cullinan's company for £150,000, as each time it was removed from the bank vault it had to be insured for over £1 million; an unthinkable price then, if not now. In the end it was decided that it would be a gift to Edward VII, and consequently the nation of the United Kingdom. South Africa was still then part of the British Empire so Edward was also their King. Therefore it was presented to His Majesty, and then sent to the world's foremost diamond cutters in Amsterdam. After examination, it was painstakingly cut into nine principal diamonds (and 96 others), the largest two of which are in the Crown and Sceptre. The other seven diamonds were set in further pieces of the Royal Family's jewels."

"You're like an encyclopaedia!" Jemima said admiringly.

"My dear, I have been here most of my life and know the story better than any others, having told it and heard it so many times."

"Yes, I can imagine." Jemima felt rather stupid at knowing so little about this famous diamond and kicked herself for spending the past week dreaming about James and not reading up on the history of it. She had been to the Tower of London as a child, where the Crown Jewels were kept on public display, but she could barely remember anything except for the funnily-dressed Beefeater guards.

"I am going to take you to the Museum now. There you can see models of the famous diamonds found in the mine, including of course the most famous when it was first discovered. There are also interesting objects saved from that era."

When the tour with Hannah had come to a close, Jemima stood outside in the sun, about to step inside one of the pretty houses which had been turned into a little museum.

"Jemima, I am going to make my way back to the office. It has been very nice meeting you and showing you around. And it is very interesting that you work in the diamond industry yourself. Do please come by on your way to the car and say goodbye, and do ask if you find you have any questions after looking around here."

"Thank you Hannah. It has been so amazing seeing it all and I am just going to mosey around here for a bit. Yes, of course I'll come and say goodbye."

"OK, divine – see you just now." The little old lady walked briskly out into the sun. Clearly doing the hour's tour of the site several times a day kept her very fit.

Jemima continued looking at various photographs of the mine and its workers over the years. There was a copy of American *Vogue* from June 1953, open at pages of the Coronation and the Cullinan in the Crown and Sceptre.

She then came to a desk with a scrapbook of newspaper articles. Always interested in history, she sat down and began leafing through them. They were mostly from the South African and British press and related to the discovery of the Cullinan Diamond in 1905, and its subsequent transformation.

However, her attention was caught by an article from the *New York*

Times, published in December 1909.

<<*Where is the Cullinan's Other Half? South Africans Still Busy in Search for Famous Diamond*

Diamond rumors are once more flying about – this time to the effect that the missing portions of the great Cullinan Diamond have been found...>>

Jemima remembered the email from the editor at the *Pretoria Post*. It seemed he could have a point after all. She felt furious with herself for not bringing it up with Mr V just because she had been so continually distracted by Danny, as she had more recently been by James. She really needed to start being more business-focused and less boy-focused if she was going to be a success in her life.

<<*When the Cullinan was discovered it bore every evidence that it was only a portion of a much larger stone...*>>

The article went on to describe how the split of the larger diamond would have happened when it was forced upwards under huge pressure, towards the surface of the earth.

<<*... possibly that the broken-off fragments are scattered over a wide space and that they may be found on the surface of the earth.*>>

Jemima read on that it had been thought that the other half of the Cullinan was in the possession of a tribe not too far from where its 'sister' had been found and, although it also spoke of a Tiffany's gemmologist denying that there ever was another half, Jemima was enthralled. This story could be the making of that new, successful, sensible her.

If she found out that Mr V had in fact bought the missing part of the

Cullinan Diamond, it would be worth much more than he had paid for it. She started Googling 'Cullinan' on her BlackBerry and quickly found its entry in Wikipedia; she scrolled down and saw that it was worth in the region of £1 billion. If the Vogel Vanderpless was in fact the other part of the Cullinan, it would be worth around the same! But if it were the missing part, how on earth had it got from tribes near here - the middle of nowhere - to the jewellery box of an old lady in Manhattan? The plot was thickening and Jemima was feeling more and more excited. It would be the most priceless gem in the world, with everyone wanting to get their hands on it.

She finished reading the piece and looked at her watch, jumping up quickly when she realised that if she wanted to speak to Hannah about this and catch her flight in two hours, she had better skedaddle. Running down the dusty avenue that had been baking in the midday sun, she dashed quickly into 'Cullinan Treasures', one of the gift shops. She wanted to buy a replica of the Cullinan and, having found and paid for what she was looking for, she left quickly and made her way back to the reception cottage, hoping that Hannah was still there. She went up the steps and into the reception to find only the brusque lady searching irately for something in the cupboard behind the reception desk.

"Hello, ummm... I was wondering if Hannah was around?"

"Why?" the lady said, turning around and looking at Jemima over the top of her dusty glasses.

"I wanted to say goodbye and thank her, and actually ask her something."

"She's on a break but I will pass it on for you."

"Oh. OK, well..."

Jemima was interrupted by Hannah, who appeared through a beaded curtain from the room behind.

"Never mind Rhonda, I'm only here. Jemima dear, how may I help you?"

"I was looking through the scrapbook of press cuttings about the mine and found one about rumours of the other half of the Cullinan. Although it also said that they were claimed as false by someone at Tiffany's?"

"Ah, yes. That is a rumour that has circulated for over 100 years. And often when a diamond of a certain size is found at the mine, the rumour reignites. It would be wonderful if it were true but I am certain that even if it had been with a tribe all those years ago, it would have appeared by now. Which it hasn't, unless someone has it and hasn't let on, which seems very unlikely as the diamond would be the most valuable in the world."

Hannah's words echoed just what Jemima had thought to herself.

"Yes, you're right of course – I just loved the thought of it. Could I quickly get a photocopy of the article?"

"Yes, we have some somewhere – let me dig one out for you." The old lady fumbled around in a drawer and pulled out a rather creased piece of paper. "We were asked to send copies of all our information on the rumour of the second Cullinan to a lady in Texas a few months ago and I copied too many so I already have some spare."

"Texas?! Americans are obsessed with diamonds! OK, thank you, and goodbye Hannah – it was so lovely meeting you and spending the morning at the mine."

"Thank you Jemima. Have yourself a safe trip home."

Jemima left for the airport, morosely imagining Fritz and Anoush had just arrived at their camp. She determined to make sure something would happen for her with someone worthwhile before too long. She couldn't help hoping that someone was James, even if he did live on the other side of the world.

16

January 2011 - Cape Town

The plane landed with an hour or so of beach time left. James had already left the club so couldn't pick her up. Jemima was actually quite relieved. She had a lot to think about. She got a taxi back to Marike's empty flat and started to type up what she had learnt.

She also had some work emails, including one from Mr V saying that he hoped that she had enjoyed the mine and that he had something interesting to tell her on her return. She hoped that the something interesting wasn't related to her Christmas fling with his grandson and replied confidently, as though there was nothing to worry about.

<<*Happy New Year Mr V! Just back from the mine, which was fascinating. Having a great time. Wishing we could relocate the Press office here.*>>

<<*Good. Mr V*>>

"Oh well, that was an OK reply!" she said out loud. "I wonder what it is he has to tell me."

She started searching for the email from the *Pretoria Post* journalist but couldn't find it anywhere, which was strange. She checked her deleted items but it wasn't there either.

Standing up and looking out of the window at the inviting beach, she decided that she deserved a cold swim. Quickly getting her things together, she ran out of the apartment building and down the hill to the beach. She couldn't wait to wash off all the dust from the mine and didn't care how cold the sea was this time.

Running into the sea, she was knocked over by an enormous wave and swirled around in the freezing water. When she got up and steadied herself enough to walk back out of the water to her towel, she saw James appearing from the road, walking towards her. She was so happy to see him and ran up to say hello.

"How was your day, except for that wipe out?!" He grabbed her big blue and white Ralph Lauren beach towel and wrapped it around her.

"Haha – yes, that was quite a wave – thank God my bikini didn't disappear! Anyway, my day was amazing! I discovered quite a cool story, or more of a mystery…"

James raised his eyebrows. "Listen, I thought we could go to a new restaurant on Cape Point with incredible views and delicious seafood. We could watch the sunset later over the ocean and you can tell me all about this mystery. My truck is in the parking lot just over there."

"I would love that. Can we pass by Marike's so that I can change?"

Jemima dried herself off and pulled her tiny denim cut offs and t-shirt back on. At the apartment she changed into a little summer dress while James waited in the car making some business calls, then they headed out on the road to Cape Point.

She chattered away about her trip to the mine, not mentioning of course her run in with Fritz in Johannesburg, and James listened intently. She told him the story of the finding of the original Cullinan Diamond, how it was now in the British Crown jewels, and how she had discovered that over the past century there had been persistent rumours of the existence of a sister diamond. She told him about the Vogel Vanderpless and, although not 100% accurate, how tests by

Bothebie's suggested that its provenance was from the same part of Africa as the Cullinan Mine's deposits.

"And you are wondering if it is the mystery stone that diamond hunters have been on the lookout for?" he teased.

"Yes. Wouldn't it be incredible?"

"Well, it seems that it would be one hell of a diamond if it was true. How can you be sure?"

"I don't know. I am sure there is a way of further tests but I doubt the Queen will let us check hers to see if they're a match! It would be interesting to see from where this Mrs Vanderpless got the diamond and why it came to auction in the rough. I've always been so interested in history and mysteries!"

"You are very sweet you know," James smiled.

"Thank you," she laughed, blushing – again wondering why he hadn't taken his flirting and kissing any further. He could be the key to ending her unhealthy obsession with Fritz once and for all.

She must have fallen asleep as the next thing she knew, they were pulling up in the car park at Cape Point. They got out of his truck and immediately a pack of baboons ran towards her. She was terrified and jumped back into the vehicle; she had hated monkeys ever since she was a little girl and had wound down her window at Longleat Safari Park. A monkey had reached through the window and tried to tear off one of her bunches.

"Come on – they're fine!" James shooed them away and opened the door.

"No way James, I hate monkeys."

"They're not monkeys, they're baboons. They will ignore you if you ignore them."

"OK," she reluctantly got out of the truck.

"Come on, let's go and get something to eat. I'm starving."

They walked up to the restaurant, which was mostly packed with tourists, although James said hello to a couple as they walked past. When they sat down he explained that they were very wealthy friends of his grandmother's who lived near them just outside Johannesburg, in a suburb called Hyde Park.

"How funny – Hyde Park."

"Yes, I know," he smiled warmly. "You should talk to my grandma, actually. She knows lots of stories about the diamond industry and she grew up near the Cullinan Mine. Actually, she's also a great one for mysteries – I bet that if there was one, she would know about it."

Jemima was starting to dread leaving James the next day. She couldn't bear the thought of returning to cold wintry London with all the memories of Fritz and Danny's temptations.

17

January 2011 - London

Her flight to London was scheduled to arrive at 6am, but Jemima was awoken by the sound of the captain's voice over the plane's tannoy telling his passengers that there was a 30-minute delay due to snow covering the runway.

Well that is going to be interesting, she thought, realising that she had forgotten to pack a jacket or jersey into her hand luggage. Her thin t-shirt, despite its long sleeves, and jeans, were unlikely to give her much warmth. *I hope this means they've ramped up the heating inside the terminal.* Jemima wrapped her pashmina and aeroplane blanket around her.

It being a cloudless morning, she could see a snow-covered England miles below. She'd had a lot of time to think since she'd last been in England and had decided that she was going to grow up and stop gallivanting around, spending money on pointless things and drinking too much. She wanted to make something of her life that would make her parents proud, instead of going to see them in the country at weekends exhausted and hungover.

Three hours later, Jemima let herself into her flat, worried about being late for work. She had told Mr V that she would be back at her desk at nine that morning but it was already almost 11am. Thanks to the snow there had been no taxis at Heathrow so she had taken the tube to South Kensington only to drag her stupidly heavy suitcase along the streets and then up the six flights of stairs to her apartment as it appeared there were no taxis in London either.

The flat was remarkably tidy and she remembered Flora was away in New York with Benjy, so she would have a peaceful few days to settle back into work. She had a lovely hot shower, thinking she had better unpack later that evening and get to the office as soon as possible. How depressing it was covering up her glorious tan after so many days in little dresses and shorts. Her Converse trainers were absolutely soaked, thanks to her trek from the tube, and she knew walking to work would be quicker than public transport. Pulling on her thick jeans, she remembered that she had a pair of as yet unworn Dior moonboots which would be ideal to wear into work. She clambered up onto her bed to reach the top cupboard and pulled them out.

Just then her BlackBerry beeped, signalling a text,

<<Will be in office in half an hour please come and see me. Mr V>>

Shit, she thought, pulling on the boots and grabbing her bag and long puffa coat. She'd never get there on time.

Jemima ran down the stairs, trying very hard not to trip or slip in the huge boots. Out on the street, the fluffy snow of an hour earlier was turning rapidly into a slushy black mess. She tried walking as fast as she could, only imagining what she looked like skidding around. Fortunately however, the streets were almost empty, with only a few people in Sloane Square and some kids building a snowman in the middle by the fountain. It actually seemed quite romantic and movie-like.

After 20 minutes she had only just got to Hyde Park Corner so replied to Mr V saying that she would be late due to the snow, knowing that he actually thought she was already there at her desk.

Walking through Green Park, she saw more snowmen and people having snowball fights. She wished for a moment that she were with them instead of going to work - she wouldn't have to face the inevitable questions from Paul Pratt and Zoe's two-faced smile. She did wonder what had happened in the few days that she had been away from the office and then decided that, as another New Year's resolution, she would stop being so paranoid about everything. Whenever she saw Mr V's or Paul's name come up on her phone display or email inbox, she got in a panic. It had to stop.

She had been focusing so hard on not slipping that she hadn't noticed she was already walking past the Ritz and would soon be in the office. Her moonboots and jacket had been a life-saver in this freeze but she was looking forward to a cup of coffee.

"Good morning," said the security man, letting her in as she pressed the buzzer. She had forgotten her Vogel security card. One of Paul Pratt's recent rules was that no one was allowed in without their card and failure to adhere to this would result in the loss of a compulsory day from their small allocation of annual holidays. This applied to everyone except the Vogel family - and of course Paul Pratt himself. For them, the door swung open immediately and without question. Luckily, Jemima was on good terms with the security guards.

"Hi, Happy New Year and thank you for letting me in! My goodness, London is quiet this morning!"

"Yes. Only Mr Vogel is here, a few others, and now you. I couldn't really not let you in."

"What?! Where is everyone?"

"Well, all the mainline trains coming into London have been cancelled due to the snow and quite a few of the tube lines are down because of signal failure. And of course no buses or taxis."

"How annoying that I live close enough to walk! How did Mr V's car get in?"

"He's been staying at the Ritz."

"Right, well I had better get upstairs and get ready as he wants to see me... I hope the lift is working and isn't affected by the snow?!"

"No, the lifts aren't affected by the snow."

Maybe she should stop trying to make jokes and just stick to pleasantries.

As the lift opened onto the press office floor, she could hear a phone ringing and guessed it was Mr V wondering where she was – no doubt he had seen her arrival on the screen in his office.

"I have just got in and will be with you in a second!" she trilled, annoyed that she wouldn't have time for a coffee.

As she took off her moonboots she realised that in her haste to leave the apartment she hadn't put any shoes into her bag. It was normally second nature as she usually walked to work in trainers and changed into heels when she got there. She got down and searched under her desk to see if she had left some under there before Christmas. The phone rang again and, banging her head hard trying to get to it, she managed to reach up and grab the handset with one hand whilst rubbing her head with the other, thanking God that there was no one there to see her.

"Sorry, I'm coming!"

"Don't apologise - I love it when you say that!" Danny!

Oh God, is he here? She hadn't replied to his text message at New Year.

"Danny – how are you? I can't talk as I'm meant to be with Mr V so I'm running down there now."

"Are you avoiding me? I am heartbroken and still in bed dreaming of you. I don't think I can face coming into work today."

"Shut up, Danny! I'm almost the only one here, I think."

"I'm sure that will earn you brownie points. I hope that your flight back was OK and you had a good holiday. See you tomorrow."

"OK, thanks, bye!"

Well there was nothing she could do except go and see Mr V in her socks and explain. It was quite annoying really; she had wanted to start the year being sophisticated and professional. Knocking her head and turning up barefoot wasn't quite what she imagined a refined working girl would do but she left the press office with her notepad and pen in hand.

18

"Jemima, I seem to remember that you only arrived back from South Africa today?" Mr V looked surprised at her shoeless feet sliding around on the incredibly polished wooden floor.

"Yes, that's right. I am sorry that I was late but I walked here as there were no taxis. Fortunately I have some moonboots but I forgot to put in a pair of shoes, sorry."

"Never mind," he chuckled. "You made it in, that's the important thing. Right, now sit down. The Vogel Vanderpless is ready to be cut; my diamond cutters have been working on it ever since we commissioned them. It will produce 39 D flawless diamonds and we are going to create the world's most expensive necklace at around 300 carats, which will be ready in early April. I have decided to auction it off at a gala event where I will donate part of the proceeds to the charity of a friend of mine."

"That is so good of you. What is the charity?"

"It is called Actioning Africa, or AcAf, and builds children's hospitals in African countries. I thought that we could unveil the Vogel Vanderpless necklace at an event that I would like you to organise for the charity, of which I am a director. How does that sound?"

He smiled, knowing she would love the project.

"It sounds amazing! When would you like the event to take place? It would be good before all the other summer events in London. How about late April, before the first bank holiday? I think the earlier the better so that it doesn't get confused with our polo day in July."

"I'll leave it with you but yes, good point. Speak to Anna about my movements around then."

"OK, I shall do. And I would have thought that most of our clients, who I suppose you will be asking, will be in London for the start of the summer season."

"Most likely. Now, off you go – I have a lot to get on with and I am extremely annoyed at those people I need to see who aren't here."

"OK," Jemima smiled inwardly, knowing it was most likely Pratt and Anna with whom he was annoyed and glad that she had managed to make it in. "Thank you for this opportunity. It will be the best party that London has ever seen!"

"Good, well don't be too ambitious. But I am sure that you won't let me down." He seemed to be half warning, half encouraging.

Back at her desk, Jemima remembered the missing email from the *Pretoria Post* and wrote a post-it note to remind herself to ask the IT department about it. She sent a quick message to Marike telling how she had arrived back to a snow-clad city and that she'd call in the next few days. She would wait to hear from James rather than contact him.

She began to Google venues in London that would be suitable for the event. The best thing would be to get an events company to sift through them all and she knew just the person to ask.

"Jemima. How lovely to hear from you. How are you? Happy New Year."

Tatiana was somebody Jemima had worked with a great deal. She listened as Jemima explained to her about the forthcoming event and that she would like her to produce it.

"Darling, that sounds perfect. It is not very far off so we should perhaps meet soonest so we can go through things. In fact why not today? It is very quiet, what with London on shut down."

"Today would be great if we can actually get to each other! I had to walk to work in my Dior moonboots and forgot to bring any shoes! Shall we say tea at the Berkeley at 5.30pm?"

"Perfect – see you there. And I'll bring some ideas – I can already imagine the kind of thing Vogel should put on."

"Brilliant – see you later!"

Tatiana was one of the most inspirational people Jemima had met. In her mid 40s with two children, she worked so hard that Jemima was amazed she had found the time to make children, let alone give birth to them. She had an events and public relations business and arranged events for some of the most high profile people and brands in London. Jemima was sure that with Tatiana's help this would be the event of the decade.

She realised she was hungry and wondered what Mr V was doing for lunch. Normally Anna got him a sandwich from Prêt à Manger if he was not eating out but of course Anna wasn't in.

"Hi Mr V, sorry to disturb you but I was just wondering if you needed me to pop out to Prêt or somewhere for your lunch – I was thinking of going there myself?"

"That is very thoughtful of you, Jemima. Let me see… well maybe we should go for lunch and you can tell me all about your South Africa trip. How about Cecconi's in 20 minutes? I am sure you can get us a good table - after all, every time I have seen you there you have a better one than me or my daughter!"

"OK, great," Jemima was flattered and pleased. "Thank you – what a treat to come back to!"

She realised she couldn't wear her moonboots to Cecconi's and had to think of something fast. Her friend and first boss Stephanie was at Gina Shoes so she called ahead and asked her to pick a pair of heels from the sale.

"Of course, darling, I'll have them waiting for you. And you can leave your boots here while you're at lunch."

"Thank you, you're a life-saver! I'll be there as quickly as I can."

With that, Jemima got her things together, pulled on her very soft and warm moonboots and headed back into the snow, which was already melting.

19

The manager at Cecconi's, Giacommo, found Jemima her favourite table in the VIP section, opposite the door. It was a banquette corner table for two, concealed from those entering the restaurant but where one could see who was coming in and if necessary hide. She had often seen a former Prime Minster hidden at the exact same table, often with tabloid newspaper editors.

As she sat down, her BlackBerry pinged:

<<running late be there soon Mr V>>

She was quite pleased as it meant she could have a cappuccino and catch up on the newspapers, which she had missed for the past couple of weeks. She liked to keep abreast of current affairs, although she was most interested in the pieces on London's social scene, and interviews with successful women like Tamara Mellon, Natalie Massenet and of course Anya Hindmarch catalysing her dreams of making a real success out of her life and making her parents proud. Although she had made it as head of PR for one of the biggest fine jewellery houses in the world, Jemima still felt she had a long way to go.

After 30 quick minutes of flicking through the *Times* and keeping an eye on who was coming in, Mr V arrived.

"A glass of champagne for you both?" Giacommo asked

"No thank you, Giacommo, but I would love a sparkling water." Jemima was determined to keep to her new resolution.

"Yes, please can we have a bottle of San Pellegrino and then we'll order in a few minutes." Mr V turned to Jemima. "So tell me, have you made any headway with the event? I really do want it to be the best London has seen. This must be spectacular."

"Yes, I have been looking at appropriate venues and have a meeting a bit later with a friend who has the best events production company in London."

"Why do we need another company – can't you do it? This is one of the reasons I employed you, Jemima."

She immediately worried that he might think she was not up to the job but remembered her other resolution. "All big events such as this would have a production company. I will manage on a day-to-day basis but we only have four months so we need someone really experienced."

"OK, well get some quotes and we'll decide. Now tell me about South Africa. You look well."

No wonder Mr V was so successful at selling diamonds; he could charm anyone. She went on to tell him all about her trip, naturally missing out anything about James.

Their food soon arrived. Jemima had chosen sea bass with fennel, while Mr V had a burger and chips.

"You must not tell anyone about this – I'm meant to be on a diet but this cold weather makes me so hungry. Help yourself to the chips."

"You don't need to be on a diet!" Jemima exclaimed, laughing. For his age, Mr V was remarkably fit and svelte. Most men in their mid-60s – especially those who were billionaires - were at least double his size.

"You're kind, Jemima, but my wife would kill me if she could see me now."

"Well, what she doesn't know won't hurt her," she pinched a chip and dipped it in the mayonnaise pot and then the tomato ketchup, not really showing off the table manners she should. "Did you know that there were rumours going around after the Cullinan was found that it would have originally been part of a larger diamond? There was an article in the mine's museum all about it."

Mr V chuckled. "I think they are just that: rumours. But it could be the most valuable diamond *if* it was ever found."

"But the VV could be it?!"

"Chance would be a fine thing. The diamond most likely comes from the same mine, but..."

"Would you get it tested?"

"It would be very hard to persuade those in charge of the Crown Jewels to let us get our hands on them on a whim." He dismissed her question and Jemima knew that her idea was of no interest to him. "Anyway, you need to get back to work, as do I. I'll get the bill."

"Thank you for a delicious lunch."

"Well, I expect you to work hard this year, Jemima – we have a lot going on. Let me know about how your meetings go with the event company, I like to be kept in the know. Right, let's go."

Mr V stopped to talk to someone he'd seen on the other side of the restaurant and said Jemima should go ahead without him. She left the restaurant tottering in her new heels back to Stephanie to pick up her moonboots. Having changed her shoes she walked as quickly as possible to make sure she was back when Mr V returned.

An email from Noémie appeared as soon as she switched her monitor on: <<*Russian Vogue shoot has been brought forward to tomorrow. I hope that you can come. It seems Sahara is in the country for only a day or two so they've had to reschedule it for tomorrow. Hoping that snow would have melted by then. I've already chosen the pieces and had them signed off by Danny last week. They're in the file labelled 'SS Russian Vogue' so if you wouldn't mind emailing Richard the images and their codes so they can get them ready for tomorrow first thing. They want us there early – 8.30am - but she is always late so no real hurry. See you in the morning. Can't wait to hear all about Cape Town. Hope you're not too brown!*>>

<<*Brilliant. I'm the only one in with Mr V and a few others. Store is open so shall call them now and send the email. Cape Town amazing – will divulge. Hope you had a nice New Year and the kids are well. See you tomorrow. Snow mostly slush now in Mayfair!*>>

<<*Ooohh exciting!*>>

Jemima went into the shoots' file and found, in Noémie's typically meticulous way, the pieces she had mentioned. Jemima was still overcome by them, even in photo format. As the shoot was for *Russian Vogue* and also one of the most famous faces in the world, Noémie had quite rightly chosen big important Vogel pieces: a white diamond and emerald necklace which cascaded over the décolletage like a waterfall and a matching pair of earrings; a pair of white diamond and ruby chandelier earrings with matching pendant necklace; a similar but much larger pendant with blue sapphires; a huge yellow and white diamond cuff bracelet. Jemima couldn't wait. She wondered if she would get to meet the famous model.

As she stepped outside into the dusk, London seemed as empty as when she had arrived. The snow had almost disappeared, however - instead there was the yellowy-orange haze of the street lights mixed with car headlights. It was freezing and she couldn't wait for a hot chocolate at the Berkeley.

Jumping on the number 19 bus outside the Ritz on Piccadilly, she jumped out at Hyde Park Corner and walked the short distance to the hotel, which still had its spectacular Christmas tree and decorations up; there was one day left until the 6th January when tradition dictated they be removed. It had been very odd seeing trees and decorations in Cape Town – they seemed so out of place in the shopping malls when it was 35 degrees outside. Jemima spotted Tatiana still wrapped up in her mink, sitting in the Caramel Room, and made a bee line for her. She was pleased to catch the waiter and order a hot chocolate, making a note to herself that as from tomorrow she must go back to not eating; she didn't want to put on the weight she had lost on her holiday diet of wine, sushi and sunshine.

"Jemima – wow, you look so tanned and thin!"

"Thin? How can you tell, parcelled up in my ski clothes? I definitely got some funny looks on my way in. How are you?!"

"Exhausted – Christmas with two kids and both sets of grandparents is never to be repeated! You might hate being unmarried, darling, but honestly, enjoy your freedom whilst you can. I'd LOVE to spend Christmas in Cape Town."

"New Year," Jemima corrected, "I had a cosy family Christmas in Dorset... anyway, it's so nice to see you. Thank you for coming."

"Of course – now I haven't got forever as I need to relieve the poor suffering nanny. Let's talk about the event." Tatiana was as ever to the point and Jemima made another mental note - to try to be more like that; cut the excess chat.

"OK, brilliant. Wow, here's my hot chocolate – and your...?"

"I know, it smells revolting – I would love one of their Prêt-a-Porteas but I'm detoxing so it is a Chinese tea which is supposed to give me more energy!"

"If you can keep it down... We did an amazing Vogel biscuit for the tea before Christmas. It was a biscuit in the shape of a flower brooch, covered in silver and multi-coloured iced balls that looked like pavé diamonds. Needless to say I brought lots of journalists here to try them and ate tons!"

"What a clever idea." Tatiana was clearly keen to keep focused.

"Right, well as you might know, Vogel bought a very famous diamond before Christmas. It was cut in a very old-fashioned and clumsy way so our guys are working night and day re-cutting it to create an amazing piece of jewellery that we are going to auction off at an event in a few months' time. Part of the proceeds will go to the charity of a friend of Mr V's, Actioning Africa, which provides hospitals for children in Africa. To be honest, I think the main point of the event is to promote Vogel and sell the necklace..."

"Yes I agree, but nevertheless it will also look good if he is seen being philanthropic. I'll come up with some ideas and we should go to look at some venues. Are you asking anyone else to pitch for this?"

"I should do but time really is of the essence, isn't it? Towards the end of April is when we'd like it and it's already 5th January! I trust you and he's given me complete authorisation."

"Immediately the venue that springs to mind is Somerset House. We've got a really good relationship there so I will be able to keep costs down. Don't worry, we'll get quotes from some others too."

Jemima smiled inwardly. She knew Tatiana was on her wavelength; she loved Somerset House and hoped they'd be able to secure it for Mr V's big event. She discussed more details with Tatiana who, as soon as she'd finished her disgusting detox tea, stood up.

"Good. Now, I have to go. I'll be in touch tomorrow about when we can do a scout around and see which other venues would work."

"Great. Thanks Tats." Jemima sat and finished her hot chocolate, watching her whirlwind-like friend collect her coat and head off to her Range Rover, and back to her family.

20

The next day, Vogel's global headquarters were back to normal. As was London, with rows of red buses clogging up Piccadilly and black cabs pulling up at the Ritz. Jemima, smiling at the ever-present green-cloaked doormen, walked past towards Vogel House.

The press office was treated a little like a periphery department and those in it significantly superfluous to the success of the company, despite their dedication and hard work. Alexa had the final say on what was produced for the press, be it a release or a piece of jewellery for a shoot. The family were very specific as to which publications they believed they should be in and which pieces they were willing to let loose into the hands of the stylists.

Noémie managed the shoots and was utterly thorough in doing so. Due to the value of the jewellery, one of the company's security team always went with her on a shoot. Most of the other houses simply sent a security guard alone, but Vogel wanted the jewellery to be handled only by a member of the press office to ensure nothing was broken or manhandled badly and that the piece was used appropriately. Once a pair of ruby chandelier earrings were used as nipple tassels on a very buxom model in a shoot, causing no end of trouble for Jemima's predecessor while Noémie had been away on holiday.

Jemima found out quickly that if there was a celebrity involved in the shoot, the civilians (PRs and guards) and even the jewellery were kept in a separate room with not much lee-way for negotiation or handling of the pieces. The Sahara Scott shoot was in North London

in what looked from the outside to be a disused prison. They had
been told by the fashion shoot coordinator to arrive by 8.30am as
there were a lot of items to get through – both clothes and
accessories – but they turned up later as the store couldn't let the
jewellery out so early. Noémie warned Jemima that the shoot was
unlikely to get underway for hours.

"Why are we the only girls?" Jemima whispered to Noémie. "And
the only PRs?"

"Vogel and Graff are the only brands which send their PRs along.
The others don't often bother. Sometimes some of them just send
pieces along on a bike!"

"Wow – we couldn't do that. I wonder if Sahara is here. Have you
met her before? She was sitting behind us at the auction before
Christmas. She is pretty amazing looking, even in the flesh, although
she has a terrible scar on the side of her face that I hadn't noticed
before."

"Yes, I remember you saying. No, I've not met her. I'm sure she
isn't here yet. She has the worst reputation for not turning up on
time."

Three hours later, after a lot of eye-rolling, watches and BlackBerries
being checked again and again, in walked one of the world's most
famous supermodels and most famous of divas, Sahara Scott, clad in
a full-length grey-blue fox fur coat.

"Mornin' everybody. What y'all waiting for?"

"You, princess," chirped one of the men but Sahara had already
swept into the next room, a huge metal sliding door to divide her and

the magazine team from the mere civilians and their jewels.

After another hour, Jemima discovered that they were not being given lunch so, after listening to the fashion team ordering Itsu sushi and sandwiches from Prêt, Jemima and Noémie decided to brave the torrential rain, which had appeared only to add even further gloom to the already dire day, and make a trip to the supermarket around the corner. Their jewels would be under the watchful eyes of all present, particularly their own guard.

By the time they had got back, shooting was already underway. The security guard informed them that the large emerald and diamond choker was with Sahara in front of the photographer's lens. However, the door to the adjacent room was being kept firmly shut, due to someone trying to sneak a peek earlier. Jemima didn't know how Noémie endured these days, sometimes several a week. She had imagined it would be interesting with such a famous model but they were being treated like second-class citizens. She wondered how many pieces of jewellery were actually sold thanks to a shoot in a magazine. It was brand awareness, explained Noémie, and *Russian Vogue* was probably the most important publication for Vogel to feature in as their best clients were either Russian or American.

Suddenly the door slid open and in walked Sahara, wearing a pair of black leather shorts at the top of her very long legs, which appeared even longer thanks to a pair of stiletto ankle boots. A brown and white fur gilet was flapping open to reveal a rather crepey décolletage, and she was holding the diamond and emerald necklace in the palm of her hand.

"Who here is from Vogel?" she called out in a low, husky voice.

Before they announced themselves, Jemima noticed the looks of frustration from the otherwise stony faces of the other security guards. They clearly wished it was their jewellery she was carelessly clutching so they could have the opportunity of talking to her.

"We are." Noémie stood up confidently and held out her hand. "Noémie - and my colleague, Jemima."

Rather than politely shaking Noémie's hand, Sahara dropped the necklace into it.

"So where is the diamond?"

Although she had a feeling as to which diamond Sahara was referring, Jemima was too celeb-struck to answer and just smiled when the yellow eyes glared at her questioningly.

"Do you mean the Vogel Vanderpless? It is currently being re-cut," Noémie unwaveringly told her.

"I'll speak to Sidney, I was there when he secretly bought it – my boyfriend wanted it, or rather I did! Right, I suppose we must get back to the diamonds here!"

Sahara hot-footed it back into the adjacent room and someone slid the door shut with a bang.

"Well – that's my girl!" came the predictable crack from one of the guards. "Always a pleasure to see her."

"I wonder why she is so interested in the VV…" Jemima mused to Noémie, "I saw her after the auction, hiding in a corner and speaking angrily on the phone to someone."

"She was probably shouting at her oligarch boyfriend for not buying it! Anyway, I hope this doesn't go on much longer. They've already shot a few of our pieces and I'm going out to the theatre later."

"Go – I can stay here."

"Are you sure? OK, I'll see next time the assistant comes through. She's very fabulous, isn't she?"

"Amazing – but did you notice the scar?"

"Slightly, now you mention it – but it was mostly covered with makeup and hair. Of course anything like that will be airbrushed out in the final photos."

"I wish I was that gobsmackingly amazing. I'm sure if I were I'd be hitched to an equally gorgeous guy."

"Darling, looks aren't everything."

"Yes, yes, I know!"

21

London - April 19th 2011

Having dreamt about Fritz for the first time in months, Jemima awoke to a mass of blond hair, which wasn't her own. In a split second, everything came back to her: James had called her to say he was in London and asked if she wanted some dinner.

It was almost four months since he had put her on the plane in Cape Town. They had spoken a few times and emailed at least once a week but she had spent the interim time keeping to her New Year's resolution of not drinking or going out too much, instead planning the event, and not doing much else. She felt she deserved a fun dinner with a hot South African who had been in her thoughts for the past few months.

However, she had definitely not intended to wake up next to him in Claridge's the day before the most important of her career. She jumped out of the huge bed, put on her clothes, which were strewn around the room, and managed to sneak out without waking him.

She smiled to herself in the lift. Her heart felt fluttery as she remembered their fun night and how nice it was to be with someone who really seemed to like her. He had taken her for dinner at Nobu on Berkeley Street and then after a night cap in the dark and secretive Fumoir bar of the hotel, they had eventually made love. Claridge's was her favourite hotel in London and making love to James was even more wonderful than she'd often imagined and day-dreamed about. Why she'd been dreaming of Fritz, she had no idea.

Back in January, just after Mr V had given her the project, Jemima caught a glimpse of Fritz and his girlfriend one Saturday afternoon on the King's Road in Chelsea. They were tanned from their six star safari and looked like the perfect couple, walking arm-in-arm with a collection of designer shopping bags on both of their spare shoulders. She knew then and there, admittedly not for the first time, that she absolutely had to move on with her life and forget him.

Consequently, Jemima threw herself into making certain that the event would be the huge success Mr V and Alexa were expecting.

Flora seemed not to know anything about Fritz's new girlfriend, which was a relief as she couldn't quiz her every other day as she had been apt to do before.

With regards Danny, except for the initial phone call on her first day back, Jemima hadn't seen or heard much from him for a few weeks after her return from Cape Town. He'd had to go the States and then on to the Far East, visiting the various Vogel stores.

Jemima had gathered from Laura, his assistant, that he had met someone in New York and they were pretty serious. Jemima had felt a pang of jealousy and was desperate to know who he was seeing.

When he got back, Danny confirmed that he was seeing someone who he thought was quite special, but didn't tell her any more. His mother had told him for the sake of Vogel he had to stop flirting with clients' children in Mayfair nightclubs and getting photographed coming out of various hotels. Jemima had kept an eye on all paparazzi photographs online and in the press but she still hadn't found who this mysterious girl was.

Now James was in London, it was more than a relief. It was exciting.

As she approached Vogel House, Jemima saw Anna speeding down the street from Piccadilly in her pristine white plimsolls. Anna always got in earlier than everyone else, so Jemima realised happily that she was also early. She had a great deal to do.

"Morning! You're here very early, Jemima?" Mr V's PA enquired suspiciously. Things had been getting worse with Anna, who seemed to be annoyed that she hadn't been more involved with the charity event. To make matters worse, Anna had been asked by Mr V to be there on the night, meaning she had to miss her ten-year-old's school play.

"I've got so much to do, with the event tomorrow."

"I would have thought you should be ready by now, with only 24 hours to go? And isn't the event production company on top of things – we're paying them enough!?" Anna said snidely.

Obviously Paul had been complaining to her about the cost of the event, which they had managed to more than make back in table sales.

"Anna, I'm so sorry that you have been asked to help tomorrow night and have to miss Tom's play. I did tell Mr V that everything was covered, as Noémie will be around, and Zoe of course - as well as all the staff from Excellent Events." Jemima ignored Anna's barbed comment.

"Thank you Jemima," Anna said in a more conciliatory, though formal, tone. "I look forward to your briefing meeting later."

"OK. Bye – see you later."

A couple of minutes later, Jemima was at her desk and on the phone to Tatiana.

"Tats, I am going to get to Somerset House for 10 o'clock, I've got a security meeting. Do you know how the setting up is coming along? Thank god for this good weather, I hope it stays!"

"They started last night as the big lorries carrying all the marquee equipment and stages aren't allowed to enter the quadrangle until 7pm when it is closed to the public. They had everything major in place before having to leave this morning. I won't be there until 11ish but Sophie is there and in full command, as you can imagine!"

"Great! I'm coming with our head of security to go through all those aspects with theirs, which will take a few hours no doubt, so let's stay in radio contact."

Tatiana and Jemima had visited several of London's top event venues before picking the one they had thought of first – Somerset House; a beautiful huge building on the north of the River Thames with a large courtyard in which they would have their marquee.

As the majority of the money raised was going to go to building a hospital in Africa, they had decided to use an Africa theme for the decoration of the marquee. Tatiana's designer had created visuals of their ideas on the computer, which had won over even Mr V, thanks to their originality. The marquee was to look like a 1920s safari camp: a huge cream canvas tent decorated inside with original safari antiques such as huge ostrich feather plumes, animal skins and pictures of desert scenes.

There would be 30 tables of ten set up like those they used in the 1920s, with canvas-style chairs and tables set with white linen table cloths. Jemima really wanted the guests to feel that they had been transported back to the golden era of travel and exploration. She hoped that the animal skins would not offend and that people would not find the theme hypocritical when the aim of the evening was to raise money for the ill and impoverished.

The invitations had been sent out as soon as the location had been decided upon and she had called the event 'An Evening of Safari during the Era of Elegance', hoping that most of the guests would dress accordingly. She knew that no money would be spared by their female guests to ensure that they were the belle of the ball. Charlie had told her ages ago that Neville's was already completely booked up with blow-dries and hair put-ups and Jemima guessed that it would be the same at all the major hair salons. It gave her a real tingle of excitement that this was all her baby.

The phone rang and she saw it was Anna on the line

"Hi Anna – have you been let off?!"

"No! But Jemima, Mr Vogel would like to see you in his office."

"OK, thanks, I'm on my way!"

"Come in," came the familiar voice from behind the increasingly familiar door. Jemima had lost quite a bit of weight in the past few months, exhausting herself running up and down the stairs between their offices so much that by the time she was back at her Sloane Square flat she could barely muster the energy to run up the six flights of stairs. She had even had to get the Marchesa dress she was going to wear taken in. It was so beautiful and glamorous, and she just wished James could come to see the event and her!

"Good Morning Mr V," she said brightly, still on a high from the previous night, before seeing Alexa on the other side of the door and worrying she was being a bit informal but Alexa smiled and greeted her. "Jemima, this arrived yesterday and I thought that you might like to see it."

She made her way over to the window, where sunlight was streaming through and a large polished wooden box sat at the end of Mr V's long desk.

"This is the Vogel Vanderpless. The most expensive necklace in the world which we will be auctioning tomorrow night."

Slowly, Mr V opened the box to reveal the most enormous necklace Jemima, and probably the world, had ever seen. An alternate combination of 39 D flawless pear-shaped and round stones ran either side to meet in the middle, with two large pear shapes attaching a large round brilliant from which hung a huge pear-shaped diamond. The brilliance of each exquisitely cut stone, which seemed like pure ice, attracting and refracting the sun, almost blinded her.

"Is it heavy?" she thought out loud.

"Would you like to see?" he said, taking the necklace out of the box and putting it around Jemima's neck. She walked over to the hand mirror that was on his desk next to the box and picked it up. As she was admiring her reflection, Mr V explained the sizes of the four main stones.

"The pear shape is 95.71 carats, the large round is 63.12 and the two pear-shape diamonds flanking the round are 29 carats each. The 35 smaller stones range from 0.9 carats to 3.2 carats. The necklace in total is 302 carats - only 2 carats more than what I had estimated." Mr V spoke proudly.

The coolness of the diamonds against her skin shocked Jemima a little but that was nothing compared to how it felt to have this exquisite necklace hanging around her neck. She wondered if a noose felt a little like this.

"Goodness – well this is a day I'll tell my children about - I have tried on the most expensive necklace in the world! How much is it worth?"

"100 million pounds." Alexa spoke coolly as ever.

Jemima noticed that neither Mr V nor his daughter had flicked an eyelid, whereas she suddenly felt that she really did have a noose around her neck and was going to choke to death.

"Wow," she said when she'd come up for air and realised that she was actually holding onto the wall. "Do you think someone will pay that much?"

"Of course!" Mr V said impatiently and motioned for her to lean down so he could take it off. "And Sahara Scott is going to model it at the event. I have given my wife the remaining three stones, which I have had made into a set of earrings and a ring."

"Really? Sahara Scott? But I have a model lined up already, do you remember – we did the casting last week? You chose her."

"Of course I remember, Jemima, but I had dinner with Sahara last night. I showed her the necklace here first and she asked whether I would like her to wear it at the event. And she is waiving her fee as it is for charity."

Of course, Jemima thought – she hadn't failed to notice how interested in the diamond Sahara had been ever since she saw her at the sale in December. There was something more to this; Sahara was infamous for not being charitable.

"Well that is great news; it will look amazing on her skin. Her ex-boyfriend is coming with his new girlfriend, that 20-year-old Latvian supermodel everyone is obsessed with."

"Sahara will be on my table. I've told her she can sit next to one of our top clients from Texas and I think that they will probably already know each other. He is much richer than the Russian so she will be happy. She probably offered to model it to make the Russian think twice." Jemima couldn't help but feel that Sahara's offer was about much more than making the Russian jealous but didn't say so.

"Now, where are we with entertainment? I would like, oh what is her name... she lost in the television singing competition... to sing."

"Memphis Brown?! But Mr V, it is tomorrow night and we already have Dame Shirley Bassey singing *Diamonds are Forever*. I think it is too late to add anyone in and not only did she lose but she really isn't in the same league...."

"Jemima, please make this happen," Mr V said in the calm but authoritative way that could freeze oceans. "She is the granddaughter of friends of ours who would like to see her perform at the event - they are coming as our guests."

Jemima didn't dare look to Alexa for help. She knew she would be fighting a losing battle. Her only chance to salvage this would be to go and see Danny.

"OK – I'll speak to her agent, if she has one, and let production know to slot her in somewhere appropriate."

"Very well. And have we sold all the tables?"

"Yes, and we have a waiting list!"

"Good. I knew £5000 a ticket wasn't too much – but we should not have a waiting list – put in more tables."

Jemima didn't even attempt to say that this would be a problem due to space. He would probably just tell her to extend the marquee, knocking down a wall of Somerset House if need be. She just nodded on her way out of his office.

22

As ever, the third floor was silent, Danny's team beavering away robotically; although a few did look up and smile once Jemima had been allowed entrance through the coded door. She was determined to muster support against Mr V's new ideas.

Laura waved to attract her attention. As Danny's assistant, Laura was in charge of checking the grading of the non-diamond precious stones, such as emeralds, sapphires, rubies and tanzanites that came through Vogel's vaults. She was also obsessed with celebrities.

"Who's coming tomorrow night?" she tried to whisper so Danny wouldn't hear. Everyone nearby perked up to listen.

"Aha, wait and see…!" Jemima winked and headed to Danny's office.

Although they'd had an intimate relationship and Danny had never used it against her, Jemima still occasionally walked on egg shells with him as she knew well that he had a reputation to change his mood and mind at the slightest opportunity. Plus he was very much in awe of his grandfather, so any criticism of the latter's ideas was unlikely to go down well.

"Morning, Jemima. So I gather you've seen the necklace? And now you are here to bribe me into buying it for you? I told you… I'm seeing someone else, you must stop pining after me!"

"Whatever, Danny. Anyway, you couldn't afford it!" she laughed.

"No, I need you to tell your grandfather that we just cannot have Memphis Brown singing alongside Shirley Bassey. Also, he wants to add more tables to enable those on the waiting list to attend, which is all well and good but there just isn't going to be any space for them.

We're pushed as it is – it'll probably be a fire hazard and the insurance won't cover it... please can you do something?"

"Calm down. As you know, when Grandpa wants something, he gets it. I'm afraid you're just going to have to make it work. I know Memphis Brown is crap, but her grandfather is his oldest friend. And she could be better since she lost in *X Factor* – had lessons, perhaps?"

"Danny, I'm surprised you're admitting to watching *X Factor*! OK, you're right. I'm going to call her agent and find out what the deal is, but the table issue is a real concern."

"Just try, Jemima. Now, I have to get on, I have so much to do as I'm off straight after the party."

"Oh how nice, where to?"

"New York for various business things, then Petra is taking me for Easter in the Hamptons."

"Very nice!"

"I know. I must remember to thank Zoe for introducing us!"

"Zoe?! My assistant?" Jemima asked incredulously.

"Yes. I bumped into her in the lift before going off to New York in January and asked her if there were any cool new bars to go to. She had her friend, Petra, meet me at the Plaza and take me out. I guess things went from there."

"Of course." Jemima felt shocked that Zoe had done this without saying anything. Leaving by the backstairs door she ran up to her office. She was running late for the security check and didn't want to field any more questions about who was going to the event. She felt uneasy, sure that there were things going on which she had no idea about.

Zoe was sitting at her desk, casually looking at Facebook on her screen, not even bothering to change pages when Jemima walked in. She really pushed the boundaries sometimes and Jemima knew that she had got in late again. Maybe when she did work experience at *Tatler* it was OK to spend the day following the lives of her friends, as they often featured in the publication, but surely few of her friends bought diamonds. Seeing the Vogel ring flashing on Zoe's finger, Jemima thought again.

She couldn't be bothered to quiz her now about Danny and her friend, and she didn't want Zoe to think she cared about it.

"Zoe, how are you?" she asked, switching to boss-mode. "Right. Today and tomorrow I need you to work fully with me on the event. Please can you find out the number of Memphis Brown's agent, speak to her, or him, saying that you're calling about the Vogel gala dinner tomorrow night. Coordinate with Tristan, at Excellent, who is running the entertainment schedule – he was in the meeting the other day, remember? Then speak to the printers re: the programmes and placement cards. The extra ones should be arriving today – of course now we have Memphis we'll have to do an insert as I am sure it is too late to do another print run for her; we've already re-printed twice. Please can you deal with that? And could you keep me posted – I've got to go to SH for the security brief with Philip Goldsmith and see what is going on there. Great, thanks." She didn't wait for an answer. "Actually I must call Philip now."

"Of course," Zoe said sweetly, although Jemima couldn't help but wonder if she had taken in all of the speech.

"Good. On a lighter note – what are you wearing?"

"Oh, my mother has sent over the dress Ralph made for me for my graduation ball last Fall."

"Sounds amazing!" Jemima replied as casually as she could. Of course Ralph had... she had become quite good at not letting Zoe's indulgent lifestyle of a designer wardrobe, multi-carat jewellery and glamorous holidays faze her, preferring to act as though she lived the same way.

She checked her phone and noticed a text from James. Her heart jumped.

<<Cinderella – you disappeared?!>>

<<I have the event of my life tomorrow night and however much I'd like to lie in bed with you all day, I couldn't.>>

<<Event of your life!? Thought that was to be our wedding?>>

<< Ha-ha. Touché. Call you later.>>

She cringed as she remembered the previous night when she had been bemoaning the fact that practically all her friends were in marital bliss. Even Flora was getting serious with Benjy and would be moving to New York at the end of the summer to be with him. After months of barely any alcohol, the several glasses of champagne had hit Jemima hard and before she knew it she was heading back to James's hotel, giddy like a teenager, and asking him if they could perhaps get married.

Oh god – how embarrassing, she felt herself blush as she remembered that particular conversation. So not cool to be having a conversation like that with someone like James.

"OK, bye Jemima..." her thoughts were interrupted by Zoe leaving.

"Yes, goodbye Zoe – call me with any questions."

"Bye – hope it is looking nice – I can't wait to see it. Oh and don't forget to call Philip!"

"Yes, I was just about to!" Jemima picked up the phone to remind the head of security of their meeting.

23

Philip Goldsmith had been at Vogel for 30 years, as he was apt to remind everyone, and 'security' was his middle name. He had been a childhood friend of Mr Vogel's in Liverpool who was very good at looking after his family and friends. Philip managed the transportation of stock around the world with the utmost vigilance and could probably tell you down to the exact GPS coordinate where each piece of jewellery was, even when it was airborne. He was a nice enough man but seemed to live on the verge of a nervous breakdown. Something which Paul Pratt took advantage of and only made worse.

"Philip, hi, are you ready? Great, I'll meet you downstairs."

Jemima took the lift down to the ground floor and waited for him outside. She hoped again that the fine weather would last for the next 36 hours. As he came through the doors, Philip already looked flustered. He was holding his briefcase and followed by the two security guards who were going to be guarding the necklace at the event. Jemima flagged down a taxi and they all got in, the two bulky guards looking more than a little uncomfortable perched on the jump seats and staring blankly out of their respective windows.

"Right, Jemima. This is the biggest undertaking in the 30 years that I have been working for Mr Vogel. If anything goes wrong, you and I will be jobless and also most likely headless. Have you made sure that the head of security at the venue is meeting us now?"

"Jamie Anderson," she informed him, "Of course, this meeting has been in all of our diaries for weeks. Jamie is going to walk us around the whole place. You must tell him what needs to be closed off and I am going to show you both where Sahara Scott will put the jewellery on, how she will walk around the marquee, and then go back to take it off."

Suddenly, the attention of the two guards turned from looking out of the windows to looking at Jemima as if to ask if they had heard her right. It was incredible the effect Sahara had on people, men and women alike.

"Mr V had dinner with her last night and she offered to wear it. She is quite tricky – I do hope that she does what we tell her to do." She immediately regretted saying that as she knew Philip would start panicking.

"What do you mean – you *hope*?" he asked nervously.

"She is a diva, like lots of supermodels, actresses and singers. They are not used to being told what to do. Particularly at her age. Even on set. I'm sure she will be brilliant, I read in a magazine that she is much happier now that she is spending more time back home in Texas and is breeding horses." Jemima spoke confidently though remembered Sahara's frosty manner at the January *Russian Vogue* shoot.

"Good. Don't worry me, Jemima. Mr Vogel should never have decided to unveil the necklace at the event in the first place. I blame you for this mad idea. In 30 years, Mr V has never done anything so risky… the insurance premium is very high just for the night."

"Philip, at the end of the day, it is his money and his choice. He knows the risks, I am sure. Right, here we are. I'll pay."

The marquee was up and already looking spectacular, even without any of the decoration. Somerset House was only closed to the public for the event the following day so the events production team would be madly carrying out all the decorating during that night and the next day but all major building inside it was already going on.

Jemima led the way through the quadrangle to the events office in a room overlooking the Thames, hoping that Philip would not want to have security on the river due to its proximity to the necklace.

"Hi Sophie, hello Polly. This is Philip Goldsmith, our Head of Security."

"*Director* of Security... hello, Philip Goldsmith," Philip corrected Jemima, formally shaking hands.

Sophie worked with Tatiana at Excellent Events and Polly was Head of Events at Somerset House. Jemima had become good friends with them both, working on the gala, but they were all looking forward to it being over and their lives getting back on track. It wasn't usual to plan an event at this level in only just over four months.

"Hello," they said in unison.

"It's looking great so far, isn't it? I've got a meeting with Jamie Anderson, your head of security now. Where should I go?"

"I'll call down."

When Jamie Anderson arrived, Jemima knew that Philip would not be happy. Jamie Anderson was in fact a woman, American, about 45 years old and dressed head to toe in beautiful designer clothes. It transpired that she had been Director of Security at The Metropolitan Museum in New York and had only recently taken this job after moving to London with her husband. Philip was immediately

157

flustered. It was well known in the company that he never trusted women with specifics such as security, and Americans even less so, having once had a security scare at the Fifth Avenue store.

"Good morning," she offered her hand to Jemima, who couldn't help but notice a ring dazzling and big enough to be a Vogel one. She saw Jemima stare and laughed. "Don't worry, it's Swarovski crystal!"

"Oh," Jemima smiled. She had enough of the label's costume jewellery herself and continued, "So this is Philip Goldsmith, our Head... Director... of Security and the two guards who will be working tomorrow night to ensure everything goes smoothly."

"It's very nice to meet you all. Now let's go through everything before we take a walk around the site. I have seen all the plans and I am confident that we can make sure your jewellery is safe, and that everything complies with the insurance company's criteria. Shall we go to my office? Coffee anyone?"

Jamie spoke with the speed and punch of a typical New Yorker and Jemima liked her immediately.

After ten minutes of discussions over strong cappuccinos, the group left Jamie's office and made their way to where the necklace would be displayed. For insurance reasons, the Vogel Vanderpless necklace had to be in the main part of the building and not the marquee, except when being modelled by Sahara. Guests would come in via the river entrance and be given glasses of champagne in The Seamen's Hall, which led to the quadrangle from the river. The hall was a picture of elegance, with classical columns and black and white marble floors - quite a contrast to the African camp beyond.

Jemima and Tatiana, along with Polly and Sophie, had envisioned this as the most beautiful room, befitting the necklace. The Vogel Vanderpless was to be encased in a glass stand, lit from below with little spotlights which would only enhance the sparkle that Jemima had been blinded by just a couple of hours earlier.

"I really do not think that this is going to work," Philip announced nervously.

"I can assure you, Mr Goldsmith, that we have had many similar exhibitions of jewellery here in the hall and never had any problem with security," Jamie said with a hint of calm impatience. Philip had asked so many questions that they were all beginning to wonder if this meeting would still be going on when the guests arrived the next evening.

"Vogel jewellery is not similar to any other jewellery, Ms Anderson. I will be surprised if our insurance covers this. I must speak with Paul Pratt, Jemima. He wanted to be here for the security brief, actually. In all my 30 years..." he began searching for his mobile phone in his pocket

"Both Danny and Alexa know what is going on. I went through everything with them. Why does Paul have to be involved?" Jemima was mortified that this exchange was going on in front of the others, including various tourists sitting in the hall.

"Why don't we go back to my office and deal with this calmly?" Jamie took control.

"How can I be calm?" Philip's face was getting redder and redder but fortunately he was already shuffling out of the hall behind Jamie. "Paul, it's Philip. I think you're right, we need you. Are you free to come to the venue for Jemima's party tomorrow night?"

"Philip, you make it sound like this is my tenth birthday party!" Jemima fought tears of frustration from welling up in her eyes.

"OK, good. Let me know when you are here and I'll somehow get out and come to find you."

"Philip, if you are going to find it hard to get out, how is a diamond?" Jemima said in frustration but knew it was a silly thing to say - someone who was going to steal something of such high value would know their escape route blindfolded.

Back in Jamie's office, Jemima was feeling calmer. If Philip wanted to panic, it was up to him. She knew she had the support of the Vogel family for all her plans. "OK, well we have got lots of other things to do so if you don't mind, I am going to go with Polly and Sophie to check on the marquee. Will you call me when Paul arrives?"

Paul was the last person Jemima wanted to see. Philip's lack of belief in her seemed something that Paul could have cultivated; it certainly sounded like it from what Philip had said on the phone. Everyone knew that Paul had it in for Jemima with this event. He was always snooping around, checking on what she was doing and trying to trip her up on things. He would have been over the moon to receive Philip's call and had probably already pre-ordered a taxi when he'd seen them leave.

She took a deep breath. She just couldn't be bothered to worry about Pratt and Goldsmith, and she couldn't believe that Paul had nothing better to do than come over. Surely he should be fiddling with figures. He had even decided to come to the event and frankly, she thought, he should worry about what he was going to wear. He must earn so much protecting Mr V's assets, he could at least spend some of it on a proper suit and shoes. How he had got Mr V to give him a ticket for free, never mind a job, she had no idea.

As they walked towards the marquee she could not help worry, however, about the price of the necklace – who in their right mind would spend that much on a piece of jewellery? Jemima knew Mr V would have a trick up his sleeve but if not, Vogel would be on every front page for all the wrong reasons. She had managed to secure an exclusive with the *Financial Times* – already entitled 'The Most Valuable Piece of Jewellery in the World' – and, unless there was a nuclear bomb (well there probably wouldn't be a front page if that happened), she was determined that it really would be that title.

The interior decoration had not yet been put up but all was going according to plan and Jemima now felt herself caught in a rush of excitement again at what she knew was going to be a fantastic evening. So much so that her spirits were only slightly dampened when her phone rang. Paul was with Philip in Jamie's office.

"I've got to go and sort this diamond display out." He really was Pratt by name, Pratt by nature. "I'll be as quick as I can."

She hot-footed it back. Thank god she was in jeans and the flats she had found under her desk – all this to-ing and fro-ing would be impossible otherwise. She had noticed Jamie's heels and couldn't help but wonder how she could walk around the courtyard's cobbles in them, let alone how she would ever catch a thief.

Jemima walked into Jamie's office to hear Paul having a go at her.

"Jemima, Philip seems quite rightly concerned that the security just

161

is not up to what it should be for something of this value or significance. I told Mr Vogel that this was a mistake but for some reason he seemed to think that you could pull it off."

"And he is right, Paul."

"Ms Anderson..." Paul turned to Jamie.

"Just call me Jamie."

"Right, Jamie – will you please show me where all the CCTV cameras are and all exits from the building, including windows."

"Paul, this building will have hundreds of windows!" Jemima protested.

"Don't worry Jemima," Jamie turned back to Paul, "we will have all the rooms off the hall locked, except the corridor to the lavatories, and I will be the only one with the key. No one can get out of that corridor and the windows in each of the lavatories are tiny – so nobody could get in or out of them either."

"I would like to see it all," Paul said to Jamie, "and I would like to have keys leading to any rooms away from where the diamond is."

"Me too!" Philip piped up, as though he was going to miss out on something.

"I'll stay here," Jemima flicked on her BlackBerry and an instant message from Flora popped up, asking what she was doing that night. She replied that she needed to take it easy. Flora replied that she too was exhausted, she'd get them some home comfort food. Jemima smiled, excited to see her friend and just relax after this annoying day - and before the big one tomorrow.

Eventually Paul and Philip came back into the office, followed by a frazzled-looking Jamie.

"Well," said Philip, "I am not 100% happy, but Paul seems to think that the cameras are sufficient. He will check them all before the event with my guards and Jamie said that there will be people manning them so they will spot anything suspicious."

"So we can carry on?!" Jemima asked Paul, who was scribbling things down in his notebook, along with what looked like some sketches. She couldn't even be bothered to wonder what they were or why he needed them. She had the go-ahead and he could sketch whatever he wanted for all she cared.

Jemima headed back to Sophie and Polly to carry on going through the marquee interiors design, making a mental note to herself to ask for a pay rise. Putting up with Paul Pratt deserved a lot more than what she was getting at the moment.

Later that day Jemima was back in her office, having reassured Mr V that everything was going according to plan. She was also able to confirm that both Memphis Brown and the extra tables for guests could be added. She then called James to say that she was sorry she had left that morning without waking him but she had so much to do and was about to go home, have a bath, and take a sleeping pill as she really needed to be up at the crack of dawn.

"Are you free tomorrow night?" she asked cautiously. One of Danny's guests had let him down at the last minute and he'd asked if she knew of someone who'd like to go. She thought James might enjoy the evening and could even make some good business contacts.

"I am supposed to be seeing the client I blew out for you last night!"

"Haha – liar! You told me he blew you out, that's why you called me!"

"I would love to come. But work comes first so I will have to let you know tomorrow if that is OK?"

"Yes, of course. Right, I am home now and heading straight to bed for a long sleep. Speak tomorrow."

She would be so happy to have a guest the next night. A few months ago she would have loved for it to be Fritz but James would be much more responsible. She would have to get him involved in the Vogel Polo Cup in the summer.

24

Flora was at home sitting on the sofa and reading the plethora of magazines she had bought, most of which seemed to be filled with what Kate Middleton would be wearing and who would be at the wedding in Westminster Abbey. The aroma of something delicious was coming from the oven in the kitchen.

"What a yummy smell!"

"Your favourite – fish pie from Waitrose!"

"Aah, how sweet of you, so nice to be at home," Jemima said. "And am I pleased to see you after the day I've had! Paul Pratt is the bane of my life. At one point I thought that I was going to have call Mr V, which I hate to do, as he'll think I can't handle things on my own. All I want to do is eat that pie, watch telly, have a bath and go to bed. I think that tomorrow will be great – as long as Paul doesn't get in my way!"

"Oh..." Flora sounded suddenly nervous. "Jem, I didn't want to tell you until after your event tomorrow but... I think you should know, Fritz is engaged."

Jemima's brain went numb and suddenly she couldn't see or hear anything. Her throat tightened so she couldn't swallow and her heart began to pound so frantically she thought she was having a heart attack. Spasms started careering down her left arm to her hand, which was suddenly mottled and tingling.

"Jem, say something. I shouldn't have told you but I have just found out that her parents are taking them both to your event tomorrow; apparently they're clients, did you know that? Fritz just called me to tell you. He feels awful but he only realised tonight that it was your party and it is too late to bail – the tickets are £5000 each."

"I know how much the tickets cost, Flora. As you said, it is my event." Jemima said with a huge lump in her throat.

"How long have you known about this?"

"Well they got engaged a couple of weeks ago but they have been in New York as her father has been trying to get him jobs. She doesn't want to live in London."

"Wow, you do know a lot," Jemima heard herself say but she didn't know from where that voice came. "And you tell me all this the night before the biggest event of my life, with a fish pie to make me feel better?!"

"Do you know what, Jemima? Get over yourself. It was over so long ago. She is a really sweet girl who loves Fritz. You haven't seen him or spoken to him in months. You have got to stop your obsession with him. And I do not want to get involved in your self-pity. If you are going to blame me for living my life then we can't be friends."

Without replying, Jemima got up off the sofa and went to her bedroom. Kicking off her shoes, she lay on her bed and gazed mindlessly at the sun setting over the green slate roof of Peter Jones. She then realised with a bittersweet relief that it wasn't Fritz getting married that upset her but that she again felt left on the shelf; everyone settling down and she was running around as a single girl. She then thought of James and wondered if perhaps he was the one for her, for the time being anyway. He was so perfect in so many ways, plus a bit older and a lot wiser; now all she wanted to do was to be with him, feeling safe. She wished she hadn't said no when he had asked her over earlier. She smiled. She would go over there and surprise him. She went into her little en suite bathroom and ran a hot bath, pouring in a very generous amount of the Chanel no 5 Bath Oil that her brother had given her for Christmas. Taking off her makeup, she smothered on a thick moisturiser, before sinking into the water with the copy of *Fifty Shades of Grey* that Noémie had given her during her dalliance with Danny; not that she'd had time to get past the first couple of chapters. She lay back, absorbing both the romance and the sex of the story, feeling inspired.

An hour later, Jemima was standing outside on Sloane Square, waiting for a taxi to pass. She had put on her favourite MiH jeans, a t-shirt, and a green Marni leather jacket with a pair of new bright white Converse trainers. She didn't want to appear slutty, turning up at his hotel at 9.30pm looking too dressed up. That was so 2010, with Fritz and Danny. A taxi arrived and she jumped in, feeling slightly nervous at her impulsiveness. Before too long, they pulled up in front of Claridge's on Brook Street in Mayfair. Her door was opened by a doorman and she stepped out of the taxi and into the beautiful black and white chequered foyer. She felt like popping into the bar for a bit of Dutch courage but she didn't want James to smell anything on her breath so she went to the lift and rode up to the third floor, making her way along the corridor to room number 329. Her heart was beating faster and faster as she got closer to the room she had left only 14 hours earlier. She knocked on the door, suddenly thinking that he might not be there and panicking that if he was he might be with someone else.

"Jemima?!" he said on opening it and although she wanted to look around him to see if she could spot someone, she didn't. She just gazed into his eyes. He was wearing sweat pants and a hoodie top and looked as hot as ever.

"Hi." She smiled then frowned in quick succession. "I missed you."

He took her hand and, pulling her into the room, he lifted her up so she wrapped her legs around his waist and as she kissed him all her worries slipped away into the ether.

James laid her down on the bed's beautiful silver silk counterpane and with her legs dangling over the edge he untied the laces and took off her Converse. He pulled her jeans off before moving his lips slowly upwards until he reached her knickers, which he pulled down her legs. With his tongue probing her, she relaxed under him.

25

Jemima opened her eyes slowly. She didn't want to wake up and for it to be another day. She wanted to remain in the bed next to James for as long as she possibly could. It was the day of the event, however, and she had so much to do.

She could see his back in the dim light that was coming through a crack at the side of one of the curtains and she moved towards him, holding him to her. She kissed his neck and he rolled over. His eyes finding hers, he smiled. "Hey," he whispered.

She smiled back, feeling as content as she had ever done.

"I want to do that all over again," he groaned and although she did too, she knew that she had to get up and get going.

"Me too but I've got to go."

"Again?!"

"Mmmm, yes!" she laughed at him as she got out of the bed and padded over to the bathroom on the thick grey carpet. The room was beautiful and the bathroom equally so. She showered quickly, using the delicious-smelling Asprey body cream before wandering back into the bedroom. She was wearing nothing but she didn't care; she felt free yet so fulfilled and confident after the past two nights with James.

"So have you everything set for tonight?" he said, looking at her as she pulled her jeans back on and searched around for her t-shirt.

"Yes I think so! Hopefully it will all go without any hitches. But you never know!" She walked around to his side of the bed, kissed him, and told him to call her later to find out if he could make it to fill the space on Danny's table.

Walking down Bond Street at 8am, Jemima decided that she would go straight to Somerset House so she walked to the bus stop and waited for the number 9 that would take her to Trafalgar Square. She thought back to the night before and Fritz's engagement. She was surprised he hadn't told her but then again he was quite pathetic like that. And to give Flora her due, they had officially split up ages ago. Jemima decided to send Fritz a text congratulating him, just to see what he replied.

Just as her bus got to where she had to get off, she heard the BlackBerry beep. She couldn't help but close her eyes, wondering what he might say. When she could resist it no longer, she opened one eye and saw that it was only an email from Mr V, saying that he wanted to re-do the speech and could she bring the original one down to his office - he would be there in 30 minutes. *Damn*, she thought already walking across Trafalgar Square towards Somerset House. She bought a soya cappuccino at Prêt à Manger and decided to walk back across the Square and along Pall Mall, past St James's Palace, to the office. She sent Zoe an email and a text, asking her to go straight to Somerset House to check on things as she had to go and meet with Mr V.

It was another lovely sunny spring morning and the rush hour was already well underway. A queue had begun to form outside the National Gallery to see the latest Van Gogh exhibition, although the gallery didn't open until 10am. She loved that people were flocking to these important museums and promised herself that when this was all over, she would take some days off and do all the things in

London that she never normally had time for. To be a tourist in her own town for a few days would be such a treat.

Jemima put all thoughts of Fritz out of her head and reminded herself of everything she had done with James the previous night, including ordering a burger from room service at midnight and falling asleep exhausted and full and, most importantly, overwhelmingly happy and satisfied.

"Good morning Jemima, are we all set for this evening?" Mr Vogel said once she was in his office with the speech printed out.

"Yes Mr V, I was actually on my way over there when I got your message about redoing the speech."

"Yes, sorry about that. I was going through it with my wife last night and she thinks that we should change it."

"Oh, I do think that this one is really good and to the point. Anyway, I'll take notes. Here is the current version."

Sidney Vogel sat down, took out his glasses and started reading, Jemima hovering and looking at it over his shoulder.

"You can't take notes breathing down my neck, and I can't bear people reading over my shoulder! Sit down over there," he snapped.

She put his rebuke down to nerves and went around to the other side of the desk, sitting down. She hoped that James would make it later so that she wouldn't be faced with Fritz and his perfect girlfriend alone.

Having taken down notes of changes, she went back up to the office where she typed up the notes, then back down to his office only to do the same thing all over again. This went on four times over the course of the morning, until she had typed up the one that he seemed happy with. She realised that it was almost identical to the one she had shown him first thing, that they had composed the previous week.

"Oh my god – you won't believe it," she said to Zoe who was sitting at her desk and made no reference to Jemima's email and text about going straight to Somerset House to keep an eye on what was happening. Jemima had imagined her assistant would be over the moon to spend time away from the office.

"What?" came the reply after a while.

"This speech that I have been re-doing all morning... it has ended up as exactly the same as the one I did last week! The one I started with this morning - except one word!"

"And what is the word?" Zoe giggled.

"Guess – diamond!"

They both dissolved into laughter. Jemima noticed her BlackBerry flashing and saw that Flora had sent her a text message:

<<*Jem, sorry for being a bitch. I'm between a rock & a hard place. Why don't I drive you to the event later, nicer than a taxi? xx*>>

<<*That's kind. Let me think about it. Might be easier just to cab it there...*>>

It was very kind of her for sure, but so out of her way. No one wanted to drive around that part of London, particularly in the evening – there was always so much traffic with people out to dinner and the theatre. Flora must be feeling very guilty but Jemima knew her friend was in a difficult position.

"Zoe, now I've got that out of the way, and you weren't able to, I'm going to head over to SH and see how it is all going. Just let me know if anything happens."

"Sure… bye," Zoe muttered breezily, face still glued to her computer and still no mention of the fact that she had been asked to go there a few hours ago. Jemima thought again of asking her about Danny and his girlfriend but resisted. She hoped it wasn't Zoe's way of ingratiating herself with Danny, with half an eye on her job.

Jemima decided to walk back the way she had just come and grab another coffee on the way. London was so pretty and she had an amazing new boyfriend. She couldn't stop smiling.

As if he could hear her thinking about him, her BlackBerry rang and she answered James's call.

"Jemima, I have managed to get out of my client meeting this evening."

"It can't have been that important if it is so easy to get out of!" she teased, thrilled to hear his voice.

"We're meeting for lunch a bit later so I can come and support you tonight if you would still like me to?"

"I would love that – thank you, James. What would I do without you?"

"I have no idea!"

26

Cheered up by her lovely call from James, Jemima spent the next few hours with Polly, Sophie and Tatiana. The time rushed by surprisingly quickly, without any hitches except for a worried Philip fretting that the necklace cabinet was too much in view through the large doors that led towards the river. Jemima wondered how many people would be sailing up the Thames with a pair of binoculars in an attempt to get a glimpse of the Vogel Vanderpless.

She left in good time to go back to the office and get changed so she would be there well before the guests began arriving at 7pm. It was looking absolutely incredible and she felt like Kristin Scott Thomas in *The English Patient*, wandering through the tents between tables that were dressed to the most precise detail.

Half an hour later, however, Jemima was still in her taxi on the Strand, having moved only about 500 metres, thanks to a burst water pipe on Piccadilly that had caused a tailback. The taxi driver didn't really seem to care; he probably earned more money from just sitting in traffic. He was listening to a football match on the radio and Jemima was getting more and more panicky. She could feel her body heating up, as it tended to do when she was worried.

"Sir, excuse me, can we try another way?" she asked, knocking on the dividing window between them.

"An' which way would you suggest that was?"

"I don't know but I am in a real hurry."

"Listen love, everyone's in an 'urry. Nuffink I can do 'bout it, WE ain't movin', NO one's movin'."

"OK, well I'll just jump out here then." She was still a good 20 minute walk from the office and had hoped to be heading back to the party in her beautiful dress by now. She made her way back along the same route she had taken twice already that day.

Exhausted by the time she got there, Jemima was relieved that Zoe and Noémie had left so at least they would be at Somerset House by now, assuming they too hadn't got caught up in the traffic. Putting her office phone on loudspeaker while she started to get undressed, she called Noémie, explaining that she would be there as soon as she could and asking if she could just find Sophie and keep Mr V cool if he got there before her.

Jemima's exquisite Marchesa dress was hanging in the cupboard behind her chair, having been delivered while she was out. Noémie must have hung it in there. She opened the door and looked at it in wonder, pleased that James would be there to see her in it. And Fritz for that matter.

As soon as she had seen the dress in the window of Harvey Nichols, she had fallen in love with it and then, at the end of last summer, found it in the sale. She couldn't believe it when she saw it on the rail and neither could the store assistant, but they had to give it to her at the price displayed, which was still way above her limit. It was very long jade-green silk with eye of peacock feathers in blue printed faintly all over. The neckline was low, like a silk negligee, which showed off her breastplate bones. She quickly put it on then brushed and put her hair up as best she could. Annoyingly it had gone a bit frizzy during the day, with all her rushing around and she hadn't had any time to go to Neville's, even if they'd had space. She hoped that her earrings would detract attention away from it.

Mr V had sent her a text earlier in the afternoon saying that Danny had a pair of earrings, necklace and a bracelet in his safe that she was to borrow. She had shown him a photo of her dress so she just hoped that Danny would provide something appropriate. She slapped on her usual going out makeup, paying attention to heavy eyeliner and shadow. She then called Danny's line but when he didn't pick up she thought she had better go straight down to his office, hoping that he hadn't yet left.

She was buzzed through and as she approached his office, she heard voices. Danny's, and a woman's with a very familiar American accent that sent shivers down her spine:

"OK, babe – I will just go and get you what you should wear from next door."

Jemima heard him go through into the room next to his. Out of curiosity she quietly peeped through the small window high in the door. She was right; she had recognised that voice – it was Petrina Lindberg! So she had got her way and found some way of getting to Danny. She should have known when he started talking about 'Petra'.

Petrina was holding the Vogel Vanderpless necklace in her hands... how could she have it? Philip should have taken it to Somerset House by now. Butterflies fluttered in Jemima's stomach and she felt something was up but there was no time to wonder so she ran back up to her office to ring Danny. She really didn't want to disturb him when he was with Petrina, who would surely recognise her. She just hoped that he would answer this time.

He picked up on the second ring. "Danny? Hi... Mr V told me to pick up some jewellery to wear tonight...?"

"Jemima – yes, I put them in the drawer to the right of your desk. Zoe didn't tell you? The key is in the paperclip box under the monitor. See you there." He put the phone down heavily before she had the chance to tell him that he needed to get the necklace to Somerset House asap, and also that a friend of hers would be on his table. She hoped that he would be nice to James, though she was sure James could hold his own amongst Danny's *nouveaux* friends.

With the butterflies still in her stomach and a lump in her throat, she unlocked the drawer. Of course Zoe hadn't told her. She opened the three green Vogel jewellery boxes and was taken aback at the beautiful pieces Mr V had lent her. She stared at them in their boxes before nervously and excitedly putting them on. The earrings were thankfully not the same huge emeralds as Sahara had worn to the Russian *Vogue* shoot but they were exquisite nonetheless. Simple emerald and white diamond two-strand drop earrings, a matching tennis bracelet and a necklace which was a very long strand of diamonds and emeralds that she was able to wrap around her neck twice so it hung down between her minute breasts. Although she had worn fine jewellery before; pieces from her family's tiny collection, she had never before felt tingling in her spine or seen goose pimples on her arms over jewellery. The coldness of the stones cooled her nerves and her flushed skin.

As she went down in the lift she looked at her reflection in the mirror and gave a little squeal at what she saw. She pulled her little MiH denim jacket around her, wondering if perhaps she should put the earrings in her pocket until she got to the event, for safety's sake. The necklace and bracelet were covered up. Knowing what Vogel jewellery cost, she guessed that she must be wearing almost £2 million and was sure she should be accompanied by a bodyguard with this amount on.

Hoping that the traffic was better than it had been 30 minutes earlier and she could get a taxi from outside the Ritz or Le Caprice. She smiled at the nice compliment from the security man at the door then went outside where she saw a familiar figure leaning against her car, chatting on the phone. Although she was still a bit annoyed at her friend's harsh words the previous night, Jemima was so happy to see Flora. Just like her, Flora was a brilliant back street driver, knowing all the cut-throughs from the main roads. She would get Jemima there faster than any grumpy cabbie listening to the football.

"Hey! Am I pleased to see you – I didn't get back to you..." she said to Flora who had just finished her call, to Benjy no doubt – they spoke on the phone all day. Their international bills must be astronomical.

"I left a message saying that unless I heard from you I'd be here waiting for you."

"Oh god, I haven't had a moment to listen to any of my messages, I am sorry – I didn't see that you'd called." Jemima wondered if perhaps there was a message from Fritz too, but stopped herself checking. Now was not the time. Besides, now she was James's.

"I'm running very late so I need you to do your magic back street driving!"

"OK, hop in – you look beautiful, by the way. Amazing dress! I recognise it. Who's it by? I haven't seen anything like it in the current collections. I could have lent you something from Stella."

"Marchesa. I got it in the Harvey Nichols sale last summer. I hid it from you!"

"Haha, good for you! Georgina Chapman is the most divine designer. It's stunning – you look stunning, those diamonds and emeralds are incredible. My goodness, I should kidnap you for a ransom!"

As they were going down yet another back street and almost there, a police car with its flashing blue lights and siren blaring came up behind them, flashing to tell them to stop.

"What the hell?" Jemima shrieked. "You weren't doing anything wrong were you?"

"It was a one way street..."

"Damn you Flora, they've really clamped down on that here in Westminster."

"I know, but the bigger problem is that I might still be a bit over the limit... I shared a bottle of wine at lunch, which we didn't have until about 2.30pm."

"Oh my god, you idiot. I am going to have to go, I'm sorry to leave but I'll have to take a cab for the rest of the way. I have all this jewellery – so dangerous to go looking for one. Oh no."

"Here he is." Flora rolled down her window.

"Good evening Miss, you do realise that you were driving very fast the wrong way down a one way street?" the very good-looking young police officer was leaning down and looking straight past Flora to Jemima whose dress was quite low cut and, from his angle, quite revealing.

"Goodness, I am so sorry – I had no idea."

"Have you been drinking, Miss? I am going to have to test your alcohol level."

Jemima felt the blood drain from her face. It was 6.15pm and she was already supposed to be there for one last run through of Mr V's speech with him. Guests never arrived bang on the invited time but this was a disaster.

Flora got out of the car, as did Jemima, who realised that she would have to leave Flora to deal with this on her own.

"Good evening Officer, I am afraid that I have to go and leave my friend in your capable hands. I have an event I am running at Somerset House and I am already late."

"Miss, it is an offence to get into a car with someone over the alcohol limit. You have to stay and wait for the results and accompany her to the police station if need be."

"But I had no idea she had been drinking – she was just being kind and giving me a lift."

"Well she wasn't kind, she was stupid." Looking at the machine it was clear Flora was over the limit. "You are only just over but you have to come with me. Both of you."

He was now looking directly at Jemima.

"Please don't make her come – she really had no idea, I've just picked her up from her office by the Ritz, I didn't think I would still be over the limit, I just had a glass of wine at lunchtime."

Jemima was practically crying by now, her makeup no doubt would be ruined.

"It must have been a very large glass. But OK, you Miss can go, but I will need to take down your details."

"Of course – thank you so much."

She wrote down her details and then turned around to go.

"I suppose we can give you a lift – how far have you got to go? It's dangerous walking around with all that money around your neck."

"Really? Somerset House." They were on a little road off the Embankment so it was not too far but she would never get a taxi down this little street and it would take her a while to hobble on her heels to the main road for one. They hopped in the back of the police car and he even turned his sirens on.

"You are quite nice after all; why don't you be even nicer and let me off?" Flora chanced.

"Drink driving is not easy to let off. You're already recorded on the machine."

Five minutes later, they were there. Jemima had texted Mr V, saying that she would meet him in the Seamen's Hall by the necklace. She hoped that Danny had turned up with it or Philip would be having a breakdown. Again she wondered about Petrina and how she had managed to ensnare Danny. She dropped her jacket at the cloakroom and as she rushed towards the hall, she could see the necklace sparkling, Mr and Mrs Vogel both looking at it intensely. She looked around to see if Danny was near but he wasn't, nor Petrina.

"Hello! Mrs Vogel, you look beautiful," Jemima said brightly. Mrs Vogel was wearing a gorgeous red silk dress that looked as if it was Valentino Couture.

Paul Pratt appeared immediately with his wife, who looked remarkably pretty and nice for someone married to such a man.

"How odd, I am sure that I just saw you getting out of a police car, Jemima. Are you in trouble?" Paul asked snidely.

"Oh. I couldn't get a taxi and managed to persuade a policeman in his car to help me."

Mr V laughed. "Only you, Jemima, would pull that off – well done!"

Jemima smiled sweetly. Paul scowled and rolled his eyes at his wife.

"Jemima," Mrs Vogel said to her, "Your dress is very beautiful, I do love peacocks – we have several in our house in Italy."

Although she was well into her 60s, Mrs Vogel was still absolutely beautiful, exquisitely and expensively coloured blonde hair tucked into a chignon and pinned into place with an enormous swan of white diamonds and rubies which matched her dress to perfection.

"Thank you! Your hair is amazing!" Jemima said, seeing Paul's scowls out of the corner of her eye. "And I hope we have a wonderfully successful night. It's so lucky that the necklace got here on time!"

"The necklace has been here since 6pm," Paul said very matter-of-factly.

"Oh but I saw it in..." she was interrupted by a text message from Sophie, saying that the first guests had started to arrive. She alerted the Vogels, who were going to greet the first 20 or so personally, before leaving the entrance and mingling with their friends and clients. Paul walked off, speaking on his phone and leaving his wife, who seemed to be straining her neck, searching for someone.

Standing at the riverside entrance to the Seaman's Hall were four waiters holding trays of champagne and cocktails. Although Paul had tried to keep costs down, Mr V wanted the best champagne served and so they had ordered magnums of Bollinger. The cocktails were either a passion fruit martini or a mojito. Jemima was not touching a drop of alcohol that night, however, as she wanted to make sure she had a very clear head. The wine at dinner was from the vineyard of a friend of hers in Stellenbosch in South Africa. There was a large selection of exquisitely prepared canapés while guests arrived.

The menu for dinner started with gravadlax and dill with a little green salad, followed by spring lamb and potato dauphinoise, then for dessert there was tarte tatin and ice cream, with cheese to finish. Jemima and Tatiana had very much enjoyed going to tastings, trying out the various dishes before choosing this menu, and she was sure it would be very well received.

As the guests came in and took a drink, they all made their way over to the necklace, sparkling in its stand. Jemima was excited to hear all the exclamations of awe from where she was standing at the door to the marquee. She even overheard a well-known hedge fund owner say that if he bought it he'd have to buy a new house, as his insurance company would not accept any more jewellery under one roof. She laughed to herself, thinking how this job had put her in a pseudo fantasy world.

Before too long, the hall was full and it was hard for people to see the diamonds in their full splendour so she asked the waitresses to persuade the guests to go into the reception part of the marquee and find their tables and dinner places. Whilst marvelling at its decoration, she wanted them to feel that they had been transported to the African desert in the era of elegance.

The celebrities were on one side of the room, mingling amongst themselves, barely willing to talk to 'common civilians', no matter that these guests were hardly 'common'. Jemima had worked hard to get Mr V to change his rule of rarely lending jewellery - except to the female nominees on Oscar night - and of course waive the £5000 for their ticket so as to get them all to come along.

Suddenly she heard all the paparazzi outside again; a storm of snapping sounding louder than ever before, as though armed robbers were attacking the place with machine guns. She knew that Sahara had arrived, fashionably late of course. Jemima texted Mr V to warn him that Sahara was on her way in so that he could go to the entrance to greet her. Scanning the room for Fritz and his fiancée, she saw James come in and her heart missed several beats. He was by far the most good-looking guy in the room and she noticed several of the models staring at him as he walked straight up to her and kissed her seductively just below her ear. He had discovered the night before that it was perhaps her most erogenous area and, even there in front of all those people, with her stomach playing havoc with nerves, Jemima melted and relaxed for a split second.

"Hey darling, you look incredible. That jewellery suits you very well. Can I bid for them tonight?!"

"I am sure you can buy them for me if you like – I'll introduce you to Mr V!" she laughed back. "Tonight there is only one auction prize, and that's the Vogel Vanderpless necklace. They're expecting over £100 million for that…" she added, whispering.

Before long it was time to be seated and slowly Tatiana's team and the waiters asked guests again to look at the huge seating plan that was erected inside the marquee at the entrance to the dining room end, and then to sit down.

"You're on Danny Vogel's table; Mr V's grandson. Do you remember that beautiful girl whom I was suspicious of at New Year's Eve? The dark one... well, can you believe it – she is dating Danny! I still think that there is something funny about her so try to sit next to her and get what you can out of her. If Danny lets you!"

"OK boss..." he winked at her and walked off to find his table.

Once everyone was seated, Jemima went to find the Vogels, who were with Sahara and the Texan oil baron, standing by the necklace.

"Is it time for us to come?" Mr V asked. "How is everything?"

"Everything is perfect. Really happy about it all; the production company have done a really great job and everyone is saying how beautiful it all looks."

"Good. Now Sahara my dear, this is Jemima, my head of Public Relations and a general dogsbody who helped me to organise this event."

He laughed and Jemima smiled through gritted teeth. Helped him organise the event! He did more disorganising than anything.

"Hi Jemima, pleased to meet you!" Sahara said disingenuously before turning back to Mrs Vogel.

"Very well. Ladies... John..." Mr V nodded at the Texan, "it is time for us to go through to the dining room. Thank you, Jemima."

"Have you got the copy of your speech? When you are ready, if you just walk up to the rostrum, I'll be there to sort out the microphone for you."

"Good."

They made their way through the mass of beautifully decorated tables and guests. Each table was named after one of Vogel's famous stones or pieces of jewellery. Mr and Mrs Vogel's 'top table' was called The Vogel Vanderpless, Danny's The Botswanan Brilliance. Others were Morning Glory, after a large yellow diamond that looked like the sun rising; Snow White and Rose Red after a huge Elizabethan ruby and pearl ring; The Star of Ceylon was a large Sri Lankan star sapphire; The Blue Star a blue diamond sold to a Chinese tycoon.

Jemima watched Mr V and his wife greet friends and family as they walked amongst the tables to their own. Sahara's Russian ex-boyfriend, who had been at the auction back in December, was there with his new 'child bride', as the papers called her. Jemima wondered how Sahara would behave. She was pleased Mr V had managed to bring along the Texan; he looked really nice – if somewhat rotund – and could definitely afford to keep Sahara in the style to which she was accustomed.

Danny and Petrina were making their way to their table. Jemima couldn't believe it - Petrina was wearing her exact dress from Marchesa, but in beautiful scarlet red silk! That girl was becoming her nemesis.

A little more than an hour later, after desserts but before coffee and the *petits fours* were served, Jemima got up to tell Mr V that it was time for his speech and Sahara that it was time for her to put on the necklace. She also had to advise Shirley Bassey, who was to be singing *Diamonds are Forever* whilst Sahara modelled the piece.

Immediately the guards were already positioning themselves around the guests. Jemima walked through the tables, pleased to be getting a lot of glances from the men. She saw James who looked up and smiled while doing a thumbs up sign. He was sitting next to Petrina so Jemima was looking forward to hearing what gossip he learnt from her. Just before she got to the Vogels' table, her eyes fell on Fritz whispering to Anoush. He looked up, smiling sheepishly. Jemima just looked away and walked on, feeling empowered by her self-containment.

As she approached Mr V, she could see Sahara looked pretty drunk.

"Sahara's drunk a lot?" she whispered to Mr V, on the other side of him to the model.

"I know. I do hope that she behaves."

"So do we all! Will you tell Dame Shirley to go up?"

"Of course." He turned to the octogenarian singer on his other side.

Jemima approached the supermodel cautiously. "Hi Sahara, I hope you're having a nice time. I need you to follow me now as it is time for the show."

"OK honey," Sahara drawled, her Texan accent stronger than ever.

Sahara got up and followed Jemima back between the tables, saying hello to everyone she passed. The recipients of her greetings looked surprised and flattered. Mr V walked up to the podium and began his speech whilst Jemima and Sahara got to where Philip was waiting nervously with the necklace. It was now in its presentation box and Jemima carefully took it out, holding it up to Sahara.

"Would you mind bending over a little, Miss Scott? I have to put the necklace on you."

"Diamond necklaces should always be put on by a man." Sahara said flirtatiously, looking at Philip, who was still squirming with nerves. Jemima hoped that he would not let the heavy necklace slip through his shaky hands as she handed it over. However, Philip did his job to perfection, even when Sahara leant over, affording him an unspoiled view of her impressive if somewhat crêpey cleavage.

Mr V's speech was going down very well and Jemima was touched to hear him thank her at the end, calling her his 'brilliant PR who no one is allowed to poach', and also adding a mention of Tatiana's company. Jemima was surprised he remembered these details; she had forgotten to include them.

As he made his way back to his table there was thunderous applause, indicating that everyone was in the right mood to bid highly for the necklace.

Once she saw Dame Shirley take the microphone from Mr V, Jemima spoke to Sophie on her mini radio, which was cleverly hidden in her dress's spaghetti strap. Sophie in turn signalled for the band to start. Sahara and the Vogel Vanderpless necklace sashayed into view of the guests, a guard almost glued to the model's behind. Philip looked like he was going to follow the guard, but instead stood next to Jemima at the edge of the nearest table to the entrance, poised and ready to run in case anything untoward should happen.

Before Jemima had a chance of going around the back to her planned position, Paul Pratt appeared out of nowhere with a glass of the ice cold Bollinger which she had so far reluctantly managed to avoid.

"Here," he said, "you deserve a glass of champagne."

Jemima took the glass in amazement – she accepted it gratefully, thankful for Paul's kindness and suddenly desperately thirsty. Although Philip was following Sahara's movements like a cat watching a mouse, he glanced over as if surprised by the kind, thoughtful gesture.

Finishing the champagne, she put the glass down on an empty side table and walked around the outskirts of the tables to watch from the other side of the room, for a better view of the auction. As she was passing Paul Pratt's table she noticed that he hadn't returned to his seat. More strangely, Petrina Lindberg was talking to Paul's wife. Jemima slowed her walking a little, looking carefully at the two women and noticing the conversation looked private – secretive, even. Petrina was bending over to whisper to Mrs Pratt, who in turn was looking pointedly at Petrina's over-large feather boa clutch bag. Petrina smiled, nodded, and walked on past the table towards the bathrooms. Jemima wondered whether she could follow her. Maybe she could find out what was happening with her and Danny and how she knew Paul Pratt's wife.

27

Before Jemima could follow Petrina, however, Michael Talbot, the same auctioneer who had carried out the Vanderpless auction at Bothebie's, began the bidding. She knew that she must watch this, the pivotal part of the evening. She would just have to track Petrina down later.

Unlike most gala events, which have a list of lots donated by all and sundry, and which become more and more uninteresting as the auction goes on, Jemima had persuaded Mr V that they should auction only the Vogel Vanderpless. The excitement was already building up in the room and Jemima had to give Mr V credit that Sahara's presence only increased it. The woman sauntered around the room between tables, sitting on some men's knees and leaning over others so that the huge heart diamond dropped into their laps. She looked like a jaguar and you could imagine her purring as she modelled the necklace as though it were hers.

"Wow! Sahara Scott really is incredible. You'd never think she was in her 60s!" Tatiana said in hushed tones to Jemima.

"I know, but my goodness she is trouble too. She is plastered!" Jemima whispered back.

"Really? Oh dear. I read she was better after another rehab stint. Anyway, do you think Mr Vogel is happy? Oh, and darling, you look amazing – I couldn't keep my eyes off you just now as you walked around the room – neither could many of the men!"

"Yes, Mr V is happy - very much so. You heard the speech? And thank you! I kind of want to run away with this jewellery but I think

I might get into trouble. Have you seen Zoe?" Jemima realised that she hadn't seen her assistant since she had first arrived.

"Yes, she was talking to that beautiful girl who came in with Danny Vogel. They were on their way to the loo. Do you know who she is? And WHO is that gorgeous man you were with earlier – on Danny's table?"

Suddenly and violently, Jemima felt very dizzy and sleepy.

"Tats, I feel very odd. Like I am drunk or something, but I've only had one glass of champagne."

As the price of the necklace increased, so did Jemima's surreal feeling of being not quite in the same room as everybody else.

"How peculiar – have you eaten anything today?"

"Yes, absolutely – I've had bits throughout the day and something just now from the kitchen."

"OK, well I'll get you some water. Sit down here."

Jemima sat down, clinging to one of the marquee posts and hoping that she wouldn't fall off the chair, pulling the whole thing down with her.

The bidding for the necklace had reached £70m and was now between John the Texan, Sahara's prospective boyfriend, and Sergey the Russian, Sahara's ex-boyfriend. The audience (which essentially the other guests had now become as there was no one else participating except the auctioneer) oohed and aahed as these two tycoons waged war on each other over the most expensive piece of jewellery in the world.

Sahara had been so obsessed with the diamond, right from the beginning, that in all her haziness Jemima was certain she had persuaded her fellow Texan to buy it for her. The bidding was going up £5m at a time and each time the Russian outbid the Texan, Sahara glared at him.

However much she tried to focus on this extraordinary exhibition, Jemima thought that she was going to fall asleep any moment. Her eyes were feeling heavier and heavier. Suddenly she was brought back to reality by the gavel being slammed down. The necklace had gone for £105 million. It would be around the necklace of Sergey's child bride and no longer that of the most famous model in the world. Sahara's face froze for a second until she managed a smile then walked like a robot through the tables in Jemima's direction, instead of back to Philip to return the necklace as she had been told to do. The guards were confused with this change of plan and were talking into their lapel microphones to each other.

Sahara was suddenly in front of Jemima, demanding to know where the bathrooms were. Although she knew somewhere inside her that she should take the supermodel to Philip to remove the necklace, Jemima couldn't think straight and didn't have the energy to argue so she simply got up and beckoned Sahara to follow her. She was sure the guards would follow on.

When they got to the bathroom, Jemima collapsed onto the bench in the corridor, closing her eyes briefly. After what seemed like forever, she realised that she hadn't heard anything and that Sahara had been in there for a while. She opened her eyes and saw a flash of red silk in the dim light of the corridor, heading towards the marquee. What had happened? Had she dozed off, or passed out?

Hearing Philip's angry voice booming at the entrance to the corridor, no doubt admonishing the guards, Jemima got up somewhat shakily, so as to appear fully in control when he arrived. She opened the bathroom door cautiously to see Sahara lying on the floor, seemingly passed out, with no necklace around her neck.

In abject panic, yet still feeling other-worldly, Jemima frantically looked around the room: the cupboards under the basins, each cubicle, each cistern. There was nobody there and definitely no £105 million diamond necklace. The only means of escape would have been through the small windows in each cubicle, which surely only a child could get through. Had someone escaped out of the door and passed her when she was asleep? That flash of red – had that been real?

Philip was knocking on the door. Jemima, panicked, looked from the door to the still knocked-out Sahara.

"Philip," she realised she'd have to let him in, there was no point delaying anything, "can you come in? There's been a terrible accident."

"What the..!" Philip burst through the door. "Dear God, please, no."

Jemima looked up at him, his face drained of all colour. This was the moment Philip had known was coming, all his working life. Perhaps this would be what finally drove him over the edge.

"What's happened?" he hissed.

"She's, I don't know, I just. I was waiting outside for her."

"Jemima!" he barked, colour now flooding his face as anger overtook shock, "why did you bring her here rather than wait for me to take off the necklace?"

"I, urgh, well she demanded I take her to the bathroom. I didn't want a scene to be caused. Mr V told me to avoid that at any cost, so I ummm... I checked inside, there was no one there, so I let her in and waited here on this chair."

She hoped there was no CCTV to prove that she hadn't actually looked inside the bathroom... at least she didn't think she had. Everything was getting so confused.

"We have to advise Mr Vogel straight away." Philip got out his phone.

"I think it is best he is told in person." Jemima spoke as confidently as she could.

"Very well, I'll go now and find him. Where is Pratt when you need him? He's normally no more than 100 yards from Mr Vogel."

"I don't know, the last time I saw him was when he gave me that glass of champagne - when I was standing next to you."

28

Philip left at a running walk to get Mr Vogel.

Jemima's heart flooded with relief as she saw James appear at the end of the corridor. She pulled him into the bathroom, sobbing.

"What's happened? That security guy just came running out looking like God knows what – and you look terrible. In the nicest possible way."

"Oh James…" Jemima let herself slide to the floor, leaning her back against the cool wall, and told him what had happened. James quietly took it all in before speaking. "You must pull yourself together. You do realise that they might very likely think you have some involvement in this? And now I am here – me even more so. I just don't understand how you could have passed out after only one glass of champagne? At least the CCTV cameras should put us in the clear and may have picked something up."

Before Jemima could answer, a familiar figure darkened the doorway. "Hello Mr V," she said nervously. He was accompanied by Philip, and Jamie Anderson.

"Jemima, tell me what has happened. Are you drunk?"

"No!"

"Mr Vogel, I believe that Miss Scott was knocked out by this chloroform-soaked cloth." James pointed to the cloth on the ground next to her, not wanting to implicate himself with his fingerprints.

Mr V looked at Jemima, his voice shaking with what could have been either fear or anger. "You do realise, Jemima, that you have got yourself into a very, very serious situation? And who are you with all these conspiracy theories?" he demanded, turning to James.

"I am a friend of Jemima's and was on your grandson's table tonight."

"Very well – you seem to be more in control than Jemima. So Ms Anderson, I presume the police have been called. Are they here yet? Where is Paul Pratt anyway?"

"I haven't seen him, Mr Vogel," Jemima said formally although Mr V wasn't listening.

"I think Miss Scott's coming round, sir," said one of the security guards, who'd put his jacket over the supermodel and had been watching her carefully.

"Right, well let's just hope she's OK. Maybe she'll even know what happened. I need all of you to listen to me now, though. This must not get out to the press. It must be contained. Jemima, I assume you can at least do that? And I want the party to continue – I don't want anyone here to know. Make sure our female guests use a different bathroom. And will someone please find Paul Pratt!" Mr V was shouting now.

"Of course," Philip said nervously.

"Mr Vogel, the police are already here and an ambulance is on its way," Jamie announced after listening to her headpiece. "I'll go and update them and let you look after Miss Scott."

"I'll come with you," announced Philip, wanting to be involved with the police from the outset and as far away from Mr V as possible.

"Philip – go and find Pratt now!" Mr V barked.

Jemima was very surprised that Paul Pratt hadn't somehow managed to work out what was happening and turn up. He'd be so disappointed to find out he'd missed the scene of her downfall.

Soon enough, the police were there and were being introduced by Jamie. A Detective Inspector Paige who looked rather like the TV detective Colombo in his brown Macintosh and thick-rimmed glasses, and a Sergeant Bankes, who looked very young.

"So Ms Anderson has updated me on what has happened; a necklace has been stolen?" Paige addressed Mr V and turned to his assistant, who was staring open-mouthed at Sahara. "Bankes, pay attention and take notes. Precise notes, please."

"Yes, sir." Bankes tried very hard to concentrate on his notepad.

Before Mr V had a chance to speak, Philip intercepted.

"It isn't just a necklace, it is the most priceless necklace in the world... I think it is Jemima you should be asking what happened?"

"Philip, I can deal with this," Mr V calmly but firmly told him and everyone present who was in control. "Where on earth is Paul?"

"I think he left; his wife isn't there either."

"He has left?! Call him on his mobile, Philip, *now*."

Jemima could see Philip nervously trying to find Paul's number in his brick of a mobile phone.

"Right, DI Paige," Mr V continued, "This necklace is of immense value. The Vogel Vanderpless has just been bought at the event's auction for £105 million." Jemima noticed Bankes now lean against the door as though he was going to faint, although Paige seemed unfazed. "It seems that when Miss Scott came to the bathroom, someone was hiding in here, knocked her out with chloroform, stole the necklace, and somehow got out of the room without Jemima, who was sitting on the chair outside, noticing. How Jemima didn't notice someone creeping out of this room with a £105 million diamond necklace is beyond me. What can you add, if anything?"

Jemima wondered if she should mention the flash of red but was interrupted by Paige clearing his throat. "I was alerted on my way here that a motorbike was spotted speeding east along the Embankment, away from this building. CCTV cameras have it recorded going well over 100 miles per hour. Unfortunately we have nothing visual showing anyone leaving Somerset House so Ms Anderson, I would like to see all the security cameras please." He turned to his sergeant, "Bankes, we'll need copies."

"Of course." Jamie and Bankes spoke in unison.

"The bike was then spotted," Paige continued, "going onto London Bridge, where it stopped and the rider appeared to drop something down to a small speedboat which was waiting on the south bank of the Thames, and which proceeded to speed up the river. The bike was found abandoned where the parcel was thrown into the boat. The motorcyclist has, of course, disappeared."

"What about the river police?" Philip asked in a panicked voice.

"They lost the boat at the Thames barrier. We tried to close it but it takes 15 minutes and they slipped through."

"Sounds like something out of a James Bond film!" Bankes laughed excitedly and all eyes turned to him.

"Shut up, Bankes. Ms Anderson, can we go to your office and look at the cameras?"

"Please follow me."

The police officers left with Philip and Jamie, Bankes having taken down the details of all those in the bathroom.

"Sahara, how are you feeling? Would you like to go home? Where are you staying?" Mr V asked kindly and Jemima wondered at the composure of this man who had just had a £105 million necklace stolen.

"I feel just awful. What happened? Why were the police all here?" Sahara asked, as though she hadn't heard a word of what had just been said.

"You were drugged and someone stole the necklace."

"Whaaat?!" she exclaimed, looking down at her chest. "Oh my... how terrible."

"I can't leave the party yet but I will find John to take you home once the paramedics have checked you over." Mr V then turned to Jemima and spoke to her in an equally gentle tone, "Jemima, you've had a rough time tonight. There is nothing more to do here. I suggest that you speak to the organisers and let them take over, then get this gentleman to take you home."

Jemima was relieved she was being dismissed for the evening, having thought at one point that perhaps she would be spending the night in gaol.

"Thank you Mr V, I promise that I did everything I could for Miss Scott."

"Yes very well, we'll obviously talk about all of this thoroughly in the morning with the police. I do not know what happened to Paul Pratt, though. He has a tendency to want to be involved in everything."

James and Jemima waited until Mr V helped Sahara out of the ladies' bathrooms.

"OK," said James, "let's go and find the organisers and then I'll take you home, or maybe you should come and stay with me."

"But..." she tried to protest.

"Jemima, your part doesn't really tie up and you'll be questioned tomorrow to the ninth degree. I want to know exactly what happened so we can get your story straight."

29

Jemima awoke and for a fleeting second, as memories of the previous evening began to flood her mind, she felt a huge sense of success. Then she opened her eyes and saw James come into the room with a cup of tea. Suddenly both a hangover from hell and the memory of how the evening had actually ended appeared with a thud.

"Hon, we need to make a very clear plan about what happened when you were outside the restroom. The police will interrogate you and they're likely to question me too."

"I know – I'm terrified they're going to think I was involved."

"No they're not, but you will be given a hard time – this isn't a theft from Accessorize."

Jemima heard her BlackBerry beep and reached for it on the floor by the bed.

<< I would like to see you in an hour >>

"It's only 7am but that was Mr V. I've got to see him in an hour and all I've got is my dress from last night. I can't go anywhere like this."

"OK, let's talk through what happened quickly, but firstly you have a shower and try to wake up a bit. Give me your keys and I'll go to your flat. I'll be back here within 30 minutes with some clothes. What do you want and where do I find them?"

"Really? You're amazing. OK, great. Flora will probably be there so I'll let her know. I need to look professional today. I have a beautiful silk Diane Von Furstenburg skirt hanging in my wardrobe... and... don't worry, I'll call Flora get her to give you some things. Thank you, thank you!"

"OK, now you get up and sort yourself out, you don't want to be late for him. We'll go through everything while you're getting dressed, OK?"

Jemima walked to the bathroom and, leaning over the basin, gazed into the huge mirror that spanned the wall of the room. The lights were very bright and there was no getting around the fact that she looked awful. Mascara and eyeliner ringed her bloodshot eyes. Her face looked red and raw.

She headed back to the bedroom and retrieved the phone from under the duvet where she had flung it after reading Mr V's text. She phoned Flora's mobile.

"Urgh. Hello?" said a croaky voice.

"Flora," Jemima whispered as though someone might hear her, "you'll never guess what's happened... but first, South African James is on his way over to pick up some clothes for me. Can you dig out my DVF patterned silk skirt - you know the one with the black band around the top and bottom? A black t-shirt and my black Dior jacket? And some flat black pumps. And I left my makeup in the office, can you lend me some which will work? Oh, and can you get my face cream and hairbrush for him too?"

"Of course but what's going on, Jem? Are you OK? Where are you?"

"I am in his hotel room at Claridge's. My life is not worth living... someone stole the necklace."

"NO! Who?"

"If I knew that, I wouldn't be so scared. Someone drugged Sahara and stole it from her when she was in the loo. The problem is that I was supposed to be keeping an eye on her but I passed out."

"Passed out? Had you been drinking?"

"No! I only had one glass of champ..." Something clicked in Jemima's mind. Paul Pratt had given her that champagne. Was it possible that he'd slipped something into it?

"Oh no my darling. Don't worry, I'll get those things together. Keep me posted."

"Just don't tell anyone as we don't want this to get out. Was everything OK with your police issue?"

"Oh yes, yes – don't worry about that! I've got to go to court..."

"Poor you, Flo. OK! I am going to have a long, hot shower and get ready for what is going to be a very difficult day. Speak later."

Jemima turned on BBC Breakfast on the large plasma television and went back to the bathroom, pulling off the t-shirt James had lent her. Without thinking to run the hot water first, she stepped into the shower as she turned it on.

"Aaaarghhhh!" It was freezing. She jumped back out and heard the news bulletin from the television:

"Last night in central London a shocking heist took place when the world's most expensive necklace, sold for a whopping £105 million, was stolen from a charity gala. Simon Ashton, outside Vogel's global headquarters in Piccadilly, has more details..."

Standing looking at her forlorn self slowly disappearing behind the steam on the mirror, Jemima only wished that she could disappear completely.

Why was it on the news? Mr V had said for it not to get out.

Someone must have leaked it and of course she would be blamed. Why did these things happen to her?

Jemima was brought back to her senses by James shouting from the bedroom, "Hey hon, I'm back with your things – how are you doing?"

"Just in the shower!" she shouted, jumping back in and frantically scrubbing at her face and body, the now scorching water bringing her back to life.

"Good. But you had better hurry up, Mr Vogel is expecting you in 25 minutes. I've ordered some coffee. Flora wanted to come but I was quite bossy and told her it was best she didn't. Wow, it's all over the news!"

"I know..." Jemima replied, coming into the room wrapped in a towel and drying her hair with another one. "I'm so scared. I always cry in difficult situations and I just know that I will each time I am questioned today. In fact I think Mr V will be the easiest one. It is that nightmare of a man, Paul Pratt, I'm worried about."

"Well you have to stand up to him. He isn't your boss, whatever he thinks. If you have Mr Vogel on your side then you'll be OK. I think that you must be completely honest with him. Tell him that you didn't check the bathroom before Sahara went in and tell him about the sleeping pills..."

"Actually James, I remembered something while you were out. Paul Pratt gave me my only drink last night. It wasn't till after I drank it that I started to feel strange."

"You're kidding! You think that..?"

"I don't know. I don't think that he'd be involved in a jewel theft.

He's too stupid for one thing. But I wouldn't put it past him if it meant me humiliating myself."

"Well look, just tell Mr Vogel the facts. Let him draw his own conclusions, for now at least. He's bound to want to know where Pratt went last night anyway."

"Yes, you're probably right." Jemima hurriedly got dressed while simultaneously drinking the coffee that had just arrived. "OK, I'm just going to do my makeup and dry my hair and I'm done."

"Brilliant – let's go back through it all one more time so you're clear in your own head. Don't worry, you'll be fine."

"Really? I wonder…"

Jemima always prided herself on how quickly, and expertly, she could dry her hair and put on her makeup, but that was without a shaky hand. Today she was shaking so much that she gave up without even trying to apply mascara, pleased that she'd had her eyelashes dyed at the weekend.

She and James reminded each other of the story she'd already told him – the truth, although to her own ears it didn't seem like such. She knew she just had to get on with the day ahead. She stood up, more bravely than she felt.

"Right, I'm off."

"OK. You look great. Call me if you need anything. I'm meant to be flying back tomorrow morning but I will probably have to stay around for police enquiries."

"Thanks, James – I don't know what I'd do without you," she said for the second time in 24 hours.

"Neither do I!"

Jemima managed a smile as she left the hotel room, her beautiful dress and shoes in the wardrobe to take away later. She got into the lift to take her away from this safe place and into what, she didn't quite know.

Barely five minutes later, she was pulling up to the office through a mass of paparazzi and police cars.

"Mr Vogel is here," the security guard on duty advised her as she swiped her card to get in.

"Thanks. I'll go straight up."

Jemima heard her voice shaking. She felt very nervous as she made her way up the grand staircase to Mr V's office.

"Come in!" She'd barely had time to knock on the door.

Inside, as well as Mr V, there were the usual suspects: Alexa, Danny, Paul Pratt and Philip Goldsmith. Danny gave her a big smile and a wink, which must have been hard considering the hangover he no doubt had, and Jemima remembered that he was supposed to be in New York with the mysterious Petrina. Even Alexa smiled kindly. Nevertheless, Jemima felt she was up against a war crimes tribunal. She started shaking. She was clearly going to get the sack, if she wasn't put in prison first.

"I'm afraid there are no more chairs... you'll have to stand," Paul said nastily.

"I'll get her one," Danny said chirpily, going into the boardroom next door.

"Thanks Danny," said Jemima as he put the chair next to his, asking Philip and Paul to move along a bit - much to their shock.

"Now Jemima," Mr V began, "Firstly I want to congratulate you on last night."

Philip and Paul sniggered in unison, causing everyone but herself to look at them.

"It was executed extremely well and looked beautiful. My wife has already asked Anna to book us on a safari..." he laughed lightly. "However, we have a disaster on our hands and unfortunately you are embroiled in it, along with your South African friend."

"But what about Sahara?" Jemima implored, knowing that she sounded like a child.

"Miss Scott will be questioned in just the same way as yourself. I would like you to tell me, again, exactly what happened. And please do not forget anything. We have both the police and the insurance company to deal with."

So Jemima began telling the panel absolutely everything that she could remember, from the start of the evening to James taking her home at the end, not mentioning that 'home' was in fact Claridge's. She adhered to James's advice of admitting that she didn't look in the bathroom before Sahara went in. She recalled the supermodel pushing past her, slamming the door.

"How long was she in there before you went in to check on her?" Alexa asked.

"I can't say for sure as I was feeling very dizzy and I think that I might have dozed off momentarily..." she added the last bit as quietly as possible, utterly ashamed of herself.

"Dozed off?!" Paul interrupted. "Or can't remember what you did? I have heard you have a tendency to drink too much."

"What?!" Jemima turned and looked at him. "Are you suggesting I had something to do with the disappearance of the necklace, Paul?"

"You said it, not me."

"Paul!" Alexa admonished.

"Honestly," Jemima addressed the room imploringly, "I only had the one glass of champagne that you gave me, Paul, before you disappeared."

"Jemima, why would I give you a glass of champagne when you were working?" Paul responded without a missing a beat.

"Paul! How can you say that? Philip, you were there too! You saw Paul give me that drink - after you had put the necklace on Sahara?" She was pleading with them and knew that she sounded over-dramatic.

"Jemima, I had more important things to do than watch you drinking champagne; one being watching Miss Scott, who had definitely had too much of the stuff. However, I find it very unlikely that Paul gave you any champagne. You're hardly his favourite person."

Jemima just sat there staring at the two men to her left and then at Mr V behind his desk, too shocked to react.

"Maybe you got confused, Jemima?" Danny suggested, clearly trying to be kind.

"No." Jemima said simply.

"Well this is very strange, but I don't want an argument over a glass of champagne," said Mr V. "You did not seem to be at all drunk when you came to collect Sahara, who definitely was. However, I would like to know HOW this is on every news channel around the world. Tomorrow morning it will be on the front cover of every newspaper."

"You couldn't buy this PR!" Jemima immediately regretted these words.

"Jemima, this PR attention has cost me £105 million. And I asked you to ensure it stayed out of the press."

"Sorry." Out of the corner of her eye she saw Danny grinning and could hear snickers from Paul and Philip. "I did not, and have not, spoken to anyone in the press or elsewhere at all. But this is such big news – it would have been impossible to contain. Anyone at the event could have found out and tipped off the press. I will not be the scapegoat for this." She began to feel an overwhelming sense of anger rising from the depths of her body. How could Paul lie so obviously? Why didn't Philip back her up? Did they themselves have something to hide? And where was Paul when it all happened?

She thought again of that flash of red she'd seen but thought better of mentioning it, afraid of being shouted at again for making things up.

At that moment, Mr V's office phone rang.

"Answer that, will you?" Mr V asked of no one in particular. Out of habit, Jemima jumped up.

"Hello?" she said, pressing the speakerphone button.

"Oh Jemima, it's you?" Anna sounded surprised, as though she had expected Jemima already to be in prison.

"Yes."

"Please tell Mr Vogel that an Inspector – no, sorry, *Detective* Inspector Paige, and his assistant, are here."

"Even Mr V can't save her now..." Paul said quietly, though well within earshot of Jemima and Danny.

209

Having been dismissed from the room, without being fired or as yet arrested, Jemima headed up to the press office. As she came out of the lift she could hear Noémie and Zoe chatting about the previous night. When they heard the lift doors close, they immediately stopped and, when she walked into the room, they were both glued to their computer screens as though nothing had happened.

"Come on! You're not fooling anyone!"

"Jemima, we don't know what has actually happened - only that the phones are ringing off the hook, there are paparazzi and police cars outside, and that a very expensive necklace has been stolen. So tell all!" Noémie said.

"Yes, please do. I tried to find you but Tatiana said you had to go home early as you were unwell – what happened?" Zoe added.

"Zoe, where were you? And how do you know Petrina Lindberg?" Jemima shot back. The feeling that something wasn't quite right with Zoe had been nagging at her.

Zoe's alabaster face went even paler than normal and she stuttered, "Oh, I ergh, know her from New York."

"OK." That was probably true. "So do you know where Paul disappeared to whilst all this was happening?"

"No – not at all..." Zoe trailed off, sounding unconvincing, and before Jemima was able to ask Zoe more about her conversation with Petrina, her phone started to ring. As she was standing near Noémie's desk, Zoe picked it up.

"Yes OK, I'll tell her..." she said, mouthing 'Paul' to Jemima's dismay.

"What did he sound like?" she asked when Zoe put the phone down.

"Normal."

"Pompous and self-important then," Jemima picked up the phone on her own desk. "Yes Paul?"

"Jemima, please come down to my office."

"Why?"

"Why do you think?"

"I don't know, Paul! To talk about why you lied about giving me a glass of champagne. Or where you were when all this was happening?" She could see Noémie's eyes and mouth were wide open listening to her. Zoe's face was expressionless as she gazed at her screen, pretending not to hear. However, Jemima really could not be bothered to have an argument with him over the phone and in front of the others. "I'll come down but Mr V wants me available for him at all times."

"He didn't say that in the meeting…"

Before he could carry on, Jemima put the phone down and got up. Mr V hadn't said anything to her but not only did she know that it would irk Paul, she thought that she should really be at her desk in case he did need her.

As she was walking around her desk to the door, her BlackBerry beeped three times in a row.

<<*Jemima, please tell me what is going on with this champagne story? I always believe you but you have to admit that it sounds very unlikely that he gave you champagne, unless he wanted to poison you… And what do you mean where was Paul during the event?*>> Danny.

<<*Hon, are you doing ok? I'm here if you need me. Police just*

called and coming to the hotel to interview me.>> James.

<<You looked amazing last night Jem.>> Fritz!

She couldn't believe it! He was the most inappropriate person she had ever met. She decided to leave the phone behind, switched to 'silent' and tucked under her keyboard, away from Zoe's eyes.

"See you!"

Noémie said, "Don't let him rile you."

"Easier said than done, the way I am feeling now."

30

As she went down in the lift, Jemima replayed Danny's text message in her mind. Yes, it was odd for Paul to have given her the champagne, but not if he had slipped something into it so that she would screw up... Why he had it in for her, she didn't understand. And again, why didn't Paul appear when Mr V asked for him?

She remembered someone spiking her drink years ago at a teenage ball and her parents banning her from ever going back to one of them. This time it would make sense. Paul was longing for her to mess up and by spiking her drink it would have been so easy for her to appear to have drunk too much and do something stupid.

This didn't explain how Danny's new girlfriend knew Paul Pratt's wife. And Zoe, for that matter. Although they may have known each other in New York, she conceded.

She could hear talking as she approached Paul's door and just before she knocked, she heard her name spoken. If Prying Paul didn't have a camera outside his door, she would have waited and listened, but she didn't want to give him the satisfaction of seeing her.

She knocked and went in without waiting to be told to enter. Of course! It was Anna conspiring with him and not even turning to look at her when she entered.

"Sit down, Jemima."

She did so without a word.

"So. Mr V wasn't very happy with you, was he?"

No mention of the lie he told about not giving her the champagne. Mr V, naturally, wasn't very happy at all. But actually, she didn't think his unhappiness was directed at her so she chose to ignore that comment, knowing that would also annoy him, and Anna, who carried on sitting next to Jemima as though butter wouldn't melt in her mouth.

"Maybe you would like to tell us what happened last night?" Paul spoke pompously as usual.

Jemima decided to answer his questions with her own. "Paul, why did you lie about giving me a glass of champagne? Unless you had put something in it?"

Paul looked at Anna, who was looking at him, and they laughed as though Jemima was being ridiculous.

"Anyway, I have just been through everything that happened. In Mr V's office."

"I would like to hear it again."

Jemima wished that she had the strength of will to say no, to challenge him about this bloody champagne and his going AWOL. Why was he lying? Instead she nervously repeated herself for what felt like the millionth time in 12 hours. She didn't understand why Paul made her feel so terrified as he was one of the most insipid, pathetic people she had ever met.

Once she had finished, he began, "So when Miss Scott came to you, asking to be taken to the bathroom, why did you not call Philip to remove the necklace?"

"I didn't want her to kick off. She was clearly pissed off that the necklace wasn't to be hers. I had been told by Mr V to avoid any tantrums."

Jemima was still trying hard not to shake with nerves but she was finding this all a complete waste of time. Not only hers but also theirs. Surely Paul should be helping the police find the thieves and not interrogating her as though she were one.

"Paul, I should go..."

"Why?" he interrupted

"Because I have the world's press calling us and I am the head of communications!"

"Anna. I think that in light of the severity of this we should ask the reception to put all calls from members of the press through to you."

Both Anna and Jemima looked surprised.

"Well... umm, OK. I had better OK this with Mr V first," Anna said nervously.

"Paul. Can I ask why?" Jemima asked.

"As I said, this is very serious. I think that you are too closely involved and if the press found out you were there they would have a field day with you."

Jemima couldn't help admitting to herself that there was an element of truth in this but she felt like she had been winded. It was really just another excuse to make her feel and look inept.

"I'll ask Mr V what I should do," she replied as politely as she could.

"Leave it with me, Jemima," Anna said as she got up to go.

Anna left but, just as Jemima was about to follow, Paul said, "One more thing, Jemima. I was doing some business for the company at the time of the theft. That is why I wasn't there. I have explained that now to Mr Vogel so there is no need to bring it up."

31

The next morning, Jemima was walking into work. Next to the Mandarin Oriental hotel, glass towers of uber-luxury flats built by the Candy brothers were going up, so the traffic in Knightsbridge was very slow. It was quicker to go by foot than by bus. She needed some exercise and fresh air, both of which she hadn't had much of in the last few days. Besides, it gave her space and time to think. She couldn't help but feel that there was much more to the situation than met the eye. Again, she thought about why Paul had lied. Paul's wife and Danny's girlfriend being friends seemed a very strange coincidence too. She must ask Danny about it.

The previous day, just after her interrogation by the self-appointed in-house Policeman Paul, she had received an email from Mr V. It was so impersonal that she thought Paul had probably got Anna to send it from Mr V's account. The email said that Anna would handle all press enquiries regarding the robbery and that Jemima's department should continue with their other normal responsibilities of organising shoots and press releases. Jemima, it said, should do her utmost to ensure that the evening's expense wasn't for nothing and that the event was featured in as many publications as possible. Of course, as the story had got out that the necklace had been stolen at the gala, all journalists wanted to write about was the heist. The fact that a necklace had been sold for £105 million wasn't having much impact on the papers as it had been trumped by the theft. Fortunately the circumstances and Sahara's involvement were still under wraps. Plus, according to Rebecca, a friend of Jemima's at the

Daily Mail, insiders of the press were saying that whenever the economy was going downhill, one of the fine jewellery boutiques was involved in a theft of a substantial amount of jewellery. It was only a matter of days before someone wrote a scathing piece about it being an inside job.

Somehow the security cameras at Somerset House showed nothing from the event whatsoever. It seemed as though someone had fiddled with them and the insurers were also dragging their heels, very possibly also thinking that it was an inside job.

Nevertheless, once word got out about the theft, several photographs had been sent to newspapers by members of the public, showing someone apparently climbing right down the outside of Somerset House. It was of course impossible to make out anything much about the person as he or she was in a balaclava and head to toe in dark clothing. However, it appeared that was how the thief had made their escape, before speeding off on the motorbike.

Jemima still wished she had seen whoever was wearing that red silk dress. The police had interviewed everyone wearing red at the party except Petrina, who had gone back to New York alone. Danny was staying to help with anything the police might need.

Just as she was crossing the road at Hyde Park Corner to walk through Green Park, her phone rang.

"Morning Mr V!" she said as sprightly as she could.

"Good morning Jemima, are you in the office?"

"Sorry, not yet – I'll be there in ten minutes."

"Not to worry, just come in and see me when you are."

"OK."

She smiled and felt a rush of relief that she wasn't in trouble for something already today. She had burst into tears quite a bit over the past 24 hours and of course had barely slept for the last two nights. She was actually relieved she was not dealing with the press on the matter as she just knew that whatever she said would be wrong in someone's eyes.

Ten minutes later she was standing once more in Mr V's office, waiting whilst he was on the phone to someone. He motioned for her to sit down and then a few moments later ended his call.

"Jemima, I've decided to offer a reward for any information that leads to the capture of the thieves. Unfortunately, from past experience I know that the likelihood of retrieving any of the diamonds is unlikely. We never got anything back from the heist at the end of the 80s. If the police are correct with what they believe was its route out of London, then the necklace would already have been broken up by the time it passed the Thames barrier. Now, only a couple of days later, the diamonds will be scattered between the four corners of the globe." He looked sad.

"How much are you thinking of offering?"

"One million pounds."

"Wow!"

"Yes. Typically people are saying that it is an inside job, they always do. But what no one realises is that these heists cost us a great deal of money."

"But what about the insurance?"

"Insurers only pay the 'wholesale' value of the stones. They do not take into consideration the design, the setting of the piece and of course the cost of keeping up the stores. It also means that our premiums will increase. This has probably cost me almost what I paid for the stone at auction."

"Oh no, Mr V. I don't believe it!"

"Well you must. Now the police are going to release this reward to the newspapers but Anna is away today ill, so you will be dealing with any press enquiries."

"Really? I don't want to be accused by Paul of saying the wrong thing."

"Jemima, don't take any notice of Paul – he is just an accountant."

She couldn't help but laugh. Thank God Mr V said that – it made her feel so much better. She wanted to ask him what Paul had been doing at the event when everyone was looking for him, to catch him out, but didn't want to push her luck.

Feeling a lot better than she had for a while, Jemima was further cheered up by a call from her friend Georgina, who was her counterpart at Asprey. Asprey had one of the most beautiful boutiques in London and they were always throwing great parties. Before she worked at Vogel, Georgina had always added Jemima's name to the guest list, despite Jemima clearly not being a client.

She had been at school with Georgina, who was now married and couldn't resist trying to match-make her single friends; she was always hopeful that one of the good-looking guest list guys she invited would see Jemima hovering by the rings and offer to buy her one then and there. Sadly it hadn't happened so far and when Jemima had started working at Vogel, she had been told she was not allowed to go to any social events of other jewellers. Alexa was paranoid that they would think Jemima was spying on them and then in turn feel free to spy on Vogel.

"Do you want to come to the launch of the new Omega store on Sloane Street tonight? Cindy Crawford will be there and I remember at school how you were obsessed with that workout video she did!"

"Haha, I was obsessed with Kate Moss! I think that I did that video all the time to be as thin as her!"

"Which worked! Anyway, come with me – we can go together and you can tell me all the gossip on the heist!"

"Ahh, that's why you want me to come…"

"No!"

"I'd love to but you know what Alexa's like… I'm still skating on thin ice, I think."

"But it wasn't your fault. Anyway, you don't sell watches!"

"You're right, and Mr V's being so nice to me… OK, cool, let's meet outside the Ritz and jump on the bus from there."

"Done. Can't wait to see you and hear all about it!"

32

Jemima saw her friend waiting for her outside the hotel and hurried up the street to meet her. They kissed and complimented each other, and moments later were on the number 22 bus.

"So, spill the beans!" Georgina said excitedly

"Not here," Jemima whispered back, "these buses are the worst places to talk!"

"OK, well then, you can tell me when we're off the bus. What is happening with Fritz? Have you seen him lately?"

The girls launched into an ultra-fast conversation that no one overhearing would have been able to keep up with, even if they had wanted to. Soon enough, they had reached their stop.

Once they were inside and they had done the rounds of the room, checking out who was there and having spotted several models and actresses, Georgina declared that she couldn't wait any longer to know the gossip of the heist. So again, Jemima told her story – this time though, the very unofficial but true version, with no holding back on the bits she wasn't meant to say. Actually, she had been told not to say anything at all but that was difficult. So far, to the few people she had told, she hadn't mentioned anything about Sahara being drunk at the dinner or passing out in the bathroom. Georgina's eyes were on stalks as she listened. She couldn't believe that Sahara had run to the bathroom only to be sedated and mugged.

"Between you and me, I've found it very odd how interested Sahara has been in this diamond – I noticed it when I went to the auction at Bothebie's in December. She asked me about it at a shoot I was on in

January, and had been asking Mr V about it too, apparently."

They were interrupted by Steven Matthews, a diary journalist from the *Weekend Post* who was there to cover the event, "Hi ladies, I couldn't help hearing you mentioning Sahara Scott."

Jemima immediately panicked and wondered how much of what she said had been overheard. Steven was a renowned hack and would stop at nothing to get his story. They all knew each other from years of events such as these but Mr V didn't like the *Post* so hadn't approved Steven's invitation to the gala. They had only sent invitations to the editors of *Vogue*, *Tatler*, *Harper's Bazaar*, *Vanity Fair* and the *Financial Times*. Georgina noticed Jemima's face burning so tried to distract him.

"Steven, how are you? Enjoying the party?"

"Yes Georgina, of course, I was just intrigued to hear Jemima talking about her apparently very *eventful* event. Which she didn't think to invite me to... What was that about Sahara Scott being so involved!"

"Steven, I am so sorry that you didn't receive your invitation. Maybe one of your assistants pinched it?" Jemima replied, trying to be polite and win him over.

"Whatever Jemima," he said dismissively, "I am actually working on a piece about the heist. This puts a whole new angle on it. We had been going to say it was looking like an inside job but if you're willing to work with me we can change the angle. This version of events would sell many more newspapers, keep the editor happy, and be much better for Vogel's reputation!"

"An inside job?!" Jemima tried to bluff past the other side of the story, "I would be very careful. We could sue you for libel!"

Jemima knew that the paper often didn't care. They were always being sued and the number of copies they would sell for scandals like this could easily cover any amount they'd have to pay out.

"Work with me, then. Tell me more about what happened to Sahara."

Jemima looked at Georgina, who raised her eyebrows and shook her head slightly.

"I never said that she was involved in the slightest! I'll need to talk to Mr Vogel."

"Do that. I'm filing my piece at lunchtime tomorrow. It'll be landing on doormats around the country early on Saturday morning." Steven walked off to ruin somebody else's evening.

"He's such a heinous person," Georgina said to a very pale and dumbstruck Jemima. "Come on, let's go – this party has gone decidedly downhill."

Jemima smiled at her friend. "Good idea."

Jemima remembered that she hadn't texted James back. Maybe he'd be free for a drink or two that night. When she wasn't worrying, she couldn't stop thinking about this hot polo-playing financier from South Africa.

"Come on, let's leave now, but let's at least get a goodie bag first."

Georgina made a bee-line for the girl giving them out, although it was a little early to be leaving.

Once outside, Jemima texted James and the girls undid the double-sided silk ribbons, which tied up the beautiful bags, and peered inside.

"Wow, some amazing things! Look at this divine Omega keyring, and this corkscrew is perfect – I might even hide it from Matt and give it to him for Christmas!"

"OK – but look, I have to get back to business! Urgh, I am dreading this call."

"It'll be fine, just take a deep breath and, most importantly, be confident – don't let him think that you fear that you have done anything wrong."

"But I did!!"

"Well, it's Steven's word against ours."

"What do you mean?"

"Well, you could say that you never said anything of the sort to me. I can verify if you like."

"Would you do that?"

"Of course! No skin off my nose. But I think we need to think how could Steven know all these things if they didn't come from you."

"I'm not very good at lying, George. I think it is best to say the truth but it's so sweet of you to offer. And at least I found out the original article was going to be about an inside job."

"Actually, yes, you're right. I think that you should weigh heavily on that. Maybe don't say anything about talking about Sahara?"

"OK, here goes." She dialled the number with dread. "Mr V, I hope I'm not disturbing you?"

"What did he say?" Georgina demanded to know when Jemima had finished the call and was reading James's reply that he was out in Ascot at the Berkshire Polo Club, having spent the afternoon playing a few chukkas on the polo field. The police had wanted him to stay in the UK as he had thought. That, thought Jemima, was good news at least.

"Well, he was pretty pissed off with me of course, but I think he is relieved to know about the inside job story so that they have 24 hours to deal with that. However, I have to go and see him again first thing in the morning. Goodness, there hasn't been a morning recently when I haven't had to go in and see him. Do I really want this job? I used to love it so much but it's taking over my life and I'm constantly on edge."

"I told you it wouldn't be easy when you started, it is never easy working for a family company. And the jewellery industry is difficult as it is!"

"I need a drink – that one glass of champagne isn't nearly enough! I can't be bothered to walk. Come on, I'll get a cab and I'm definitely going to expense it this time!"

"OK! There's one!" Georgina started madly waving her arm in the air to hail the cab and when it stopped, the girls jumped into the back.

33

The next morning, Jemima found herself yet again in Mr V's office, fortunately without the panel this time. He wanted her to repeat what she had said the evening before. She was getting thoroughly fed up of repeating herself.

"But were you drunk, Jemima?"

"No, of course not! It was 7pm!"

"Very well. You should not have told anyone – not even your mother or father – about Sahara being drunk or passing out in the bathrooms. Between you and me, she is being kept an eye on by the police."

"Why?!"

"Her story doesn't quite add up, apparently. According to the police."

"Goodness. Well, she has been very interested in the stone since I saw her at the auction back in December. She asked me about it at the *Russian Vogue* shoot."

"Don't start making up conspiracy theories. We need to deal with the matter at hand. I have my lawyer dealing with it already. Even the *Weekend Post* would not dare to print a story about it being an inside job. This happens every time anybody is burgled: rumours that it is an insurance scam."

"OK. I'd better get back upstairs. We've suddenly had a plethora of shoot requests."

"I don't want you focusing on those – waste of time. And from now on I only want us to feature in the top magazines from Condé Nast and in the *Financial Times*. You should be spending your time getting interviews about all the good work that we will be doing following the event. We must move away from this heist. The police are dealing with it now."

"But Sahara's ex-boyfriend can't have paid the money if he didn't get the necklace, so we can't go ahead with the donation. Unless... maybe you should make a donation to show that this heist hasn't stopped your charitable stance, and that you are still doing what you can to help these children? That is a good story to run."

"Jemima, well done – this is why I continue to employ you."

Mr V's praise was bittersweet; maybe a little more bitter than sweet, but anything to distract him from her gossiping the previous night.

"The police have yet to release the news about the reward. This could be a double whammy. Not only are we offering a million pound reward but you are going to donate... how much?"

"How much will I have to donate for this to be worth it?"

"I think that it would be amazing to announce that you still intend to donate some of the profits from the auction, so why not donate the money we made from the tickets?"

"Once I have paid the bills. OK, put together a release and I will speak to Paige to sort out the reward announcement. Perhaps it is best that it comes from us."

"It would make more sense. We should get someone to do an exclusive – maybe you should offer to be interviewed. The *Evening News* has been trying for months and I'll say you'll do one if it goes into tomorrow's paper before the *Post* arrives on Saturday.

"Good. Now run along – speak to who you have to and get someone in before lunch."

As she was running up the stairs to her office, Jemima smiled to herself. If she could pull this off then her skin would be saved. Would she be able to get somebody in before lunch?

With a bit of persuading from Jemima, by lunchtime the *Evening News* had sent somebody in to interview Mr V and would run the story in the final edition of the day, thereby pre-empting the *Post*'s Saturday morning piece. Clearly Mr V's lawyers had dealt with the *Post* as she hadn't heard from the vile Steven Matthews and she didn't want to ask her boss any more about it as he was so happy with her new idea and thought that the interview had gone well.

At 5.30pm, when the final edition hit the newsstands, Jemima ran down to the newspaper seller under the Ritz's covered walkway on Piccadilly. Sure enough it was on the front cover:

<<*"AFRICA'S CHILDREN WILL NOT SUFFER"*

Sidney Vogel, Chairman of Vogel Diamonds, has pledged to honour his word by donating all the proceeds from tickets of his charity auction towards building a much-needed hospital in Johannesburg. There is also a reward of £1m for information pertaining to the £105m necklace heist.>>

The article spoke of Mr V's achievements, what he had felt when he discovered his precious diamond had been stolen, and how one million pounds was little in comparison to putting whoever was responsible for the theft behind bars for a very long time. The story was then picked up and ran on the BBC1 and ITV News that evening. It would no doubt be picked up the world over, hopefully killing any story Steven Matthews thought would make his name.

34

After her first good night's sleep in what seemed like weeks, Jemima opened her eyes slowly. She remembered that the *Weekend Post* was out and she must get a copy. She leant up and looked around the bedroom for her BlackBerry so she could download the piece straight away.

She eventually located it in the kitchen, only to discover it was completely drained of battery. As she plugged it into her charger she noticed underneath a copy of the *Guardian* the unmistakeable script of the *Weekend Post*. Hesitantly, she pulled it out with a sense of foreboding. Bang on the front cover was a huge photograph of the Vogels greeting Sahara Scott outside Somerset House.

<<Drunk Diva Loses the World's Most Expensive Necklace>>

This was the less than flattering accompanying headline with an indication to turn to page 3 for the full story. So the *Post*'s editor had deemed it scandalous enough to be on the front cover and the subsequent next facing page. Jemima already knew what it would say without putting herself through the pain of reading it. But read it she did – of course.

<<The news of the disappearance of the planet's most expensive necklace has provoked conspiracy theories, rumours and sightings the world over in the few days since it was, apparently, stolen at a high profile charity gala in London on Monday night. But in a twist I have since uncovered, it seems that this all could have been prevented if the infamous Texan supermodel Sahara Scott had enjoyed one, or two, fewer glasses of the Bollinger champagne that

was flowing more freely than the Niagara Falls at Vogel's charity gala in Somerset House. All the more interesting because it comes from the horse's mouth, as such – no one could accuse the glamorous Head of Public Relations at Vogel of being in the slightest bit horsey, in fact the closest she has probably ever got to a horse is the Dior Saddle bag that was hanging from her arm on the night in question.>> As Jemima had grown up riding her own horses this was a huge insult. *<<She has raised a lot of questions as to how this necklace disappeared from the ebony neck of Miss Scott who was, according to our source, passed out cold inside the lavatories of the former riverside palace. Did the diva really pass out from too much champagne or, bearing in mind that she is renowned for her love of jewellery, has she done what so many clothes horses do and simply forgotten to hand it back after her job? Maybe she was paid to do just that and if so, it looks like Vogel might be closer to getting caught for an inside job than ever before.>>*

Jemima looked blankly up from the newspaper and noticed that her BlackBerry had turned itself back on with enough charge. It was flashing red, signalling a new message. As she was about to pick it up, Flora came in.

"Oh hi, Jem. Benjy's going to make us a fry up, having been a darling and gone and bought us breakfast and the papers, but…"

"Flora. My life is over."

"Really? What did you do – call Fritz?!" She sat down next to Jemima on the sofa.

"No. I don't care about him. The paper. I didn't tell you last night as you were out. Here, read it."

"OK – look, here's Benjy. Benjy Boy – give Jem a mug of strong coffee, she's had a real shock."

"Oh, yeah – I didn't read the article Jemmy but the headline is pretty shit. Have this," he handed her a mug of steaming, strong black coffee.

"Thanks, Benjy. Thank God you two are here. I just want to run away."

"No, you must not do that. This is bullshit – I bet Mr V will sue the paper over this."

"I don't know if I want to hang around to find out. I haven't even checked my messages and I know they're coming in as my BlackBerry's been vibrating non-stop." She moved to the table to retrieve it and saw several missed calls, two texts, and an email from Mr V. Danny had called, as had James.

She read Mr V's email in dismay. He said that this was worse than worse. She must have lied to him about what she said and she had ruined the reputation of the company which he and his family had built over the past half a century. And would she call him. Now. 'Now' was sent at 7am; four hours ago. No wonder he had continued to call. She didn't really know what to do – should she call him first, or Danny?

Before she had a chance to decide, her BlackBerry vibrated and she saw that it was Mr V again calling her. She decided to answer it.

"Jemima, I presume you have seen the *Weekend Post* and that is why you are failing to get back to me despite my calls and emails."

"Errr no, not at all," thinking fast, she said, "I am at my parents' house in the country and I was out doing things with my father. I left my phone behind." Flora was doing the thumbs up sign and nodding.

"I have seen it just now, yes. It has upset me a great deal. All those things they said about me. I thought you had your lawyers working on it all of yesterday?"

"You never told me yesterday that you suggested that Ms Scott could have been involved in stealing the necklace. Her lawyers have been on the phone and want to sue me for slander, as well as the newspaper for libel. You have brought down her name and, more importantly, ours. You should never have told anyone she was there when the necklace was stolen. Particularly at a party where you could have been overheard, which I'm guessing you were - unless you actually told the journalist himself? Why did you not tell me that you had said this?"

The smell of Benjy cooking breakfast teamed with the shouting in her ear was making Jemima nauseous.

"Miss Scott has said that she will withdraw her case if you leave Vogel, however I am sending you on a month's suspension pending further action whilst the investigation is still ongoing. Please do not come in on Monday and do not continue this conversation with anyone. It might be best if you stay there with your parents, away from causing any more trouble in London."

He hung up before Jemima had a chance to respond. She had never heard him so angry.

"So?" Flora and Benjy said in unison, neither having touched their delicious-looking breakfast.

"He's suspended me as of now, for a month." As she told them what Mr V had said to her, her eyes welled up and tears starting to pour down her cheeks.

"Flora, what am I going to do?"

"I think that you must call James. He sounds like he'll know what to do. We need a plan of action. I also think that there is more to this Sahara Scott story than meets the eye. Why should she worry about what a mere PR girl thinks... no offence!"

"None taken. You're right. To be honest, I do wonder why she is so adamant about my dismissal. And I am starting to think that Paul Pratt really does have something to do with this too. Me being suspended. Why did he lie about giving me champagne, and where did he disappear to? I wish I had asked Mr V what he was doing but it's too late now. Do you think Sahara is worried about what I might know?"

"If that is true then you could be in danger. If you're right and she is capable of stealing a £105 million diamond necklace then the sooner you are out of the way, the better. Maybe you really should be at your parents'?"

"Yes, maybe. I'll call James now and ask his advice. Maybe I can go and hide in South Africa with him! Plus, I can do a little bit of digging too. There is something I want to investigate at that diamond mine I went to over New Year."

"Good for you, Bond girl! You've always wanted to be an undercover agent – here's your chance!"

"Haha! Right, I'm going to call James. I just hope he's OK with this."

35

James was still in the UK, at Heathrow in fact, having been given clearance to leave by the police. He was waiting to board a flight to Nice to see a client who lived in Monte Carlo and had seen the newspaper in the airport lounge. He told her to get out to South Africa as soon as possible. He was going to be travelling a lot but she could use his house and should there be any problems, his grandmother was in the same neighbourhood. He even used his air miles to buy her ticket, saying that she needed to keep all the money she had in case she really didn't have a job to come back to in a month. Despite herself, Jemima smiled.

Although she'd been told not to go in, on Monday morning Jemima was standing at the entrance to the Vogel head office. She wanted to go to her desk and pick up her personal belongings. She was determined to hold her head up and let no one know just how angry and hurt she was at being made the scapegoat in all of this. She knew she'd spoken out of turn at the party – or at least carelessly, but really, that was one of the more minor problems which Vogel was facing. Yet nobody else was being held accountable for any of the other events which had taken place.

"I am afraid your security card has been stopped and I am not allowed to let you in," the security guard said when she asked why her card wasn't working.

"What?! I have things upstairs in my desk and I'm only having a month off until things calm down." She saw Anna coming down the stairs.

"Anna. What's going on?"

Anna asked her for her BlackBerry and security card. Jemima could detect a slight smirk on her lips. "I was told you were with your parents, out of London? Mr Vogel does not want you entering the building, Jemima, so I will need to take these and they will be returned, if you return, in a month's time."

Anna seemed to over-enunciate the 'if' but maybe Jemima was being paranoid.

"This is ridiculous. Maybe I should have kept my mouth shut and let the *Post* print the inside job story."

"I think you should have kept your mouth shut, full stop!" Anna replied and waited until Jemima had left before scurrying back to her office.

Walking back up past the Ritz and getting the circadian smile and 'Good Morning' from one of the regular doormen, Jemima felt very sad that this was how everything was turning out. Maybe she just got too involved in things but she loved Vogel and felt it was such an honour to work for Mr V. Anyhow, at least she was getting out of London. It would still be nice weather in Johannesburg, so she managed a smile and decided to go to Top Shop in Oxford Circus to buy a couple of new bikinis.

By 6pm that evening she was sitting in her economy seat and laughing to herself about how different it was from when she was sitting in the Virgin Upper Class. But she couldn't think about that now. Her mind had turned back to the mystery of the Cullinan Stone and she still couldn't shake the feeling that the Vogel Vanderpless and the Cullinan were somehow linked. She wished she could work out why Sahara was so interested in the diamond. It was more than just that the diva loved diamonds.

"Hi!" came a voice that she didn't recognise. Jemima prayed that it wasn't someone she knew who was going to ask her all about the Vogel heist. Looking up, she vaguely recognised the very made up face looking down at her. "Of course, you don't remember me. Sorry…"

Jemima thought that she did look vaguely familiar and read her name badge. Oh yes – Debbie!

"You flew with us a few months ago, well just after Christmas, but in Upper Class. I couldn't help remembering you as you were so funny, pretending to be carrying a million pound ring in your handbag!"

"Oh god, of course, and I got so drunk you had to help me off the floor!" Jemima laughed, not minding that the woman next to her looked shocked.

"I'm sorry that you couldn't go in Upper this time but the top deck has been taken over by a celebrity so we have less opportunity to upgrade…" the flight attendant said excitedly and Jemima loved that she assumed Jemima would only be comfortable in Upper Class.

"Who?"

"Well, I am not meant to say but…" she leant forward to whisper. "Sahara Scott."

Alarm bells started ringing in Jemima's head. This was a coincidence too far.

"Really?" she said then, realising that she sounded too interested, "Wow, how exciting!"

Jemima's exhaustion soon caught up with her and she fell into a deep and much needed sleep. Waking nine hours later to a dark cabin, she made her way to the back to use the bathrooms. As she was standing in the queue, she heard the cabin crew gossiping amongst themselves.

"So... Sahara just woke up in a fit. She said that someone had stolen a box she had with her. She demanded they search the whole upper deck of the plane before it was found above her in the locker. One of the stewards had put it up there when she was asleep. She was a real bitch apparently."

"Wow – I wonder what it was that was so important and how on earth could someone have stolen it? She probably just forgot where she put it! She drank a lot too, apparently."

"Yes, it was just a flat box or something, with a padlock."

"Really? Can't have been that interesting or those dogs at security wouldn't have let it through."

After a couple of cups of coffee, Jemima's brain was working overtime. It was hard to believe it was nearly time to touch down. She couldn't help thinking about Sahara upstairs and almost didn't notice the morning sun shining brightly through her little window. She turned on her phone and after the customary 'Welcome to South Africa' text messages, she got a message from Rosemary, James's grandmother, saying that she would be waiting for her after Passport Control. Jemima was so looking forward to meeting her. If she was anything like her grandson then she would be a treasure.

It took ages getting off the plane as they had to wait for Sahara upstairs to disembark first with all her paraphernalia, including the mystery box. Jemima was careful to make sure that she wasn't spotted so she pulled a baseball cap hard down on her head and put on her sunglasses, feeling as conspicuous as a celebrity. Once in the terminal, she retrieved her luggage quickly off the carousel and immediately saw who she thought must be James's grandmother, waiting for her as the automatic doors opened. She had the same bright aquamarine eyes and wide smile as James but was very petite.

"Hi! You must be Rosemary? Thank you so much for coming to meet me – it would have been so easy for me to have taken a taxi."

"Of course not, it's a pleasure – you must be exhausted after your flight and James said you've had an awful time of late. I didn't want you adding to that with an unfriendly taxi driver!"

"That is so kind of you! James has been my knight in shining armour recently – I bet he didn't tell you that, though!"

"No, but I know my grandson particularly well and now that I have seen how pretty you are, I can guess!"

Jemima laughed bashfully and didn't say anything as she had no idea what James had told Rosemary of their relationship. She still wasn't really sure of it herself.

"Right, let's go. My station wagon is parked just outside."

Within half an hour of chatting about this and that, they drove through the entrance of a gated community in the wealthy suburb of Hyde Park, and up to an attractive white house.

"I don't know if James explained that this was his parents' house but they both died a few years ago. His mother was my daughter and they bought me my house when my husband died so we'd all be near each other. Sadly I was only here for a year before they were killed."

"My god, he never told me – what happened?"

"Yes, it was a tragedy. They were shot when some kids hijacked their car at a robot about a mile or so away."

Jemima had heard of this happening, when stopping at a traffic light in a nice car at any time of day, but particularly at night.

"I'm so terribly sorry. That is simply dreadful."

"It is. Thank you. I live eight houses away from James, at number 14. If you have any problems, call me. And you must have a swim – James has a very pretty heated pool. Now, would you like to come for lunch today after you've settled in?"

"I'd love to come for lunch if you really have nothing else to do. You've already been so kind collecting me."

"I've nothing to do until bridge at 5pm, which frankly I am tiring of! Here we are. I'll just show you around and then I'll be off."

When Rosemary had gone, Jemima explored the house. This was the most amazing place; not as big Stuart's where they'd spent New Year, but all white with incredible art on the walls and a pool just big enough to do lengths in without getting annoyed at turning around every five seconds. The master bedroom was huge and had a lovely view of the garden. The bed was also huge and Jemima wished that James was in it.

She quickly unpacked her belongings, having, as ever, brought much more than she needed. With her bikini on, she went downstairs, stepping out into the sunshine. She would have a swim then sunbathe awhile before lunch, trying to put the past week into perspective and decide upon an action plan.

36

"Jemima dear, did you have a nice morning? Would you like a glass of Chenin Blanc? It is from a friend's vineyard in Constantia – down on the Cape."

"Heavenly morning thanks and yes please – I'd love one! Just the one though, please. I've got a lot to do in the next few days."

"Here you go. James said you're here for a holiday as you've had such an awful time, so what have you got to do?"

"I don't really know where to start…"

"Start with a large gulp of wine – that usually helps me!"

Jemima smiled. She was already so happy here with this lovely lady's soothing company. She did as she was told, took a large gulp, and then a deep breath, and began to tell Rosemary the whole story, from her suspicions about the Vanderpless Vogel being the missing part of the Cullinan Diamond, to her suspicions about the world famous supermodel and her creepy colleague Paul Pratt.

"So the long and short of it," she got to just under quarter of an hour later, "is that I think Sahara Scott has stolen what I believe to be the infamous other part of the Cullinan. But I have no way of proving it. They have the same gemmological origin but there must be more to it than that. Why was Sahara so interested in this particular stone? She has known Mr V for years and has bought several pieces from Vogel. There is something about this diamond that she wants. I thought that if I could find the connection then I might have a motive. Then the hardest part will be finding the proof. Oh, and there's Petrina Lindberg, who I can't help but feel suspicious of, but maybe she really is just interested in Danny Vogel... I don't know?"

"My dear, you do realise that there have been rumours about the existence of another part of the Cullinan Diamond ever since it was found, at the beginning of the last century? Geologists have always denied such an existence."

"Yes, I know. The thing is that the Vogel Vanderpless stone appeared from nowhere. I just have a hunch... My friends would laugh as I have always wanted to be an undercover agent or something!"

"And are you trying to find out what happened?"

"Mmmmm..." Jemima laughed. "I know Sahara is involved and I want to prove myself right. I just don't know *why* she is involved."

"But why would this stone be the other half of the Cullinan?"

"It must sound ridiculous but I received an email the day after Mr V bought the stone, from the editor of the *Pretoria Post*, saying that it was the missing part of the Cullinan. Anyway, I didn't know about a missing half of the Cullinan and so I didn't think again about it until I saw the articles in the museum at the mine. The odd thing is that I cannot find the email anywhere and I would never have deleted it. I wish I knew why this man thought that the VV was it."

"Well we can always call the paper and you can speak to him?"

"Yes, that is a good idea. But even if he says why he thinks it is, the only way that I can truthfully prove it is to have it tested, which is impossible. The necklace is missing and I've been effectively fired - because of this feeling I have about Sahara. She knows that I suspect her and that is why she demanded Mr V get rid of me. Why would she worry about me if she had nothing to be guilty about? And that incident on the plane is so odd and so suspicious, don't you think?"

"It all sounds very odd. I can't help but remember an incident that happened years and years ago…"

"Yes?" Jemima said rather too loudly, scared that the old lady would wander off rambling, as she was already opening a second bottle of wine and hadn't produced any food yet. Jemima was starting to feel a little hazy herself after the flight and lying in the sun for a few hours earlier.

"My grandparents had a farm, not far from the Cullinan mine, near a small town called Rethabiseng. My father worked in the government so we lived in Pretoria, but on weekends and the holidays my mother, brothers, sisters and I would go for weeks to the farm. We all loved it. The next door farm belonged to a couple the same age as my parents and they had a daughter, Marta du Plessis, who was an only child. We became friends when I was about 13 or 14 and spent a lot of time together. She was a little younger than me and her mother home-schooled her so I used to give her my old school books. Marta was a really sweet girl and when I wasn't around she spent time playing with the daughter of her mother's maid. The two became quite good friends, I believe, much to Mrs du Plessis' annoyance. She felt that her pretty white daughter shouldn't be playing with the black servants' children.

"Then in 1953 - I remember the year as it was the year of the Coronation and I had met my future husband - one sunny spring day when Mrs du Plessis was sitting on the veranda with my mother, drinking tea, I overheard her talk about a strange incident involving the brother of her maid. He had turned up out of the blue to try to convince Mr du Plessis to buy what he professed to be a diamond from him for quite a significant amount of money. The man started to get angry when Mr du Plessis said that he wasn't interested. He said that he had found it and that it was the other part of the Cullinan Diamond that Queen Elizabeth of England had. Mr du Plessis said that was an old myth which wasn't true, and told the man to leave."

"Oh my goodness! It does, or rather did, exist!" Jemima was fascinated.

"I'm sorry to put a dampener on your thoughts and hopes but I do think it is one of those old wives' tales."

"But how did someone like that even find a diamond that could have been the Cullinan's other half?"

"As I said, if it even was a diamond... anyhow, a day or two later, we heard that he had come back and shot and killed his sister in front of her daughter. It was all very sad. He was found a few days afterwards in a nearby farm, stood trial and was hung for the murder."

"What happened to the du Plessis family?"

"Well the strange thing was, the family left very quickly after this incident. I forgot to mention that my mother never really liked Mrs du Plessis; not because she didn't come from a very good family. Mr du Plessis was not very wealthy but of good breeding and a real gentleman, but Mrs du Plessis treated him and the staff very badly. She was a snob and very much looked up to my mother, who was English."

"Where did they go? And what happened to the poor little girl whose mother was killed?"

"Well, the family disappeared into thin air. As did the little girl. No one knew what happened to her. My mother thought at the time that they might have gone to America. A cousin of Mrs du Plessis had moved there after the war and Mrs du Plessis spoke about it a great deal from the letters she was sent."

"This is amazing... I mean, if they didn't have much money how would they be able to afford the fare to New York? I know lots of people moved to New York after the war but I can't imagine that she would move somewhere that her life would be worse off than the one she left behind?"

"Yes, you are right – to be honest, I never really gave it a moment's thought. I had met my husband, Frank, by then – I was 17 or 18 – and was very consumed by him. The farm was left abandoned. However, in the mid-70s Frank and I went to New York on holiday to visit James's mother. She was working for Christian Dior in their New York press office."

"I worked in Paris in the press office for a while."

"How marvellous – oh, what a shame Daphne isn't here. She'd have loved to compare notes with you. Well, we were in New York and having breakfast in our hotel, reading the papers. I remember that I was reading the gossip pages in the *New York Post*, not that there was much point as I wouldn't have known who any of the people were, and the pictures weren't very clear. Daphne came in to meet us and when she saw me reading the *Post* she was excited, saying that a very important client of theirs was supposed to be in the society pages. She was photographed wearing one of their couture designs at a gala opening from the previous evening. I remember the lady was a

Martha Vanderpless and I recognised her. Although the photograph wasn't very good, I was certain that she was my childhood friend."

"Mrs du Plessis must have altered their names to sound grander."

"Yes. I mentioned to Daphne that I would love to meet her and see if she really was the same person. Goodness, my poor daughter was mortified, saying that they were the crème de la crème of Manhattan society and of course they had probably never even visited South Africa. So I dropped it at the time – it had been such a long time since we'd been friends and maybe I was mistaken – the photo had been very bad."

"But you had definitely thought that it was Marta du Plessis? Having moved very high up in the world?"

"Yes, and later I realised that it definitely was her. The next day we waited for Daphne outside the store to take her for dinner and I clearly saw the girl I had known as Marta du Plessis coming out with several Christian Dior bags. She was of course 20 years older but she had exactly the same features. Very unusual eyes – one was green and the other brown."

"And did you go and say hello?"

"No! Daphne had made it quite clear that I shouldn't – they were not allowed to talk with couture clients so I didn't want to ruin anything for her. And anyway, what would I say? We had nothing in common any more."

Not about to let her theory go, Jemima jumped up excitedly. "How on earth did they go from being out-of-sorts farmers in South Africa, abandoning their farm, to being Dior clients in Manhattan - unless Marta had married extremely well? And society then would not have condoned such a marriage! I bet that they took the stone, knowing all the while that it was a diamond. New York was not only far enough away, with little if no contact with South Africa, but also has a thriving diamond industry."

"But then how would it have come to auction still as a rough diamond, almost 60 years later?"

"According to that article I read from the *New York Times* in 1909, the 'other half' of the Cullinan was said to be huge; even bigger perhaps than the original one given to Edward VII, which was itself over 3000 carats. I bet that they took it to New York and rather than get the whole thing cut and polished, which would cause too much interest, they probably managed to get someone to cleave a bit off it."

"Ahhh. Well yes, that sounds probable, from the little I know of diamonds. After all, appearing out of nowhere to sell a diamond which you say may have been very large would have caused more than just eyebrows to rise."

"They would have had to find someone willing to do it, possibly for a cut of the profits once it was sold. If it was the other half of the Cullinan then no matter how big the 'cut off' was, it would have been worth a great deal of money as it was such a wonderfully high standard diamond. If only we could find out who did the job for them. But we don't even know if it was done here in South Africa, or in New York."

37

After lunch, Jemima and Rosemary moved to the conservatory with a pot of coffee.

"Jemima, I have an older cousin in Johannesburg who used to be in the diamond business, with De Beers I think. Perhaps he could shed some light on who might have cut this diamond."

"Yes, he might be able to look up who the diamonds cutters were in the 1950s. There can't have been many? Thinking about it, I am sure Mrs du Plessis would have taken it to New York to have it done there. It would be too obvious here."

"I will call him just now. Why don't you call the *Pretoria Post*? Do you remember the name of this editor?"

"Thank you. Yes, sort of, it was Walter something."

Rosemary handed Jemima the portable telephone while Jemima was looking for the number online on her BlackBerry. She still couldn't understand where the email had gone, unless someone had hacked into her account. Paul Pratt sprang to mind. She dialled the paper's offices and asked to speak with a Mr Walter, hoping that would be enough. It was but he wasn't in so she said she would call back later.

"I wonder what happened to that little black girl," said Rosemary wistfully.

"I wonder if she took her with them to New York, thinking that if she had a maid she would look the part, but quickly discovered that it wasn't possible to keep the little girl."

"She was about 13 years old, so not so little. She also would have been too much of a connection to South Africa. I do wish I could remember her name – I recall that she had a distinctive birthmark on her face. Maybe she left the city and went south to where she would be more employable?"

"Texas perhaps?"

"Possibly."

"And Rosemary – what was the mark the little girl had on her face?"

"It was terrible pigmentation on her right temple; I remember finding it difficult not to stare, actually. But she was very pretty otherwise, even as a little girl."

"Sahara Scott has a scar on her right temple. It is always airbrushed out in photography but faintly visible in real life…"

"And I seem to recollect she is from Texas?"

"Yes, and the first black supermodel."

The two women looked at each other. Jemima felt a huge sense of relief, and excitement, as finally the thoughts which had been churning around her mind for months started to fit together and make some kind of sense.

"Well my dear, it looks increasingly likely that this Sahara Scott was the little girl I knew when I was a child myself. Did she steal the necklace because it had been the diamond that Mrs du Plessis stole from Sahara's mother, leading to her murder? She must have known when a diamond came up for auction as the Vanderpless diamond."

"Maybe they are still in contact? Marta and Sahara?" Jemima wondered. "And I suppose Sahara believes the diamond is rightfully hers. Perhaps she expected the money from the sale?"

"I am sure Sahara doesn't need the money. I agree that she believes it is rightfully hers, though."

"I think that we need to find out what Martha Vanderpless is doing now and maybe you could try to make contact? Without cutting too close to the bone, it is not as though it will bother your daughter now."

"Yes you are right, and she would be much happier that we sorted out this problem – she was such a fan of detective stories and more often than not would work a mystery out within the first five or ten minutes," Rosemary said with sadness in her voice.

"Oh Rosemary, I am sorry. She must have been so young."

"Yes, she was – they both were. Now, I've missed bridge but I have a tennis lesson at 6.30pm and after all that wine, I shall need a snooze before."

"Gosh – I must have overstayed my welcome ..."

"Not at all, this is so exciting, but the days of lengthy wine-filled lunches followed by sets of tennis are long gone for me. I suggest that you go back to James's house and have a rest too – you can't have slept well on the flight. Make notes of what we have been talking about and then tomorrow morning we will drive to the mine. You said that you have been there before. Let's see if we learn anything else to satisfy us that this really could be the second Cullinan."

"Do you think we should tell James?"

"NO! He will think his grandmother has gone mad and be angry that I am encouraging you when you should be resting. Let's wait to see if we learn anything concrete tomorrow."

"OK. He did say how you knew lots of mysteries about the mines! Enjoy the rest of your day. I'll come over after breakfast."

Jemima left, deciding to cool down in the pool before crashing out in her very comfortable bed.

38

Jemima awoke at 2am with a thumping headache. After lying in bed for a couple of hours, unsuccessfully willing herself to sleep, she got up and pulled on a bathrobe, making her way through to the kitchen. At the fridge she opened a mini can of Schweppes Tonic Water, pouring herself a glass, and then another.

As she sat on the veranda, looking up at the full moon and sipping her drink, she started to think back over the conversations of the day before. She hadn't made any notes, of course; she was always being told off by Mr V for forgetting her notepad. If something interested her then she would always remember it and, fortunately, most of what he said did. Paul was another matter. He was so monotonous that she could easily and happily forget anything he told her.

However, what was as clear as the sky above her was that, before they did anything, they needed to find out if the Vanderpless diamond was indeed the same one that was left with a maid at a farm near Pretoria in the 1950s. The only person who could verify their supposition was the then Marta du Plessis, now Martha Vanderpless, who had put it up for auction. They had to find out where she was. If she was still in New York then why hadn't she auctioned it at Bothebie's there? Going inside, Jemima pulled out her laptop and logged on to James' Wi-Fi.

'Martha Vanderpless' she typed into Google, amazed she hadn't done so before the auction. Immediately, lots of entries came up on the screen and Jemima was very surprised that she hadn't heard of her previously. Martha Vanderpless had once been very much a New

York socialite. She didn't seemed to have changed her name and there was no mention of a husband or children. Jemima clicked on to see if there was anything recent about the woman and found several pieces about a refuge for single mothers that she was opening in Brooklyn. Apparently she was hoping to open several more across New York in the next few years. There was to be a fundraiser cocktail evening the following night at the Plaza Hotel in Manhattan.

"Well that is a sure fire way of pinning her down," Jemima said to herself out loud, before looking at flights between Johannesburg and New York for herself and Rosemary. Although it all sounded like exactly what her mother would call a 'wild goose chase', and an expensive one at that, it was the perfect opportunity to find out about the diamond face-to-face and she hoped that Rosemary was still as keen on helping her with the mystery when she had a clear head. She would put the flights on her credit card and somehow pay it off later; after all, she might even win the award Mr V was offering. The mine re-visit could wait.

Jemima sent an email to Tamsin, one of her best friends who lived in New York City and who was always invited to these events:

<<*Hey hon, I am hoping to be in your city tomorrow night, would love to see you and wondered if you're going to the fundraiser at The Witney – aren't you on the museum's young person's committee?*>>

Looking at her computer's clock, she thought that it was around nine or ten in New York so no doubt Tamsin was already out on the tiles. With a bit of luck she would catch the email while in a taxi and, being someone who subscribed to every type of messaging possible, would probably reply within minutes.

Jemima got up to stretch and make a cup of tea and by the time she was back at the computer she had indeed received an email from Tamsin, who was very excited to think she might see her. Jemima smiled contentedly and went back to bed with her tea. Exhausted from all the excitement and lack of sleep she fell quickly into a deep slumber.

Waking with a start a few hours later, Jemima dressed and wandered over to Rosemary's for breakfast and to fill her in on the latest nocturnal discoveries, hoping that she wasn't aghast at the suggestion of flying across the world to track down her old friend. It wasn't going to be a cheap trip and in the clear light of day, Jemima had not much idea how she was going to pay for it, or pay off the rest of her already large credit card bill - unless she did get that reward.

"Good morning my dear. How did you sleep?" Rosemary asked, looking very sprightly.

"Not very well. It must be the time difference and all that travel. But I did manage to make use of my insomnia. I found that tomorrow night in New York, Martha Vanderpless is holding a gala event to raise funds for a woman's refuge in the city."

"Oh, well done you. How useful the internet is. Did you learn anything else about her?"

"Not very much at all – there was no mention of a husband or children. Nor of her parents. But they must be dead by now. I think that she might be a bit of a recluse. This must be quite a big thing for her."

"We must go!" Rosemary exclaimed determinedly.

"But it is tomorrow night and we are two long haul flights away!" Jemima said, trying to contain her excitement. She'd had a feeling Rosemary would think as she did.

"My dear, there is nothing like a bit of adventure in life."

"OK, well I can pay for the flights with my credit card but they are not cheap."

"You save your money. I can cover the flights, and our stay at The Carlyle. My husband would have me stay nowhere else."

Within the hour, Jemima and Rosemary were booked to fly that night out of Johannesburg, with a brief stop off in London for breakfast, landing in NYC the next day 'in time for tea at The Carlyle'. Jemima couldn't quite believe that she was going to New York, courtesy of James's Miss Marple-like grandmother, and they were perhaps closer to solving the mystery. If only she could get concrete proof.

"What a jet-setting, investigative couple of days we have in front of us!" Jemima exclaimed excitedly that evening as they were waiting in the queue to check in, after a day in the sun. "I do feel guilty, however, not telling James. He'll be furious that I am dragging his grandmother to the other side of the world on a whim."

"Jemima my dear, I feel young again doing this."

"You don't cease to surprise me! OK, here we go; our adventure begins!"

They had arrived at the check-in desk and Jemima put both their passports on the counter.

"Good morning. And how was your journey to us today?"

"Yes thank you, fine." Jemima smiled, loving Virgin's American-style welcome.

"Mrs Von der Haye and Miss Fox-Pearl, you have been upgraded to Upper Class. I can check you in here but you are welcome to use our Club check-in desk in London for your on-going flight to JFK. And obviously our lounges."

"Upgraded?" Jemima and Rosemary exclaimed in unison.

"Yes – hold on, let me see who... Debbie Peters, she is one of the flight attendants. She must have noticed your names on the passenger list."

"Oh goodness – she is so sweet. How nice of her. Thank you!"

"It's our pleasure!"

Having proceeded through the routine of checking in their baggage, they moved through the gates and to the departure lounge for a drink.

"That was a quick trip!" a shrill voice came across the bar and Jemima once again saw her flight attendant 'friend' who was heading towards them, pulling her suitcase.

"Hi – thank you so much for the upgrade – wow – I didn't think that was possible nowadays?"

"The flight is not too full so it's at our discretion."

"This is..." Jemima was about to introduce Rosemary.

"Must be off – I'll be in trouble for chatting." Debbie turned to Rosemary, "Do excuse me and enjoy your flight, I'll see you in there." She trotted off on very high heels, pulling her little red suitcase behind her.

"She's like something from a *Carry On* film!"

"Isn't she just!" Rosemary laughed and they got up to board as Upper Class was called. "I haven't flown anything but economy class since business trips with my husband and then it was always British Airways Business Class."

"It's amazing. The only annoying thing is it's so nice to sleep when the chairs become beds but then you miss all the great movies!"

"I would sleep over modern movies any day!" Rosemary said as they settled down into their seats and the hostess came around, offering everyone champagne.

"I am going to be good and not drink. I need a good sleep after my insomnia last night," Jemima said determinedly.

"Well you did a lot of research and it's thanks to that we're on our way to New York!"

"Yes but what I can't quite work out is that, even if Sahara stole the necklace, she will never be able to wear it, and I can't imagine that she would dare to approach anyone to re-set the stones, or even cut the larger ones, for fear of being caught. All Vogel's diamonds over 0.8 of a carat have 'Vogel' engraved on them, although it's only visible using special laser light."

"Maybe she will use the same diamond cutter who cut down the original diamond back at the beginning of this mystery."

"Haha – that would be too convenient! He or she would be doing well to still be working now! Oh, did your cousin tell you anything?"

"How stupid of me. Yes, he called just as I was leaving the house. He gave me the details of an old De Beers colleague who moved to join his family in New York in the 50s. My cousin says he won't be working as he was a good few years older than him, but apparently he had a son who was born in New York City, so perhaps he is also in the diamond industry. They are Jewish and his family originally escaped from Antwerp just before the war, taking their trade with them."

"Maybe this is one of those families which passes on their trade through the generations. Hopefully we can track them down."

"Here's his information. He said something about a diamond district. I wonder if we'll have time to pay them a visit." Rosemary handed Jemima a piece of scribbled-on notepaper.

"I'll make time. I can't believe that a diamond this large stayed completely out of anyone's knowledge for so long," Jemima said, excited about this new line of enquiry. She tucked the paper into her jeans pocket. "Another point I am wondering about is that, even if Martha Vanderpless confirms our theory of the connection, how would Sahara have been able to carry it off? She can't have been acting alone – she'd have had to hide the necklace and then chloroform herself. Anyway, that person was seen climbing down the wall. There can't be many people small enough to squeeze out of that tiny toilet window, and experienced enough in climbing to achieve that feat. Most importantly, how will we prove that Sahara has the necklace? At the moment all we have are theories!"

Jemima took a deep breath after her monologue and saw Rosemary smiling at her.

"I agree, my dear – but I believe that all these things will find a way of proving themselves to us. Now you must excuse me - the past couple of days have been exhilarating but exhausting. I must eat this delicious-looking food and have a long sleep. I can't imagine that we will sleep on the way to New York!"

"Goodnight Rosemary – thank you for everything."

Jemima decided to watch a movie to help her drift off and before she knew it, she was being awoken by the friendly flight assistant who offered to make her bed back into a seat while she freshened up in the bathroom.

Heathrow Airport, London

"Good morning Jemima, did you sleep well?" Rosemary said, leaning over the partition. "Now we have a big day ahead of us so make sure you have a big breakfast. These scrambled eggs are surprisingly good for an airline and there is even a slice of smoked salmon!"

Jemima smiled at Rosemary's perkiness.

"The kind stewardess told me that it is raining in London. So instead of traipsing into town, why don't we go to Terminal 5? I would love to see it."

"Yes OK, good idea. It's pretty amazing. It only opened a couple of years ago."

They made sure their bags were being taken care of then found the shuttle to take them to the other terminal. Although Jemima was starting to think she really might be in with a chance of getting that reward money, she was sure Paul Pratt would somehow find a reason as to why she wouldn't be allowed to keep it. He'd say they should donate it to charity or something in order to raise the company profile. She decided that she would just window shop and let Rosemary do any buying. She could at least buy her benefactor lunch in one of the many terminal restaurants, however.

After an hour of following Rosemary around, Jemima remembered that actually she needed to buy another bottle of her favourite scent, Chanel no 5. Agreeing to meet Rosemary at Gordon Ramsey's Plane Food restaurant, Jemima made her way to the Fragrance and Beauty section.

"What about this?" said a voice that was so unmistakable she almost knocked over a display of promotional products. Before she was spotted, Jemima hid behind the makeup stand.

"Do you think that she will like it?" a female voice replied in a similar accent.

It was Paul Pratt and his wife. Jemima was again surprised at how attractive Paul's wife was. They must have been going to visit family in the States, although Jemima was surprised that Paul would take a holiday at such an important time for Vogel. *Please don't let us be in the same plane*, she silently begged. He was the last person she wanted to see – but she did want to see where he was heading.

"I have no idea what she would like, Barbara. Now hurry up or we're going to miss our flight."

Jemima managed to catch a view of them as they were leaving the Duty Free area and, staying a good distance behind, she followed them to their gate, hoping Rosemary wouldn't spot her and shout her name out loud.

She had to hide behind various objects and people several times;

Paul was so naturally suspicious, he seemed to be looking around as though he knew someone was following him. Although what he had to be suspicious about in the middle of an airport, Jemima had no idea. Eventually they got to their gate, having stopped at one of the many TV monitors hanging in the terminal. Jemima couldn't believe it – they were flying to South Africa! Johannesburg at that. What were they doing going there? A holiday, she supposed - hopefully it was a safari where he would be eaten by a lion.

Jemima realised that Rosemary would have been at the restaurant for at least ten minutes so she turned around and hid herself in the crowds, racing back to their meeting place.

39

Manhattan, New York City

Jemima had arranged to meet Tamsin on the steps leading up to the Plaza, then they would all go in to the party together. She had mentioned to Tamsin that she had an older lady with her who had grown up with Martha so Tamsin was excited. It seemed that Martha Vanderpless was quite the person to be associated with in New York. Jemima hoped that she would be able to blag their way in as of course they weren't on the guest list.

"Hey!" Tamsin exclaimed, "Jem, you look awesome! And hello..."

Jemima was wearing a hot pink lace Alice by Temperley dress she had ordered online at Net-a-Porter's sale site Outnet before they had left Johannesburg. She had managed to get it delivered to the hotel for when she arrived as she hadn't taken anything suitable with her to South Africa. She almost couldn't believe it when she opened the door to her room to see the big white bag with 'The Outnet' in big letters.

"Rosemary, this is Tamsin Littlewood; Tamsin, Rosemary Von der Haye."

"How lovely to meet you, my dear. What a pretty dress you have on."

Tamsin was looking as sensational as ever in a pre-order knee length charcoal dress by Azzedine Alaia and a pair of black patent strappy sandals, her blonde hair clearly having had a professional finish.

"That is so kind of you, Mrs Von der Haye."

"Do call me Rosemary. You must join us for dinner after the event."

"Rosemary, thank you, that is very kind but I have a couple of other events to go to after this one."

"Tamsin is one of the most invited girls in New York and regularly has three or four parties a night!" Jemima laughed enviously; not that her London life hadn't been sociable before she'd embarked on the gala event. She did miss running around town.

"Goodness me! How do you do it?"

"Well, it is part of my job being in PR and events to know who is out and about and what is going on. Fortunately my work pays for my cabs and I don't need to be in until 11am, but also I don't drink during the week." Tamsin's enthusiastic voice hinted at an American accent which she must have picked up quite recently.

"Oh dear, well I can't wait for a drink. We've had a very long way to come for this!" Rosemary said, already walking up the steps.

"Oh?" Tamsin asked, intrigued.

"Yes - from South Africa!"

"Oh my god – no way!"

"Yes – I'll tell you later but come on, let's go and find her a glass of champagne!" Jemima scampered after Rosemary.

The event was in the hotel's Terrace Room so they made their way through the beautiful foyer to an ornate room buzzing with hundreds of people. Jemima spotted lots of people she recognised from *The New York Social Diary*, which she followed avidly: Ivana Trump, Oscar and Annette de la Renta and Barbara Walters, to name just a few. Rosemary's breath was taken away when she looked up at the ceiling, reminiscent of the Italian Renaissance with figural paintings.

Huge, exquisite chandeliers hung down, picking up the colours of all the figures below.

They saw Martha welcoming guests who were being introduced by an assistant and again Jemima saw that Rosemary's eyes were on beanstalks, this time looking at her childhood friend. For a moment Jemima panicked that she would be overcome when talking to Martha. She grabbed a glass of champagne for them both and began looking around for Tamsin, who had already disappeared. She finally spotted her in the middle of a group of glamorous people, laughing and chatting. Tamsin looked up and motioned for Jemima to come over.

"Rosemary, I think it would be best if I leave you to it with Martha. We have worked out what you are going to say."

"Yes, very well. She looks so grand and important standing there greeting all those people, I do feel nervous."

"Oh Rosemary, I am sorry for making you do this."

"No, you aren't making me do anything I don't want to do, and it is good for me. I haven't been outside of South Africa for ages and I needed the excuse. We can't come all this way for me to chicken out. I'll go over now."

"OK, well I am going to join Tamsin with her friends but I will keep an eye on you to make sure all is OK."

"Thank you."

"Good luck!"

Jemima watched as the elegant old lady, dressed in a royal blue silk shift dress, approached the evening's hostess, having not seen this now incredibly glamorous and important New York socialite for more than 60 years. She thought how amazing Rosemary was. They had only met a few days ago and immediately James's grandmother had taken on her cause and now would no doubt be on the way to finding out the mystery.

Jemima kept glancing over from the group of Tamsin's friends and she realised that Rosemary was just about to talk to Martha. She could only see her friend's back but she had a perfectly uninterrupted view of Martha's face which, on hearing who Rosemary was, went momentarily yet unmistakeably pale before she quickly recomposed herself, looking as though she couldn't be happier to see Rosemary and that they really were lifelong friends. Before Jemima knew it, Rosemary was heading towards her with a huge smile on her face which wasn't just from the champagne.

"How did it go? She looked shocked to see you! I could see her face fall from here and I bet she has had work done to prevent just that!"

"Do you know, I didn't really notice, though her assistant looked at me as though I was an imposter, particularly when I called her Marta, and without my glasses I found it quite difficult to focus on her face. However, I am invited for tea tomorrow afternoon when I shall plug her for information and the story, if there is one."

"Really?! That is amazing. Let's hope that she doesn't cancel."

"Oh, she won't. I believe that she has a large secret to hide and she knows that I know part of it. Who knows, perhaps she'll feel like opening up to me."

"Brilliant! Oh thank you, dearest Rosemary. Shall we have a look at the exhibition? There is about to be an auction and they're always fun to watch – unless you happen to have organised it and an enormous diamond necklace goes missing!"

"Maybe I should buy something, as a goodwill gesture?"

"Good idea – let's get an auction catalogue."

As they were walking over to pick up a catalogue from a table near the auctioneer's podium, Jemima glanced back at Martha who had been looking at them; well, Rosemary really. When she saw Jemima look over she quickly diverted her eyes back to the next person in line to meet her. Jemima froze. It was Petrina Lindberg's father, who she recognised from the Bothebie's auction before Christmas. He was, after all, one of the most dashing men she had ever seen. He leant down and kissed Martha incredibly familiarly, almost on her lips, and his hand rested on her arm just that bit too long. Jemima felt a fast pounding in her chest and once again wondered what the connection between Petrina Lindberg and the Vanderpless Diamond was. Did Petrina and Sahara know each other too?

40

The Carlyle was not far from the Plaza on the Upper East Side. Rosemary had booked them into two of the hotel's beautiful bedrooms. Jemima awoke excited about what Rosemary might learn from Martha and looking forward to her day in the big and buzzing city that she had always loved. Opening her beautiful pale blue silk curtains, her eyes were dazzled in the bright sunshine. Springtime in New York! She decided to go for a run around Central Park to loosen up her limbs after the past two days of long haul flights.

The freshness of the park with its cherry blossoms already out gave her hope after her very odd month. What a scandal it would be – 'Diva steals Diamonds' would be again on every cover and news channel in the world. However, this time she would not let that irksome journalist Steven Matthews near her story.

Of course Sahara must be that poor little girl who had lost her mother and was shipped away from everything she knew by a cruel social climber. Could Petrina be related to Martha somehow?

Jemima came out of the Park and ran down Fifth Avenue for a bit, then crossed along 60th Street to Madison Avenue, slowing down to a walk so she could gaze into the windows of the jewellery stores which framed the street. Cartier, Bvlgari, Graff, Damiani, Georg Jensen. The sales staff were filling the windows with jewels for a day of sales. She wondered what she would buy herself if Mr V gave her the reward... it would be nice to have some money to spend on herself for once. Maybe she could even put down a deposit on a flat – if they gave her the whole £1 million award she could buy a flat outright.

As she arrived back at the hotel and was riding up in the lift, she thought that she must look up Rosemary's cousin's contact and go to see him that day. She arrived back at her room and found a note from Rosemary slipped under her door.

<< 9.30am. I tried knocking a few times and no answer so I don't know if you are still asleep or not, my dear. Martha left a message for me to go to her house for lunch, which will be nice. I am heading downstairs for breakfast. I will be there for a while no doubt.>>

Jemima was happy to see it was only just after 10am so she wouldn't miss Rosemary. She wanted to give her the Dictaphone for her to record the conversation so they didn't miss any little clues. Looking at her BlackBerry, she noticed an email from James, teasing her about jetting off with his grandmother. Rosemary must have said something to him and she kicked herself for not being the one to have told him. There was also one from Danny asking her to call him. It was the first time she had heard anything from anyone at work since she had been suspended, and she recognised the little butterflies fluttering in her stomach that she realised she hadn't felt for a while. She'd call him later; she had no reason to jump when the Vogels called; not for the time being, at least.

Jemima showered and lathered her body with the complimentary Kiehls' body cream then got dressed in her jeans and a white Anne Fontaine shirt. She wanted to look business-like if she was to meet this guy. She felt for the piece of paper with his details on and Googled his name and address on her BlackBerry:

<<Sam Goldberg 458 West 47 Street>>

Annoyingly, nothing came up but then she wasn't too surprised as she knew that, despite the glamorous boutiques, diamond dealers were very private. If he was a cutter then he probably didn't have anything online. She would just go to the address and remembered that he was in what was called the Diamond District. It was probably quite a different diamond district to Madison Avenue. She decided that she would go straight after breakfast so she took all she needed with her and went back down in the lift.

The breakfast room at The Carlyle was exquisite; very English, with hunting scenes adorning the walls and plush chintz upholstery. Rosemary was sitting by a window, engrossed in the newspaper.

"Jemima, hello, how are you?" she asked as Jemima leant down to give her a kiss.

"I feel great! Amazed that I managed to go to such a great party and wake up without a hangover! I have just been for a run around the park and down Fifth Avenue."

"Goodness, well done you! It doesn't cease to amaze me how the young run; I am sure we didn't go for runs. We just played tennis, swam, and rode horses."

"Wow, I would much prefer one of those options each morning but living in London, or New York for that matter, doesn't really make any a viable option!"

"No, of course not! Now look, here is the Page Six write-up on last night, with photographs."

"Oh! Can I look at those photos? I want to see if there is a photograph of a man I saw kissing Martha. He seemed to be more than just a friend, but I saw him in London with who I was sure were his wife and daughter. I wonder who he is?" Jemima was leaning over Rosemary's shoulder, looking at the newspaper photographs, but she couldn't see him.

"She really is very glamorous isn't she?" Rosemary mused. "So different from the little shy tomboy I knew in Africa! I am quite sure I looked very much the poor relation last night. I wonder what I should wear for lunch – I don't know if I have brought the right things."

"Oh Rosemary, you looked divine and I think she looked as though she has had some work done on her face and neck. After breakfast let's go and see what you have with you. What time has she asked you?"

"12.30 for one. I asked the concierge and her apartment is very close so it will take me no time to walk it. Now I think that we need to work out what I am going to let on to her."

"Yes, definitely. I was going to go straight to visit this diamond cutter. It is a shame that his father isn't still working, as this Sam Goldberg might not have the first idea of where Mrs du Plessis went with her rock. But you're right, we need to work out what you'll say. Let's do it in your bedroom – we don't want to be overheard and I have a Dictaphone I would love you to take with you so we don't miss anything. Hope you don't mind that?"

"Gosh – I hope I know what to do. Would you like me to come with you to see that man?"

"No, you relax and get ready for your lunch. The Dictaphone is very easy, don't worry."

"Wonderful! We can exchange our information this afternoon when we're both back. Now, what are you going to order?

41

An hour later, Jemima went back down in the lift for the third time that morning and walked through the reception with its plush auburn sofas and a floor so polished she could almost see her own reflection in it. She said hello to the doorman, who pushed open the heavy revolving door, and left the peaceful buzz of the hotel for the busy street outside.

Jemima started down Madison but realising that she was taking too long - no small thanks to the distractions of the stunning shop windows - she hailed a cab which took her across to Fifth Avenue and sped downtown. Getting out at the corner of 47th Street, she started towards the Diamond District. There were shops all down each side - both small-fronted ones and larger ones with double windows. The buildings were very high and the street was narrow so no natural light was able to be reflected from the innumerable pieces of jewellery and watches in the windows. Instead there were bright lights shining out of all of them. The signs were very basic, some of them with lettering which looked more akin to those on cinema billings in the 1950s. Jemima realised that many of these shops had been there and not changed for 50 or 60 years.

Many of the people she passed had black caps and beards and she could hear Yiddish being spoken around her. It could not have been more different from Bond Street or Madison Avenue where the other spectrum of the diamond clientele bought their jewellery. She carried on walking until she got to number 458 and saw that there was no sign with 'Sam Goldberg' above the door but rather 'R. Gowlsky'.

She went inside and asked if there was such a person around.

"Oh yes, Sammy – he has the upstairs. Have you got an appointment, Miss?"

"No, I don't. Is that a problem?"

"Might well be. He's a busy man and he might not even be in, I've not seen him today."

"Oh dear. Have you a number for him?"

"Yes. You from England?" the small man said, picking up his mobile phone from under his long grey and black beard which was resting on the glass top of his cabinet.

"I am. Yes." She smiled, wishing he would hurry up and call his friend.

He spoke into his telephone in Yiddish, all the while looking at her.

"What is your name?"

"Oh! Jemima Fox-Pearl."

He nodded and repeated her name into his phone before nodding again and ending the call.

"Come back in ten minutes and he will see you."

"Thank you so much for your help. I'll be back in a bit."

The man nodded again and went back to his papers.

Jemima went back into the street, wandering aimlessly before heading back to meet Sam. She was thinking it was about time to go back when she saw none other than Petrina Lindberg walking into the store on the opposite side of the road. It just looked like a regular jewellery shop and she wondered what Petrina was doing there when she could surely get Danny to ply her with jewellery. However, she didn't want to miss her appointment with Sam Goldberg.

Damn! This girl was so mysterious. It unnerved her but again, following Petrina would have to wait.

When she went back into the shop, the old man pointed a crooked finger at a door at the back of the room. Jemima opened it and went up the small wooden staircase to another door on which she finally saw 'Sam Goldberg' and 'Cleaver' engraved on a small plaque. She knocked on the door and went in.

Sam Goldberg looked like he was in his mid to late 40s, was overweight, and needed to wash what was left of his hair as it was greased to his balding head.

"Hey, how can I help you?" he said in a voice that sounded to Jemima like Woody Allen's.

"Hi Mr Goldberg."

"Call me Sammy. Mr Goldberg is my old man. We're both Samuel."

"OK, thank you Sammy. I was really hoping that you might be able to tell me anything about a large rough diamond that would have been cut somewhere in this district in the 1960s? It may be a long shot but I was in New York and I am doing some research on diamonds for a novel." She thought this sounded as unsuspicious as possible. She didn't want to raise any questions about why she wanted to know about this diamond.

He laughed. "Girl – do I look that old?"

"No. I am sorry – maybe your father would know. A South African lady brought a large rough diamond to New York to have a bit cleaved off. I heard your father is South African so thought she may well have come to him."

"Yes, you should ask my father about this – he did work here then and you're right, he is from South Africa. He may know about this story. Bearing in mind he is a diamond cleaver by trade."

"How could I speak with him? Does he live around here?" Jemima probed while looking around the room. The walls were covered with pictures of famous diamonds with their names written underneath: Dresden Green, Florentine, French Blue, Tavernier Blue. Next to the photographs was an identical photograph of each stone with 'Replica' written underneath.

Her attention was brought back to the room by Sam, who had been talking into his phone in Yiddish.

"Hey you, what's your name? Forgotten?" Sam spoke suddenly harshly, in a brash New York accent.

"Oh umm, Jemima Fox-Pearl."

"Right. I have just spoken to my father. He said that he knows nothing about what you want. Anyway, I am busy. You should leave."

"Oh, OK – I am sorry for wasting your time. Sam, before I go..?"

"You really need to leave, Miss." He seemed to be getting angry.

"I'm going, but what is that store opposite with all those big pieces of ornate jewellery in the window?"

"That is Simon Schall. My rival in making replicas of famous diamonds."

"Oh, is that what these photographs are? You make replicas?"

"Yes I do, Cubic Zirconia replicas, and that man is taking my business away thanks to being able to afford the most up-to-date machinery - unlike me. Now go. I am very busy." He opened the

272

door and practically pushed her out and down the stairs.

Jemima gathered herself together and walked down the steps, wondering what Sammy's father had said that made him change so suddenly. Just as she was about to leave the shop, having thanked the bearded old man, she saw Petrina walk out onto the street with a large bag over her shoulder and an equally large smile on her face. When she had walked far enough out of sight, Jemima slipped out and ran across the street to the store, opened the door, and went in. A man was sitting at a desk with a pile of paperwork, on the top of which were two photographs. One was of the Vogel Vanderpless necklace and the other of the four large diamonds: the heart shape, the round, and the two large pear shapes.

What was going on, and what on earth had Petrina got to do with the theft? She was certainly involved somewhere. As the man looked up from the photographs, Jemima turned around and left the shop.

42

When Rosemary returned to the hotel and knocked on her door after lunch, Jemima was snoozing on her bed, exhausted from walking all the way back. It took her a moment to gather her senses but then she got up and opened the door.

"Rosemary, how did it go?"

"She was extremely nice and humble actually; but... is everything OK my dear?" Rosemary asked kindly.

"No, I'm fine - just exhausted from everything. I am sorry. Do tell me..." Jemima smiled.

"Well, it was all very enlightening and confirms much of what we thought," Rosemary said happily, "and I think I remember enough without your Dictaphone but I've recorded it nevertheless. Marta du Plessis and her family left South Africa shortly after the conviction of their maid's brother for her murder. Of course the story was printed in all the local papers and people came digging around the farm, looking for the diamond, but they had no chance of finding it – Mrs du Plessis was a step ahead of the game. It appears that she had always believed in the story of the existence of the Cullinan's pair diamond - Martha remembered her mother talking about it after an article she had seen in a local paper – and suddenly there was a big chance that this elusive and mysterious stone was actually in her house. She had taken it from her maid, saying that she would get rid of it, but instead it seems she kept it. She had a younger cousin, Louise, who had met an American GI whilst working as a nurse in a field hospital in France during World War II. They fell in love and she moved back with him to America. Mrs du Plessis had longed to emigrate too and now she had the perfect opportunity. America was not only far enough away for them to hide from the scandal but New York City was a prominent part of the diamond industry. She wanted her daughter brought up as a lady and not to end up marrying a simple South African farmer like she considered herself to have done."

"She sounds such a terrible social climber!" Jemima gasped.

"However, there was the complication of the maid's daughter, who Mrs du Plessis obviously felt some responsibility for – quite rightly, as it was her actions that led to her being motherless. So they sold the farm and with the money it generated, they were able to buy the boat passage across the Atlantic, thereby removing any suspicion as to how they could afford to leave the country. They took the girl with them as their maid. Marta's father apparently knew nothing about the diamond, but had been convinced by his wife that they could make life in America work. He was a farmer, but what had once been a good profitable farm was now costing him more to run than it was worth so he was happy to sell up and get out of it. The murder and ensuing scandal had rocked him badly. Marta says she doesn't know what he had expected to do with himself to look after his family as he was only experienced in agriculture, but they set themselves up in a down market place in New York City. Very early on, Mrs du Plessis visited a South African diamond cleaver. She felt that he might be trustworthy, being the same nationality."

"Sam Goldberg," Jemima whispered. "His son, also Sam, was quite odd today when I met him. I will tell you in a moment."

"Yes, Samuel Goldberg. Well, she went along one day to his tiny shop with the hope of finding out what this 'rock' was. She promised the gemmologist significant compensation, should it prove to be real, if he didn't ever speak of it to anyone. Even if it wasn't the Cullinan's pair, and this gemmologist wouldn't have been able to prove it was without doing a series of tests, it was a very large diamond; one which would no doubt garner international attention. Mrs du Plessis did not want anything leading back to South Africa, the scandal, and their old life there. After all she was, indirectly at least, the reason two people had died."

"How did Martha know all of this? Do you think her mother eventually confessed to her from where all their money came?"

"No, no, she said she had no idea until after her mother died last year. But I will get to that," Rosemary replied patiently, smiling at Jemima's question. "So anyway, not long after, the gemmologist confirmed to Mrs du Plessis that it was a diamond of exceptional quality. She asked him to cut off a section and make it worthy of selling. The man cut and polished the part that he had cut from the larger diamond, leaving the latter as a rough from which another part could be chipped off at a later date. When Mrs du Plessis went back to pick up the polished diamond, she was amazed at the beauty of the stone. Since arriving in New York, she had browsed the jewellery stores to get an idea of what she might be able to sell the diamond for and had seen gems she would previously have not imagined could exist. However, she never conceived that hers would turn out so beautifully. To her the diamond was like a crystal ball – just by looking into its depths she saw a new life, whereby her daughter would grow up as far away from the rundown farm in which she had been born several thousand miles away, 14 years earlier."

"My goodness, she sounds as much a dreamer as me. But I've never had a crystal ball, let alone a diamond, I can look into!"

"Oh my dear – all good things come to those who wait," Rosemary said but Jemima had heard that phrase too many times.

"With the help of the gemmologist-cleaver, Mrs du Plessis sold the cut and polished fragment of the diamond and put the remaining larger part of the original in a safety deposit box in the bank. She never told anyone except Louise, who had by then moved to Virginia as her husband was to run his family ranch. Louise took Sarah, the black child, with them. Yes, Sarah is Sahara's real name. A year after they arrived in America, the newly named Mrs Vanderpless told her husband that she had come upon a great deal of money and they would be moving to a better district in the Upper East Side. Their lives were about to change and their names too. He didn't ask why – he hated his new life in the city and his job at the New York Farm Bureau wasn't making him happy. He was a shadow of his former self. His wife's news meant that he would not need to work at all but, although he was still young, he began to deteriorate rapidly and died after only a few years in the city. Martha (by now her mother had changed her name to what she considered a more elegant version) missed her father so much. She hated what her mother had done to him and the new life they were leading, away from the freedom of South Africa. She quickly went off the rails; going out every night at parties, albeit with eligible young men, just the sort her mother wanted her to socialise with and eventually marry. However, within a few months she was pregnant but the boy, also 17 years old, wasn't quite the right one in her mother's eyes. Mrs Vanderpless was furious that their new life might be ruined by her daughter's out-of-wedlock 'mishap' as she apparently called it. Martha was sent to Virginia to stay with Louise; out of the way of anyone in society finding out about her pregnancy. Louise had been unable to have children herself so she and her husband happily agreed to adopt the baby - Sarah would become the nanny. Martha had a little girl who was looked after by her adoptive parents with more love than any little girl could have wished for, and looked after by Sarah, who herself was turning into a beautiful young woman. Martha was sent back to New York and Mrs Vanderpless forbade her to keep in contact with Louise or Sarah. Although she was terribly sad, Martha was young and believed her mother when she had said that it was for the best. She stayed friends with the boy, though she found out later that her mother had paid him to leave her alone. He was there last night, apparently. Martha only told him about their child after her mother's death. The two of them went down to Virginia with Patrick's other daughter last year."

"Oh my god – this just gets weirder and weirder, my head is spinning!"

"Anyhow, back to the diamond… the money from the sale of the small part of the diamond kept Martha and her mother housed and clothed in the best of the best Manhattan had to offer. Martha never married but she didn't need to, from a material point of view at least. She still knew nothing about how the money had appeared and she never questioned it - after all, by now she could barely remember her life back in South Africa and having seemingly endless money had become her reality. Nevertheless, with her mother's constant social climbing, Martha became depressed and lonely. She was increasingly sad that she never knew how her daughter was growing up and she didn't even know her name. She never heard from any of them down in Virginia and she didn't dare go behind her mother's back by going there and seeking out her daughter."

"This old Mrs Vanderpless just gets worse and worse! She sounds like something from a Danielle Steel novel!" Jemima said, her eyes wide open.

"Sarah, on the other hand, was everywhere. There was no avoiding her. She was no longer a maid but a model." Rosemary smiled and continued. "Through magazines and newspapers, Martha followed her rise to top supermodel with both pride and jealousy. She seemed to have become successful and admired in her own right, with no mother controlling her every move. Sarah had been spotted by a scout for a new modelling agency that had just set up in New York - Wilhemina Models. They already had one successful black model, Naomi Sims, and were looking to capitalise on her breaking of barriers. Her name was changed to Sahara - referencing her roots, although no one recognised that the Sahara Desert was a long way from South Africa – Scott, the name of her former employer, Louise Scott. So the years passed and, as we know, Sahara Scott became one of the most famous supermodels in the world."

"Oh my goodness, this is all fitting together like a jigsaw!" Jemima exclaimed, feeling her heart beat in excitement, instead of the usual nerves.

"Although beautiful and a constant fixture on the party pages of all the right publications, as I said, Martha never married and she had no more children, much to her sadness. Instead she became devoted to worthy causes. Last year in May, Mrs Vanderpless died suddenly of a stroke. When the lawyer informed Martha of the will, she discovered that her mother had left a safety deposit box at The Bank of America on Fifth Avenue but no details as to what was inside. Martha discovered what looked like a large lump of rock and beside it a note with details of the diamond cleaver, our Mr Goldberg. There was also a letter to Martha confessing everything - how Mrs du Plessis had 'come upon' the diamond in South Africa and that was why they had all this money. She also said how sorry she was about making her give up her daughter. Martha couldn't take it all in. Her life ever since they had left their farm when she was a girl was based on a lie, and a murder. However, before she did anything with the diamond, she decided to speak with Louise in Virginia. She called on the pretence that she wanted to tell her about her mother's death. After some hesitation, Louise explained everything from her side of the story. Martha was relieved that Louise apparently had no idea how Mrs Vanderpless had come to have a diamond that size. Mrs Vanderpless had given Louise money, which had enabled her and her husband to have a good life, and most importantly they had adopted this beautiful baby girl when they had been unable to have one of their own. Martha got in touch with Patrick, her childhood sweetheart, and they went together to meet Barbara.

"Martha decided that she would get rid of the remaining (still large) rough diamond. She wanted nothing more from it and felt that it had in fact brought about a lot of bad luck. Her father dying so young, having to give away her baby; not to mention Sarah's mother's murder. She already had quite enough money and thought that with the money she raised from the sale, she would open a home for single mothers who couldn't afford to raise their children alone but didn't want to give them up. Martha took the rough diamond along to Bothebie's in New York, who became very excited. Their team of experts had never seen anything of such quality or size."

Rosemary rose to pour herself some water from a bottle in the minibar and continued, "Well, she said that the diamond was christened the 'Vanderpless Diamond' and it was valued at £20 million. The team at Bothebie's began an intense marketing agenda, with the diamond travelling the globe. They wanted Martha involved and kept asking about how she came about the stone. She quite firmly said that she wanted nothing to do with it and that it was best sold in London, well away from her.

"However, one day Martha received a phone call from Sahara Scott. She had known of course that Sahara would hear of the sale; Sahara was known for her love of diamonds but what did she know about the Vanderpless? She had been so young when her mother had been shot and it had taken this long for Martha to find out about the diamond herself. However, it seemed Sahara knew plenty. *'The diamond you are selling; I am presuming it is the same 'lump of rock', as your father described it, that my mother was killed for?'* Martha said she didn't know how to answer this but Sahara was apparently very aggressive, accusing her of living off the proceeds of her mother's death. Something in Martha flipped. She was not going to let this woman bully her as her own mother had for years. Had they not given Sahara a chance in rescuing her from a life of servitude in South Africa? She was now one of the most famous faces in the world, worth as much as this diamond, she didn't doubt. Martha didn't want Sahara to bring up the incident that had happened so many years previously – in another life and another world, both so far from where they were now. She told Sahara in no uncertain terms that the diamond had been given to her mother by a boyfriend she'd had when she was a widow. Sahara was having none of it. *'I do not believe a word that you are saying. And this is not the last you will hear from me. That diamond that you are selling is stolen. And it belongs to me.'* And with that she hung up the phone."

43

"Wow, what a bitch!" Jemima gasped.

"Well sadly, Sahara was right. But Martha was so ashamed of the whole incident and, not wanting to drag up events some 60 years old, she just came up with the story. She also felt that if it hadn't been for her parents bringing the then Sarah to the United States from being a poor black orphan in South Africa, her life would not be what it was now, which is probably true, though doesn't really excuse what happened. However, Martha is most concerned that now Sahara will spread the truth about her daughter. She doesn't want this girl's life ruined by whatever vendetta Sahara might consider she has."

"So it really seems it would have been Sahara who stole the necklace? She thinks that it is rightfully hers. We still haven't any proof, though."

"My dear, yes. Although I believe Martha, this would be one old lady's word against another's. I wonder how the police are coming along with their enquiries."

"Yes... maybe they have already caught the thief and we're wasting our time. Although I am sure we would have heard on the news. If only we could catch Sahara with the necklace - or find out who she managed to con into helping her steal it... Who was the person who climbed out of the window?"

"I fear it is going to be very difficult – what would she do with the necklace? She can't wear it."

"Maybe she has already had it broken up and made into pieces of jewellery for herself. No one would think twice about it as she already wears huge diamonds anyway!"

As they were both thinking hard and fast, Jemima's BlackBerry started pinging, indicating an instant message.

<<Where are you? Call me… X>> Danny.

Damn, she hadn't called him back but why was he sending her an 'X'? That was a first! And he hadn't exactly stuck up for her when she had been suspended.

<<What's going on? I am in NYC!>>

<<Pratt's gone…>>

He knew that would make her call - but what was the urgency? When she'd seen Paul and his wife at the airport, they must have been heading to South Africa on an extended holiday. Had he been fired? He never would have resigned – he liked the power that he wielded over Vogel's employees too much. Damn it, she was going to have to call Danny.

"Hi - thought that would make you call!"

"You know me too well. So what has happened? Did Mr V fire him at last?!"

"No, he handed in his resignation with immediate effect about a week ago. No one knows why."

Jemima wasn't sure whether she should tell him that she had seen Paul with his wife at the airport. It seemed pretty irrelevant and, like his grandfather, Danny hated comments with no relevance – which Jemima was very inclined to make.

"So what are you doing in NYC?"

"Just seeing some friends… What's happening there? Are the police any further towards finding the thieves?

"I can't believe that you are not more excited about Pratt leaving – it means when you come back your life will be easier!"

"Danny, you are kind – I don't know if I am wanted back, or if I even want to come back – no doubt Mr V has someone in my role already, if Zoe hasn't taken it for herself. And you didn't do much to stick up for me."

"Jemima, you caused such mayhem - Sahara Scott was going to sue the company! And anyway, Zoe left yesterday to get married. She only did a few days' notice."

"Really? I can't believe that!" Jemima said, feeling a tinge of disappointment that no one had bothered to tell her. She had only been away for a week. "Anyway, the journalist completely twisted my words. They were also said in private."

"Well they think it must have been a guest at the party who stole the necklace. There was a black tie, suit and shoes found in one of the rubbish bins by a back exit but so far they've not managed to track who they belonged to. He must have changed into something to steal the diamond before he made his escape on the motorbike. I don't know – to be honest, I am so bored of it all. When are you back in the UK? You're expected back in a couple of weeks, I think – my grandfather was saying that only the other day."

"Was he? I haven't heard anything from him since before I left."

"He wouldn't contact you – he is pissed off with you. Just play it cool like you would with a boyfriend… oh, you're not good at those games are you?!"

"Thanks for that. Anyway – gotta go – things to do, people to see…"

"Well let's have a drink when you're back."

"That would be nice." She smiled into the phone.

Jemima hung up, her mind running away with her. She still hadn't worked out what Petrina had been doing earlier that day. That girl was appearing in too many places for it to be pure coincidence. Maybe she should have asked Danny. And how convenient that Zoe had left just now; she wasn't supposed to be getting married until Christmas. She had definitely never mentioned anything about leaving, in fact quite the opposite...

"I take it that was someone from work?"

"Yes, Mr V's grandson, who's very nice when he wants to be. Not much to report except my nemesis has left the company - and what's funny is that I saw him and his wife at Heathrow, heading to Johannesburg."

"Oh, it seems Johannesburg is the place to go!"

"Hopefully we won't bump into him."

"Why didn't you get on with him?"

"He always had it in for me – I have no idea why. He treated me as though I was an idiot. He'd spent a lot of time in the States apparently and had a really annoying pseudo-American accent, even though he's really Irish, which used to drive me mad."

"Oh, Martha said her daughter is married to an Irish-American – she met him at university in Virginia, but now she lives in the UK. So sad for Martha as she'll never now get to know her - but at least they did get to meet last year."

"What do we do now, Rosemary?"

"I'm not sure, dear. I must admit though, I could do with a snooze. You look tired, too. Why don't we have a rest and meet up a bit later?"

"That sounds great. Sorry, Rosemary, this is all a bit tiring for you! I bet it's nice to have met up with Martha again, though. It sounds like she really needed to talk to somebody. You're a good listener, like your grandson!"

Jemima was glad of some time alone. Her mind was spinning and she wanted time to try and put it all straight, make sense of everything. Although she hadn't said anything to Rosemary, the moment that Martha's daughter's husband had been mentioned, Jemima had thought of Paul Pratt. An Irish-American man with a degree from Virginia University, now living in the UK. It was too much of a coincidence, surely? Now it really was all starting to add up. Paul had only started working for Vogel a short time before the Bothebie's auction and everyone in the industry knew that Sidney Vogel would buy that diamond. Had Sahara managed to get him the job at Vogel so she would have someone on the inside? She had, after all, known Mr V for a long time and could easily have said that she knew Paul very well. Maybe she did. After all, she had been his wife Barbara's nanny all those years back. Paul would have been able to tell her what was going on all the time and probably gave Sahara the nod to offer to model the necklace at the charity gala. Then it hit her. The Pratts weren't going to South Africa for a holiday. They were going to meet with Sahara, no doubt to get their fair share of the loot.

She thought again about seeing Petrina in the Diamond District.

What was her part in all this? Jemima was convinced she had one, especially now she knew what she did about Paul Pratt's wife. The two of them had seemed very familiar with each other that evening at the auction. What had she been doing there? What had Petrina been doing with the VV before the auction? Maybe she should call Danny back and warn him about his girlfriend. She needed proof, though. She had already lost so much credibility, she was sure that nobody would listen to her unless she could prove what she was saying.

Jemima suddenly felt overwhelmingly excited about her theories and wanted to go and tell Rosemary but the old lady had looked so tired, perhaps she should wait. She thought the only way that she would relax in the meantime would be to watch a movie so she got onto her bed and flicked through the hotel's selection on her TV.

"*How to Steal a Million*! Well that would be pretty apt... and Audrey Hepburn! I'll watch that." She lay back on her huge pillows where she managed to fall asleep, awaking just in time for a conversation between Peter O'Toole's character and his companion, a wealthy American tycoon. She was struck by the lines about paying huge amounts of money for something that could never be exhibited, or even acknowledged. The response was apt – the ownership was all that mattered. The ability to take it out of a vault, all alone, and to know it was his. Other people didn't really seem to matter.

That was it! Sahara wouldn't have split the stones up. It wasn't the money she was after – after all, she had no need for money. She would keep the necklace hidden and just take it out, put it on, and gaze at herself admiringly. Perhaps that was the way Sahara felt that justice had been done.

Despite her concern for Rosemary's fatigue, Jemima raced out of her room and knocked on her door.

"Come in!" a surprisingly bright voice called.

"Rosemary – have you ever seen that Peter O'Toole/Audrey Hepburn movie – *How to Steal a Million*?

"Oh, probably years ago – everyone was in love with those two."

"Well at the end, this American tycoon is intent on getting his hands on the most famous sculpture in the world. He doesn't care that it is stolen and that he can never display it, even in his own house. He says he just wants it and to know that it is his... I think that is what Sahara will do with the Vanderpless. She wants to know that she has it back, maybe as a revenge for her mother's death."

"Goodness, I suppose that does make sense."

"And," Jemima continued, almost breathless with excitement, "You know I said I saw Paul Pratt and his wife, who is called Barbara by the way, at Heathrow - heading for Johannesburg? I bet that they were off to meet Sahara to get their share. Maybe they think that she is going to break up the necklace and give them one or two of the diamonds. Sahara must have got them roped in. I think Barbara is Martha's daughter. I bet Sahara told her the story and together they made the plan, placing Paul in the company to keep an eye on things. It all came together when Mr V bought the diamond. Of course that was a gamble but Sahara knew Mr V wouldn't let a diamond like this slip through his fingers."

"This is so exciting! How on earth are we going to find them?"

"The paparazzi will find Sahara, I am sure. I'll Google her and I am sure we'll be told which hotel or whatever she is staying at."

"Well done. Then I guess our next move is back to South Africa. I have to say that however exciting these days have been, I am looking forward to being back in my own home."

"You're right. I am going out of my mind sitting here. Are you up for a walk? I can show you the Vogel store!"

"That sounds divine. I'm going to let Martha know we're leaving New York too. I do hope she'll keep in touch now that we've made contact again. I feel like she needs a few real friends in her life."

44

Sure enough, the paparazzi found Sahara. Jemima picked up the *Daily Mail* during their connection at Heathrow airport, which had a hazy photo of Sahara on page 23 - she was not of any particular interest at that time. The picture showed her not only in South Africa but holding a shopping bag from the shop where Jemima had bought presents for Flora and Marike - the Cullinan Treasures Boutique. Sahara was getting out of a black Mercedes at what looked like a hotel entrance but sadly there was no sign visible and Rosemary didn't recognise it. Jemima realised that Sahara had been at the Cullinan Mine, probably reading the same newspaper articles that she had herself read some six months previously. So Sahara did believe that the Vogel Vanderpless diamond was the missing part of the original Cullinan. Should all this be true, not only would Jemima be solving the whereabouts of Mr V's diamond but she would also be unravelling one of the biggest mysteries in the diamond world.

By the time she was back in James's house, Jemima was exhausted but she couldn't rest. She was living off nervous energy with the feeling that she was so near to catching her diamond thieves, she couldn't take her eye off the ball or, more accurately, diamond.

"Hello, may I speak to Hannah please?" she asked whoever had answered the phone at the reception for the Cullinan Mine tours and immediately knew it was the same offhand lady who wouldn't help her months earlier.

"Who may I say is speaking?" the woman said, as though Jemima was asking to be put through to the Queen.

"Her granddaughter."

"She doesn't have a granddaughter!" Jemima could hear a hand being put over the receiver: "... someone saying that they're your granddaughter!"

"Really? Don't worry, I'll take it... Hello, this is Hannah."

"Hannah, hi – this is Jemima Fox-Pearl. I'm sure you won't remember me but I remember how helpful you were when I came months ago in January and you gave me a lovely tour of the mine."

"Oh yes my dear, I do remember you – though I'm a bit surprised to find out you're my granddaughter!"

"Gosh, sorry about that – I just wanted to make sure I could get to speak to you!"

"Yes – what is it, my dear?" Hannah laughed.

Jemima needed to know if Sahara had been at the mine. How should she broach the subject?

"You know that I was interested in the story about the other half of the Cullinan? I was wondering if there was any chance of you copying that article about it from the *New York Times* from 1905 and faxing it to me – I am staying at a friend's house in Johannesburg."

"It's strange that you ask about that again today."

"Why?" Jemima replied, feeling sure that Hannah was about to answer her question without any further probing.

"Someone was in earlier this week asking about the story too – she asked to take a photograph of the model of the Cullinan in its original rough state."

"Oh really? Who was it - a school child doing a project?"

"No, an extremely beautiful black American lady. She had the most

292

extraordinarily long painted nails. I couldn't help but notice when she got out a pen to write down something."

"I wonder why she was interested? Do you think it could have been the same person who was asking for information back in September?"

Jemima was trying to keep her voice steady and not start squeaking. She just knew it was the same person; Sahara - or Sarah. Maybe Hannah could even tell her where she was staying. Of course this lovely old lady had no idea who the beautiful black American lady was – she had probably been stuck in the little village her whole life.

"Goodness, what a memory you have! Yes, now you come to mention it, I think it probably was the same person. Well they did both have Texan accents - I remember as I recognised them from my days of watching *Dallas* and we don't have many Texans calling us. Let's see..."

Unless it was Barbara Pratt who had been the first person to enquire back in September, it must surely have been Sahara.

"The lady who came here said something about her mother having some connection to the Cullinan. Yes, it was quite extraordinary really as everyone believes it to be just another diamond myth. She wanted a copy of the same article but I had none spare. I had to go up to the museum to get the piece and copy it here but she was in a hurry to leave so she asked me to fax the document to her hotel room. She did look very out of place in our humble village – not like you when you came."

Jemima couldn't help wonder what she meant by that. "Wow – I bet someone like that stays somewhere amazing!"

"Yes, she is staying in the penthouse suite at The Rembrandt Hotel in Rosebank, lucky lady – I believe it is a stunning hotel!"

"Yes, I have heard of it – how nice. Anyway, maybe you could fax the article to me too?"

Jemima couldn't believe her luck. Having given Hannah the fax number, she said goodbye and raced around to Rosemary's house. The old lady was dressed for tennis. Jemima marvelled at her stamina.

"Jemima, hello! You look very excited – have you found out where they all are?"

"Through a stroke of genius, if I may say so myself, I have found out that Sahara is staying at The Rembrandt in Rosebank. I just now need to catch her and the Pratts with the necklace."

"The Rembrandt! Why, Robert - James's brother - is the General Manager there. How strange that I didn't recognise it from the photo. I can't think why I didn't think of asking him before if he knew where she was staying – I think they host most of the visiting celebrities. Oh, but I am going to be late for tennis. Ah, never mind..."

"Really – this can wait..." Jemima said unconvincingly.

"Nonsense – we've been half way around the world for this! I'll tell the other three to play without me. Maybe they can rope someone else in from the club. I'll call Rob now and we can go and see him. He'll know what to do – I have very smart grandsons!"

"Thank you!" Jemima smiled, at the same time starting to feel nerves setting in. This was it!

She jumped into the passenger seat and thought how she really must call James. She was about to meet his brother, and had been hanging out with his grandmother in business class cabins and posh New York hotels, but had hardly been in touch with him! A few months ago she would have been constantly on the lookout for new messages from him, and worrying over the slightest detail.

As they arrived at the hotel, Jemima's confidence started to falter. "What if she sees me? She might recognise me and know something is up. Paul definitely will if he is here too."

Rosemary pulled off her white baseball cap, which matched the rest of her white tennis outfit. "Put this on and pull it down over your face!"

"God, this is ridiculous – like some comedy caper, I feel like a character in a movie... who gets caught!"

They went into the reception and Rosemary asked for her grandson, who arrived quite quickly and could not have appeared more different from his brother James. He was very thin, with dark hair, and looked very serious.

"Hello." He kissed Rosemary then turned to Jemima. "How are you? I've heard lots about you."

"Oh really – good, I hope?!"

"Most of it! James is heading over this weekend."

"Is he?" Jemima exclaimed, surprised and happy to hear the news.

"Oh dear – that was supposed to be a surprise," Rosemary sighed.

"Anyway, you two – I haven't missed my tennis to chat about your weekend plans... Robby darling, can we go somewhere private?"

"Sure – let's go to my office."

The Rembrandt, being an old hotel, was a rabbit warren of corridors behind the scenes. Jemima followed Rob obediently through them, thinking she would never find her way out on her own. Once in the office the two women explained the situation.

"So you're telling me that we might have the world's most expensive necklace in this hotel? I've seen a lot here, Sahara isn't the first celebrity, but this... what do you want me to do? Get one of the chambermaids to go into the room and retrieve it?"

"I don't think we should do that," Jemima, thinking hard, missed Rob's sarcasm. "Otherwise we're just stealing it back from her. What we need is proof that she has the necklace. I do not want to be calling in the police squad to find that she doesn't have it on her.... There is no way that she would be stupid enough as to leave the necklace hanging around in a drawer... she must have it hidden somewhere. *I* need to get in her room when she is not around. I just hope that it isn't in the suite safe – which would of course be the obvious place!"

"My dear, what about the gentleman from your office and Martha's daughter?" Rosemary asked.

"Rob, can you see if a Paul Pratt has checked in?"

Rob moved to his computer, clearly well used to obeying his grandmother's commands.

"Yes, we have a Mr and Mrs Pratt staying in one of our basic standard doubles. They arrived yesterday."

"Typical!" Jemima laughed. "Even though he is expecting to land a windfall, he still stays in the cheapest room! I wonder where they have been. They must have arrived a few days ago if I saw them at

Heathrow on our way to New York? Is there any way to find out if the three of them are in the hotel right now? It would be perfect if they were all out and then maybe you could issue me with a maid's skeleton key card so that I can go and rummage around...?"

Rob's eyebrows raised so high that they almost reached his hairline. "I can't just let you into our guests' rooms!"

"Robert," Rosemary said firmly, "You need to do this. Trust me."

"Well OK, I'll call Reception and ask if anyone has seen them leave."

Having established that no one had, or seen any of the trio around the hotel, Rob called Sahara's room and then the Pratts'. No one answered.

"Rob," Jemima asked, "I know it feels wrong, but can I get into her room? And could you keep an eye on the CCTV cameras in the corridor to warn me if she comes back – or, even better, waylay her until I manage to get out... is there another exit?"

"Well, it is a large three bedroom suite, so you will need some time to search it. There are a number of places in which she could have hidden the necklace. There is also a private pool terrace, from which you could exit by climbing over the wall and jumping to the garden below – it's quite a drop though. I should maybe have somebody there waiting to help."

"Goodness, this all sounds incredibly dangerous," Rosemary was worried. "I really can't let you do this. Rob, can't you do it instead?"

"I don't mind – what can they do? I am 99.9% sure that it is there with her and that Pratt will want to get his hands on either some of the stones or cash. The best thing would be to catch them all in there together!"

"But what will you do if you DO catch them?"

"Maybe you should call the police here just in case?" Rosemary suggested to her grandson.

"No!" Jemima exclaimed. "They'll be spotted. I have an idea. Rob, can you lend me a chambermaid's uniform and maybe check the hotel's CCTV cameras to see if anyone is on the terrace by the pool..."

"We don't have cameras up there so that the guests have privacy."

"OK. I wonder where the Pratts are – after all, Sahara should be close to Paul's wife, having been her nanny all those years ago."

"Rob, you go and get Jemima a uniform so she can change and we can get this over with," Rosemary said nervously.

"This is more than my job's worth, you know," Rob grumbled.

"Look, don't worry about your job. This hotel wouldn't run without you, as you know damn well. You're helping solve the crime of the century, you'll be a hero!"

Rob looked at his grandmother, then at Jemima. Then back to his grandmother once more. He sighed.

Ten minutes later Jemima, dressed in a maid's outfit, was pushing a trolley along the corridor. She heard a voice coming from round the corner that she couldn't help but recognise; it was Paul Pratt saying that they had to find someone before it was too late. The voices were coming from the direction she was going so perhaps they too had been trying to get into Sahara's room.

"We have to find her and get what is due. She couldn't have done all this without my help – she planted me, for god's sake. Making me move back to the UK and be nice to that stupid old billionaire who treated me like I was just an accountant."

"Oh Paul – you ARE an accountant. I never wanted to go along with this – you should have said no to her, she has always been tricky."

"Barbara – you have been conspiring about something with that sister of yours. Don't act all innocent with me."

"I don't know what you are talking about, Paul. Anyway, I am going back to the room – you deal with Sahara."

The voices started getting louder as they approached. Jemima pulled out the key card and knocked on the nearest door. Hearing no answer, she quietly opened it and slipped in, leaving the trolley outside and the door slightly ajar so she could tell when they had walked past. Stepping into the room, her stomach sank as she noticed in the mirror that the room was occupied – and its occupants were making love! *Damn.* She just hoped that they were so occupied with each they wouldn't see her.

She heard footsteps outside and when they had gone past, Jemima opened the door a crack and saw the Pratts walking in the opposite direction from Sahara's suite.

"Honey – I think there's someone in our room!" she heard.

"What…?"

"There's someone in our room – I just saw in the mirror…"

Before she had a chance of being thumped, Jemima slipped back out and pushed her trolley as fast as she could towards what she hoped was Sahara's suite. She knocked on the door but there was no answer so she let herself in, leaving the cumbersome trolley outside again. Thinking quickly, she wondered where on earth the necklace would be hidden. She'd heard those flight attendants describing a very plain, long box. She tried to think of where she herself would hide things... The most obvious place in a bedroom would be under the mattress. It seemed unlikely that Sahara would go for the obvious, but she had to start somewhere. She started to lift up the huge, heavy mattress in the master room but couldn't see anything. Then she opened the wardrobes and couldn't believe the dresses Sahara had brought to one of the poorest countries in the world. She could quite see why Hannah had said that she looked out of place in the little mining village of Cullinan.

Putting her hand into anything that looked like it had a substantial lining and pockets, Jemima found nothing. She then lifted up all the boots to see if it could be hidden inside any of them. She opened drawers and carefully lifted all the clothes in turn. She even checked the ice compartment of the fridge. She had to keep reminding herself that this was a huge necklace and not easy to conceal, remembering with a pang when she had tried it on. Before everything went wrong.

She checked, without any luck, the subsidiary bedrooms and bathrooms and, having pretty much searched everywhere in the palatial penthouse suite, Jemima went towards the main bathroom, which came off the master room. It was then that she noticed the door was slightly ajar. Now there was singing coming from inside. Her heart almost in her mouth, Jemima crept slowly towards the door, thinking that if Sahara did see her, at least she was well disguised as a chambermaid, her uniform complete with frilly cap which she had tucked her hair into. Edging closer to the crack in the door, she realised that Sahara was in the bath. She could hear the occasional splash of water but she couldn't gauge where the bath was in relation to the door.

She was as close as she could be when the suite's doorbell rang. Her first thought was that it could be the real chambermaid and that Rob hadn't thought to put her off, but of course she couldn't call them on the walkie-talkie that she had tucked away; Sahara might hear her. She hoped that Sahara would ignore the bell and carry on luxuriating in her huge bubble bath.

"Why won't these people just leave me the hell alone?!"

Just before Jemima had a chance to move away from the door, Sahara got up out of the bath. Through the crack in the door, Jemima saw in the mirror that the world's most expensive necklace was nowhere else but around Sahara's neck, bubbles and foam dripping off it into the bath. Jemima pulled her BlackBerry out of her pinny and, turning it to camera mode, she managed to take a photograph.

"Sahara, I know you're in there!" came Paul Pratt's voice whilst he banged on the suite's door.

Jemima scuttled away from the bathroom and towards the French doors, which led to the terrace. Opening them as quietly as possible, she slipped out. She positioned herself out of sight but with a good view of the suite's door and saw Sahara, wrapped in a white towel robe, go to open it; the necklace still around her neck, reaching into her crêpey cleavage.

When the door opened, Jemima saw that Paul was alone and looked shocked to see Sahara standing there in only a towel with £105 million worth of diamonds around her neck. He pushed in before Sahara had a chance of inviting him.

"What is going on? We've been here for three days, as you instructed, and you have avoided us. We want what is due to us so we can leave and get on with our lives."

"Oh Paul, I've told you. You and Barbara will get what you deserve. I will get my manager to transfer money into your account. Where is she anyway? You been bullyin' her again?"

Jemima thought back to Paul and Barbara's argument. What did he mean when he accused her of conspiring with her sister? Who was her sister and what would they have been conspiring about?

"Oh shut up, Sahara, you know that wasn't the deal – we agreed on some of the diamonds. I didn't sacrifice my old life and suck up to that old man for a bit of cash."

"I know but really, I think it would be best for them to stay together as..."

"As what? You can't do anything with the necklace as it is – so there is no point in keeping them together! You said that we would split it up, you'd sell what you didn't want and we would have four of a considerable size."

"Paul dahlin'..." Sahara started, "Barbara's real mother told me on the phone that she thought this necklace brought bad luck – I would hate to pass such luck on to you both. Louise would never forgive me."

"No one is going to forgive you when they find out what you have done!"

"What *we* have done, Paul. I go down – you both go down and, unlike you, I can afford the best lawyers. No, I have decided to keep it together, as it was when it was taken from my mother 60 years ago.

Of course it looks much better now Sidney has played with it."

She gazed down at the necklace on her chest.

Jemima felt like she was in a movie – she couldn't believe what she was hearing. She managed to take photos of them together and decided to text them to Danny before she got out of there. Her job was done and she wanted to stay alive to claim her prize.

She moved back behind the wall, towards the edge of the terrace, so she could firstly send the close-up photo of Sahara standing in the bath with the necklace, hoping that he would know how to react. She then thought that he was often preoccupied with organising his nights out or berating his team for something mundane, so with a deep breath she sent it to Mr V too, along with the two pictures of Paul and Sahara. Almost before she had clicked the keypad-lock button on the BlackBerry, her phone rang. *Shit*. She rejected the call but it was too late.

"Someone is on your terrace. I heard a phone ring." Paul spoke agitatedly.

The next thing Jemima knew, there was the sound of footsteps running towards the windows and for a fleeting second she was frozen to the spot. She was still out of view but realised that if she moved further back she would fall into the pool, so she decided to move as quickly as possible to the balcony on her left and climb over it. She hoped that the drop wasn't too big and that Rob had organised someone to be there to help, as he'd said he would.

"Oh Paul. It's only one of the maids!" drawled Sahara.

"Jemima?" shouted Paul, disbelievingly.

"That is that bitch who worked for Sidney!" screeched Sahara, staring too.

Jemima had reached the balcony in the few seconds that it took for them to realise who she was and she looked over the side to see that it really was a big drop – but there was a flowerless Jacaranda tree that she thought she could reach and climb into.

Paul was already pulling open the French windows in hot pursuit, followed by Sahara - still in her towel robe with the £105 million around her neck. Jemima climbed over the balcony's balustrade, trying very hard not to look at the ground below. White-knuckled, she edged along a bit, keeping half an eye on Paul. He was running around the pool towards her. Once she got to the tree she held onto the balustrade tightly and, sticking her left leg out, felt for the branches, cursing the fact that she had swapped her Converse for the flimsy maid's shoes.

She found a branch with her foot and grabbed on to the higher part, managing to heave herself onto it, shaking it so much that if there had been any of the beautiful purple Jacaranda flowers, they would have heaped onto the ground below. She wasn't very heavy but the tree wasn't very strong and she knew that if she wasn't quick she could easily break it. Nearer the trunk, the branches became more like a ladder she could climb down.

Paul was already over the balustrade on to the other side of the balcony but Sahara had retreated just inside the French windows, the Vogel Vanderpless around her neck, glinting in the sun.

Jemima glanced back at Paul and saw that it looked like he wasn't going to bother with the tree and would just jump to the ground to cut her off. Then he seemed to turn into Spiderman, shimmying down the wall. Jemima couldn't help but stare, realising then that it was he who had climbed down the wall of Somerset House. She recalled now his droning on about wall climbing at weekends. One more piece of the puzzle slid into place.

When he wasn't looking, she threw her phone into a bush to safeguard the evidence. She had a moment of panic as she realised she still hadn't turned off the ringtone and wondered what on earth Rosemary, Rob and his team were all doing. Surely they were keeping an eye on the CCTV cameras and could see what was happening? She was almost at the ground when they appeared around the corner, along with several police officers. One of the policemen caught Paul as he was trying to run away and another held up his arms for Jemima to jump into. Once she was safely down, she was hugged by Rosemary.

"Well done my dear, I was terrified that you would fall and break something. Did you find the necklace?"

"Yes, she was wearing it! But what shall we do – Paul's caught, but Sahara was just upstairs. She will be trying to escape. I don't know where Barbara was, either – she wasn't with Paul when he came into the suite. I heard her earlier saying she was going to her room instead."

"Don't worry, and calm down if you can. We sent some officers upstairs to stay outside the suite when we saw him going in after you, but you're right - where is his wife? And how did he climb down that wall? I was terrified both of you would break your necks!"

"Well we know now who it was climbing down the side of Somerset

House!" Jemima retrieved her phone from under the bush. "I'd evidently blocked out his boring climbing stories but I do remember now how he likes to brag about how great he is at it. He couldn't have got through the window, though - Sahara must have passed it to him then put the chloroform cloth over her mouth herself!"

45

As they were walking back through the gardens into the hotel, Paul in handcuffs, Mr V called, adding to Jemima's nerves.

"Mr V, hello."

"Jemima. I am on my way."

He hung up, no 'well done' or 'thank you'. Jemima heard one of the police officers suggest that Sahara and Paul Pratt be temporarily imprisoned in Sahara's suite. They were clearly keen to keep everything as low key as possible, until they were sure of what had happened.

It seemed that Barbara Pratt had already disappeared, however. She was nowhere to be found in the hotel and the police discovered that all her clothes, her passport and handbag had gone. The police would want to talk to her about her involvement but Security had not seen anyone of her description leave the hotel.

Meanwhile, Jemima went with the two police officers to retrieve the necklace from Sahara. She suggested to the senior police officer present, Captain Adlam, that he call Scotland Yard and speak to a DI Paige, who was handling the investigation. Jemima knew that Paige would be shocked beyond belief that she, the emotional PR girl from the party, had foiled one of the biggest diamond heists in the world, and she couldn't help but smile.

"How long will we be in here for?" Paul asked Captain Adlam nervously as they approached the door.

"Until we can work out what to do with you, as you will be extradited to the UK to face charges there of course."

"But where will we sleep?"

Jemima couldn't believe he could ask such a stupid question!

"Paul, you're in the one of the most expensive hotel suites on the continent of Africa. You have the choice of three huge beds, although I am sure Sahara has already taken the best!"

"Shut up Jemima, I should have known you would have had something to do with this."

"To do with what? You stole one of the most important pieces of jewellery in the world from your boss and endlessly tried to get me in some way implicated. You turned off all the security cameras at Somerset House, and deleted that email from *Pretoria Post* suggesting the Vanderpless's possible connection with the Cullinan Diamond! You even cleverly got me out of the company when I started working things out. I am just pleased that it was me who caught you. Where has your wife gone, anyway? I wouldn't wonder that you have something else up your sleeve."

"OK," the more junior officer said to Jemima, "We'll take it from here. We need to get the necklace to the hotel safe for the time being, sir." He addressed Rob, who nodded his approval.

Captain Adlam walked over to Sahara and began to remove the necklace from Sahara's neck. Jemima was amused to note that even this senior policeman, who had no doubt seen all manner of things in his time, could not prevent his hands shaking – whether from the value of the jewels or being in such close proximity to Sahara Scott, she wasn't sure.

"Honey, I can do it," Sahara said with great effort and handed it over. Despite the woman's huge wealth and success, Jemima couldn't help but feel a little sorry for her, whose whole life had changed the day her uncle arrived at that farm not so far from where they now were, with a rock he believed to be a diamond. She wondered if they would now do tests to establish the rock's provenance.

"Well girl, here we are again," Sahara turned to Jemima. "How did you know I had taken it?"

Jemima felt a wave of emotion run over her and sat down on the edge of one of the plush sofas.

"I learnt about the mystery of the Cullinan's other half when I was here on holiday in January and it captured my interest. I then saw you at the *Russian Vogue* shoot. Remembering seeing you at the Vanderpless auction before Christmas, I realised how interested you were in the VV. But I knew for sure that you had something to do with the theft when you tried to get me sacked. Rosemary told me all about the du Plessis family and everything seemed to tie up. Maybe I have read too many Agatha Christie novels but I guess I was just lucky in the end."

Later, in Rob's office, Captain Adlam reported his conversation with DI Paige.

"He was amazed, Miss, and wanted to know how you'd done it. I said that maybe they should ask you that so he wants you to call him as soon as possible."

"OK, thanks! They'll probably think I'm in on it too!" she joked back with a slight fear in her stomach – she hadn't thought about this before but she wouldn't put it past Paul to bring her down with him.

"Don't be silly!" Rob said behind her, "You have saved the day! And now for some champagne. I think that the hotel can pay the bill as long as in your no doubt countless media interviews you don't forget to mention its name."

"I couldn't think of anything I would like more!" Jemima sighed, the pounding in her chest settling somewhat.

Rob made a call and shortly one of his staff appeared with a bottle of champagne in an ice bucket and three glasses. Rob popped the cork and with the fizzing champagne frothing up and out of the bottle neck, Jemima felt an overwhelming sense of relief.

"Well, I really have missed out on all the fun, haven't I?" James said, walking in through the office door. "Where is my glass, or shall I go up and get another bottle?"

"Another bottle please!" Rosemary jumped up in joy.

"OK, but then I want you to tell me why you are all drinking champagne and not working. Rob?" He kissed his grandmother and gave his brother an enormous bear hug.

"The only job Rob has for the time being is being keeper of the Crown Jewels!" Jemima laughed, standing up to kiss James hello.

"What?!"

"I'll tell you later. Come on, let's go and get you a glass." Jemima took him by the hand, reluctant to let him out of her sight.

46

On receiving Jemima's photographs via his BlackBerry, Mr V, who had been on his way to New York, had instructed his pilot to turn his Gulfstream jet around mid-Atlantic and fly straight to Tambo Airport in Johannesburg.

As soon as he arrived the following day, he called Jemima again, wondering why she hadn't been there to meet him. He wanted to do a quick turnaround and head straight back to London with both Jemima and the Vogel Vanderpless necklace.

"You left it in a hotel safe, Jemima?" he had bellowed into her ear whilst walking through the airport to his car.

"Yes," she croaked, curled up in bed with James, barely awake. "The police insisted and they've got it well guarded. Don't worry Mr V, it is one of the top hotels in South Africa, with the utmost security."

"What and where is this hotel?" he asked abruptly.

"The Rembrandt in Rosebank, your driver will know."

"Very well, I am on my way. I will see you there very soon." He sounded more relaxed.

Jemima threw her phone down on the bed and stretched her tired body, looking at James who was still fast asleep. Her heart jumped at how gorgeous he was. Thank God they had stayed at the hotel so she didn't have to hurry too much to get to Mr V in time.

Guessing she had about an hour, she started kissing James all over his strong, tanned back. Climbing on top of him, she rubbed her breasts along his shoulder blades until he stirred and, half asleep, rolled over. Straddling him, she leant over, hoping to wake him up with her mouth and what she knew was her expert technique. He groaned. Once he was fully awake she walked towards the bathroom to shower, leaving him wanting more.

Jemima turned on the shower, needing to wake herself up after their late night drinking alcohol and making love. She took her time in the hotel's incredible power shower, lathering her body with the luxurious gels provided, day-dreaming about the night before and what she would do now she was about to receive the award Vogel had offered.

After Rob had left and gone back to his wife and family, dropping their grandmother back at her house, James and Jemima had stayed up chatting, and she'd filled him in on what the two sleuths had got up to over the past few days.

"So my darling clever girl," he had said when they were sitting on the suite's balcony, drinking yet more chilled champagne and eating succulent crayfish and salad, "what are you going to do now?"

"Well, I am sure I can have my job back if I want but I have enjoyed this more than anything. So much more exciting than sitting in a press office organising jewellery shoots and acting like Mr V's personal PR. I have been thinking about perhaps becoming a private investigator..." She laughed nervously, wondering if he would think she was mad.

"What a great idea! I think that you would be very good but you have to change your life a little. Less drinking, no more passing out at parties. And you'll need to get some formal training, even having pulled this off!"

"I know," she was embarrassed that he thought of her as such a frivolous person but she knew there was a huge element of truth in what he was saying. "I am going to use some of the money I get from the reward to put myself on a proper course and also learn self-defence. I can kind of see myself as a real life Lara Croft!"

"Don't laugh at yourself – I can totally see you as that." James pulled her onto his knee and kissed her. "My god, I have missed you."

"Have you?" Jemima asked mischievously, her heart thumping like never before.

"Of course. I am so proud of you. What a change from that love-struck, heartbroken girl I met six months ago."

"I am still quite love-struck," she winked.

"Really? Let's see how much."

They had walked inside, falling onto the bed whilst ripping off the few remaining clothes they each had on.

When Mr V arrived half an hour later, Jemima was in the hotel lobby waiting for him, beaming after her romantic night and looking forward to receiving his congratulations.

"Jemima, who is guarding the Vogel Vanderpless?" Mr V snapped, looking hot and bothered.

"Hotel security is patrolling the grounds of the resort and of course the hotel itself on a 24-hour rotation. Apart from the policeman standing outside all night, no one other than myself, the hotel manager and my friend James were…"

"What was he doing here again? He sounds too involved, Jemima."

"It is a long story Mr V, but I can guarantee that the necklace is in one piece and very secure in the hotel manager's safe."

"Very well. Let us go and get it and get straight back on my plane to the UK."

Jemima nodded and led him through the reception to the office, where Captain Adlam was waiting.

"Hello sir. I'm going to need some identification to prove you are the rightful owner of this necklace."

Mr V looked insulted but submitted to the request.

"Very well," Captain Adlam ordered one of his officers to open the safe, "I trust you have adequate insurance and security for travelling with something of such value, sir?"

"Yes thank you, I have done this kind of thing before!" Mr V snapped.

Unwrapping the necklace from the towel, he started checking the stones. He then turned around, got up shakily, and instead of giving Jemima a congratulatory kiss, he scowled at her. He was shaking with anger.

"Jemima. This is not the whole necklace."

"What do you mean?" she asked, almost wailing with disappointment. It looked like the necklace to her.

"These aren't diamonds." He pointed to the four large stones.

"They're not..? Well what are they?"

"They are CZs. Cubic Zirconia replicas."

"What? Fakes? But how can they be?"

"Someone has swapped the real stones for these. I can see that they were prised out of the platinum and replaced."

For a second, Jemima was amazed and wondered if he could be mistaken, but if anyone could tell, it would be him.

"They are a very good copy and I think that there is only one person who would have been able to do these, but I don't know how he would have been involved. Where is Sahara? I want to speak to her now." Mr V spoke more calmly.

"She is in her suite. I can take you there, sir, as I'd like to know what she will say to you," Captain Adlam offered.

"Let's go."

With the necklace back in the safe they made their way up to the suite.

"Jemima, I am sorry I snapped at you. I cannot deny that you have done a tremendous thing here. You have, after all, found most of the lost stones, but I am sure you realise that the most valuable are not here. They together are worth more than half the value of the whole piece. Who has the heart, the round and the two pear-shaped diamonds? That is what we now need to discover."

Jemima didn't know what to say so, for perhaps the first time in her life, she decided that it was better to say nothing at all.

47

Sahara Scott's Suite, The Rembrandt Hotel, Rosebank

The door opened and Mr Vogel, Rob and Jemima walked in to see Paul and Sahara lying by the pool on the terrace, sipping juices. Although it was autumn in the Southern Hemisphere, there was a bright sunshine, even that early in the day, and they were catching what rays they could before their indefinite time behind bars. Paul's alabaster body looked almost like a corpse next to Sahara's endlessly long black legs.

"So much for being under arrest," Mr Vogel said as he stepped through the French windows and onto the terrace. Paul jumped and sat up straight whilst Sahara hardly flinched.

"Good morning Sidney," she said brightly. "I do hope that you are pleased to have your necklace back. Although quite rightly it should be mine. You have a clever girl working for you."

She turned to Jemima, "You worked it all out; why it really is my necklace, didn't you?"

"Ummm..." Jemima didn't really know what to say to that particular question. "Well, until the stone is matched with the original Cullinan, there is no proof. I think it is one person's word against another. But nevertheless, you stole the necklace."

"We are currently having that theory tested as her Majesty and the Tower of London had to give approval. However, that is by the by, isn't it Sahara?" said Mr V.

Jemima was thrilled to hear that finally they were having her theory formally tested but she was surprised that Mr V had said nothing to Paul. He had not even acknowledged either his former company secretary's involvement, nor indeed the fact that his puny shock-white body was lying mere metres away from him.

"What else do you need, Sid? You have the diamond that was stolen from my mother and uncle half a century ago."

"This is not all of it. Where are the four major stones?" For the first time since she had met him a year previously, Jemima heard panic and impatience in his tone.

"What do you mean, Mr Vogel?" Paul asked, standing up and finally covering himself with his hotel bathrobe.

Still not looking at Paul, Mr V said to no one in particular, "The large stones in the necklace downstairs are not real diamonds. They are Cubic Zirconia replicas and I can't think who could have made such masterpieces, except Simon Schall. He does all our replicas and Danny was arranging one of the Vogel Vanderpless for an exhibition."

"Huh!" Jemima exclaimed, "I knew it!"

"Knew what?"

"I saw Petrina Lindberg in his store in Manhattan two days ago. I also saw her with the necklace just before the gala. She was also wearing a red dress. I saw a flash of red outside the bathroom before we found Sahara."

"Petrina?" Mr Vogel asked.

"Yes - Danny's girlfriend. In fact, I saw her talking to your wife, Paul, for a long time at the gala just before the necklace disappeared."

"Petrina Lindberg is my wife's half-sister!" Paul said. "I knew they were up to something."

"Up to what, Paul?" Mr Vogel said, finally looking hard at Paul.

"After old Mrs Vanderpless died, Sahara tried but failed to get her hands on the diamond. Martha Vanderpless wouldn't relinquish it and insisted it only ever brought bad luck anyway. Sahara got in touch with Barbara and me and told us all about what had happened in South Africa in the 1950s. Sahara said that if we got the diamond back we would get a large portion of it that should be Barbara's. When Barbara's birth mother and father came to visit, they brought along her half-sister, Petrina. Barbara hoped that she might be able to make Martha see sense about sharing the wealth but it was not to be. The diamond auction was already being arranged anyway and Martha insisted that everybody was better off without it. So Sahara helped me get a job with you, Mr Vogel..."

"Aah, I always wondered why you were so keen on this jumped-up accountant working for me, Sahara," Mr Vogel said, nodding his head.

"With me knowing what was going on," Paul did his best to ignore the insult, "we could devise a plan to get to the diamond. I do remember something that I found strange... Barbara never really wanted to go along with the scam originally. It seemed to be after she'd spent more time with her sister that she changed her mind. They went out to dinner together one night in Houston and then from the next day she wanted to know all about it. Planning the move to London and always asking me how things were going when I started working for you, Mr Vogel. I was a little surprised at first but her interest and enthusiasm gave me the confidence to carry it out. She was also very meticulous and was the mastermind behind the night of the gala."

"Ha!" Sahara laughed. "She was not meticulous one bit, from the day

318

she was born, Paul. You barely knew your wife. She was a dumb and gullible child."

"Well she planned how we carried it all out!" Paul argued back.

"No she didn't," Jemima said. "Petrina Lindberg did. I knew from the moment that I met her that she was up to something and that she was incredibly clever. She's a very successful lawyer, don't forget. Sahara did you see anyone in the bathroom when you went in there?"

"Yes there was a beautiful girl in there at the basins. I thought I would have to wait until she left before I passed the necklace through the window to Paul. Then the next thing I remember was waking up having used the chloroform on myself."

"And the girl was in a red dress right? So the flash of red was her leaving with the four diamonds in her oversized ostrich feather clutch bag!" Jemima smiled that it was all fitting together. "Petrina knew about the plot because she devised it! She persuaded Barbara to go along with your plan to steal the Vanderpless that night out in Houston. I always wondered why, Paul, you wanted to know every detail of the gala but you were telling your wife who in turn, unbeknown to you, was being fed the plot masterminded by Petrina. She was always one step ahead of the game, using you all. She found out from Danny, who she was desperate to meet, what the diamond was going to be – a necklace and that the four major stones were worth more than half the value of the whole piece. She probably also learnt from Danny about the Cubic Zirconia imitation necklace which she could use to replace these four diamonds. I saw Petrina go towards the bathroom when Sahara was modelling. She found the bottle of chloroform placed there before the event by

Barbara which she knew you were going to use on yourself having got rid of the Vogel Vanderpless. You didn't do it - she put you out with the handkerchief soaked in chloroform which James found by you. I bet somehow she made sure her DNA wasn't found on it. Once you were out cold she swapped the stones with the fakes from Simon Schall and passed the necklace through the window to you, Paul, just as Sahara was supposed to have done. When I saw her in New York a few days later she was getting new Cubic Zirconias from him to replace the ones that she had put into the necklace to then give back to Danny. He couldn't go to New York because of the heist so sent her along to do it for him, unknowingly with an imitation necklace missing the four CZs which she took out of their settings when she was in Danny's office before the gala."

"Jemima, it seems you have worked it all out. I am amazed I have to say. I am going to speak to Danny. We need to find out where these two women are with my diamonds. Jemima, we are going to go back to London on my jet now. Where are your things?"

"Oh, uh, at James's house."

"OK, you go and get them. I need to speak to the police here and Paige in London, as well my daughter and grandson; particularly Danny. How he got involved with this girl, I don't know. I will meet you at Tambo airport."

As they walked back through the French windows into the suite, Jemima heard Sahara say cattily, "It looks like you've been double-bluffed by your wife, Paul."

Jemima didn't wait to hear his reply but she couldn't help smiling to herself.

Epilogue

Vogel House, London April 29th 2011

It was the day of the Royal Wedding and hardly anyone else was in at Vogel House but Jemima was looking forward to watching it on TV later that morning.

She was sitting in Mr V's office, looking at the new addition on the wall behind where was he was sitting. It was a huge oil painting of the Vogel Vanderpless - before it had been cut into the 39 pieces. It was amazing and, staring at it, Jemima couldn't help but feel an overwhelming sense of pride at having rescued this diamond, which had caused so much upset over the years. Well part of it, at least.

"Now, Alexa and Daniel are on their way with DI Paige," Mr V said, putting down his phone.

"Oh good. OK." Jemima couldn't help but feel the old butterflies and wondered about the reward. Mr V hadn't mentioned anything about it on the flight back to London. In fact, he had spent most of the flight in his bedroom. She wished that she was back with James and Rosemary and not sitting wondering what was going to happen next. James had taken her back to his house where she had packed her things and said goodbye to Rosemary, then he had driven her to meet Mr Vogel, who was already waiting for her in the private terminal.

"I do want to thank you for what you have done, and apologise for doubting you in the first place. Although, having said that, this really is all a rather extraordinary, unbelievable state of affairs. Your story about the diamond is incredible. We will find out shortly its connection to the Cullinan, however I also want your help in finding the other four parts."

"Mr V, I would be honoured, but I really have no formal training and I think that a lot of my success was down to luck. Amazing that James's grandmother knew Martha Vanderpless and the story of the murdered maid from her childhood."

"Be that as it may, you have proven yourself capable of duties far beyond those of a press officer and I think you'll work out how you can go about finding the rest of the diamond."

Jemima took all this in. Only the previous day she'd been saying to James how much she wanted to be a private investigator!

Alexa and Danny walked in with Detective Inspector Paige and, having congratulated her, they sat down.

Mr Vogel began. "Thank you for coming in to see us, Paige; particularly today when I am sure you are wanted on Royal duty. Now, I gather you have been briefed by my grandson about this Petrina Lindberg who, along with the wife of Paul Pratt, we believe has the four large diamonds. They were removed from the Vogel Vanderpless necklace and replaced with four very good replicas, as Jemima told you from my jet yesterday.

"Yes Mr Vogel, that is correct. Miss Fox-Pearl's story all adds up and it would appear she's solved the case almost single-handedly. We have no proof as yet that this is what happened, however. So Miss Fox-Pearl," DI Paige continued, turning to Jemima, "you were suspicious of Sahara – and rightly so. You say you were also suspicious of Petrina. Why was that?"

"I met her back in South Africa, at New Year. She was very strange at the party – always asking me questions about you, Danny, and things about Vogel. I also heard her on the phone to somebody, mentioning my name and Vogel. She seemed to know quite a bit about diamonds and jewellery. She had a huge Cartier Panthère ring on her finger and that beautiful watch which covered a tattoo."

"Yes, she had a tattoo of a snow leopard," Danny said. "Quite out of character, I thought."

"That was what the ring looked like – a snow leopard! It was the white gold and diamonds with black onyx – I remember it seeming huge on her thin fingers."

"We did a DNA test from a nail varnish she left at young Mr Vogel's apartment," Paige continued. "Through her mother, who is from Montenegro, Petrina is related to one of the most notorious members of the Pink Panther jewel thieves - Nicolai Poparic. She also goes by the name Petra Poparic and operates under a different rival gang – the Snow Leopards."

"Yes." Jemima said confidently. "I read once about an offshoot of this gang that turned against them and operated in competition. Unlike the Panthers, the Leopards steal mainly from private individuals, collections and mostly historical pieces. They're fairly new on the scene."

"Jemima," Mr V spoke up at last, "Paige has already gone through this with me and we have agreed that you are to work with him in tracking this girl down. You will undergo formal training. From what Danny says, she was going to be at the Monaco Grand Prix in three weeks. Danny, I want you to continue this relationship…"

"She ended it a week ago." Danny sounded almost embarrassed.

"Don't worry – I've been to the Grand Prix, I know how it works down there. I have friends in Monaco and I'm fluent in French and Russian; I can infiltrate." Jemima spoke with a growing sense of self-confidence. "Leave it with me."

Acknowledgements

Firstly I would like to thank my mother, Trisha Goodbody, to whom I have dedicated my first novel. Without her teaching me to read and write, and buying me novels at every possible opportunity, I would not have the love for books that I do. Her generosity allowed me the dream of writing my own.

My amazing father, Mark, for being at the other end of the phone, encouraging me to keep going and doing what all fathers do best. My brother, Alastair, for designing the most beautiful and perfect cover. Kirstie Farquhar of Garrard, whose technical drawing on the cover depicts the Vogel Vanderpless necklace exactly how it was meant to be in my mind and with whom I had such fun 'commissioning' the ultimate piece of jewellery.

Katharine Smith of Heddon Publishing who has edited and published this book with more patience and support than I could ever imagine; a publishing house I am proud to be part of.

So many people have both advised and encouraged me that to include everyone by name would mean another book but you know who you are and I am beyond grateful.

Penultimately, Bebe Rivera for loving me, looking after me, and being there over the past two years whilst in South America.

And last but definitely not least the love of my life - Milo, my Jack Russell/ Dachshund cross, who made the trip over the Atlantic with me and keeps me smiling, happy and fit every day of my life and who makes his first appearance in Jemima Fox's next mystery.

About the Author

Josie Goodbody grew up in Dorset, studied French Literature and Language at Exeter University and having spent a year working in the fashion industry in Paris moved to London. For over a decade she worked in Public Relations for several international luxury brands, after which she spent a year in Monaco.

She currently lives between England and Uruguay and is already working on the next novel in the Jemima Fox series.

If you have enjoyed *The Diamond Connection*, a positive review on Amazon, Goodreads or any other literary site would be very much appreciated.

Lightning Source UK Ltd.
Milton Keynes UK
UKOW02f0108100315

247582UK00004B/293/P